PROTEGIMUS - A Henry Knox Story

PROTEGIMUS

A Henry Knox Story

By

Pete Briggs

ISBN: 9798310701120

ACKNOWLEDGMENTS

Writing a book is never a solo endeavour, and there are a few people without whom this journey wouldn't have been possible.

To my wife **Courtney** – Thank you for your unwavering support, patience, and belief in me, even when I was lost in the world of Henry Knox. Your encouragement has been my anchor, and your love reminds me that the best stories are the ones we write together.

To my daughter **Alix** – You inspire me every day with your curiosity, kindness, and boundless imagination. This book may not be a bedtime story, but I hope one day you'll read it and know that you were always part of the journey.

Chris and **Kate** – thank you for helping me shape this story, your input and support have been invaluable.

And to every reader who picks up this book—thank you. This is just the beginning.

CHAPTER ONE

The town of Oldham wore its despair openly, the scars of time and indifference etched into every brick. Each terraced house along the battered streets bore the marks of neglect: countless windows were boarded up, hiding hollow interiors from both prying eyes and thieving hands. Soot-stained chimneys, the relics of a once-thriving industrial age, now pointed toward a perpetually sullen sky.

Amid this decline, Henry Knox navigated a battered former military Land Rover Wolf 1-10 down a forgotten mill-town street, the growl of its tired engine echoing like distant thunder, an elegy for a place on the brink. The green-and-black vehicle, scarred from its own service, fit seamlessly into these desolate surroundings. Finally, Henry parked outside a dilapidated terrace house whose facade was peeling, the flaking paint like skin over old wounds about to split, revealing the deep marks of time and disregard.

Knox swung open the Land Rover's door, the heel of his boot hitting the ground with a solid thud. A cold wind nipped at his face, lacing the air with the chill of a long-forgotten grave. Standing over six feet tall, his stocky build commanded the narrow street, lending him an unmistakable air of authority. Salt-and-pepper hair framed a broad forehead, and his angular, square jaw was softened only by the deep-set blue eyes that swept the area with the trained vigilance of a seasoned soldier. He wore a dark T-shirt, combat trousers, and polished Alt-Berg boots, the same practical uniform he'd carried over from his military days.

Henry had seen much in his life, from the poverty-stricken streets of his youth to the deserts and war-torn villages he'd traversed in service of his country. Now he fought a more elusive war: one waged for personal survival and moral justice in these neglected pockets of civilian life.

His private detective agency, Knox Investigations, operated from the same Land Rover now parked outside the derelict terrace, was a comparatively new venture, a calculated risk of being employed outside of Service without a boss. Even though business had been slow, Henry's resolve had been strong and unwavering.

In the forces, persistence had always reaped results, he hoped it would now, but he had found out quickly, that being outside the Army's safety net, left him feeling exposed and alone.

As Knox moved toward the door, the street seemed to hold its breath. A suffocating silence pressed down, and the air felt stale, as though all life had been wrung from it. Somewhere in the distance came the slow, rhythmic thud of a bass drum, like the fading heartbeat of a dying town.

When he reached for the door handle, rust flaked beneath his fingertips. The metal felt unnervingly cold, as though the house itself had succumbed to the surrounding lifelessness. Henry knocked, his closed fist sounding a sharp, echoing note that pierced the hush like a death knell.

The door rattled under the impact and drifted slightly ajar. Splintered wood ringed the lock, and the hinges looked warped, barely clinging in place. Someone had kicked this door in more than once. Knox took a step back, scanning the length of the street.

The signs were everywhere: cracked doors, bent frames, broken locks. This was no isolated incident. The entire neighbourhood looked systematically torn apart. A war zone, Knox thought grimly. These feeble doors never stood a chance. Whoever was responsible had done it with brutal intent.

A gust of wind tugged the door open with a groan, drawing Henry's attention back to the threshold just as an elderly man emerged from the shadows. The man's face was carved with deep lines, each wrinkle telling a story of hardship. A thin halo of silver hair clung to his temples, the last traces of youth refusing to vanish entirely. He gripped the door frame with trembling hands, his hesitant movements hinting at frailty. Yet despite the cloudiness of early dementia in his eyes, a momentary spark of recognition ignited when he saw Knox.

Knox kept still, taking in both the man's posture and the dimly lit interior behind him, waiting for something, anything, to crack the silence.

Henry's mind flickered back to the phone call that had led him here. Earlier that morning, he'd been sat in the driver's seat of his Land Rover, parked in a quiet corner of a public car park. His mobile vibrated against the dashboard, and an unknown number glowed on the screen.

"Knox Investigations," he answered in his usual guarded tone.

The voice on the other end was tense, laced with desperation. "Mr. Knox? My name is Lila Alderson. I'm calling about my father, George Alderson. He lives alone in Oldham..." Her voice caught, the weight of distance pressing through the line.

"Go on," Henry prompted, instantly alert.

"I live in Canada, and I can't get home right now," she explained. "My dad... he's in the early stages of dementia, and some thugs have started targeting him.

They robbed him and now they keep harassing him. He's terrified, and I don't know what else to do. I need someone to help him. Please, Mr. Knox, can you help? I'll pay whatever it takes."

The urgency in Lila's voice had struck a nerve. Her plea for help tugged at Henry's sense of duty, that same protective instinct that had guided him through years of service.

"I can do that," he'd said, the decision as natural as breathing. "I can be in Oldham within the hour."

Lila exhaled, a shaky sound of relief bridging thousands of miles. "Thank you, Mr. Knox. He lives on Kipling Street, number ten. I—I really appreciate this."

The old man's voice drew Henry back to the present. "Mr. Knox? Thank heavens you've come," he murmured, his tone a fragile thread of relief and despair. He gestured for Henry to enter.

Stepping inside, Henry's gaze swept over the modest hallway: overturned framed photographs with shattered glass, broken furniture strewn about, the silent aftermath of repeated vandalism. This frail man, George Alderson, had been living in constant fear, tormented by local youths whose brutality seemed to mirror the decay of the entire neighbourhood.

Moving farther along, Henry first caught the sharp odour of fresh paint, which struck him as odd, as George clearly hadn't hired any decorators for some time. Then he grimaced at a foul acidy stench, that threatened to overwhelm him. He scanned the corridor, and his gaze landed on the wall near the living room door, which was marred by ill-spelled graffiti in jarring red spray paint: "Tommy's boy." The lettering sloped unevenly, each character clumsier than the last, and below it, the carpet was discoloured and stained with urine.

George's dishevelled appearance spoke volumes. He

looked as though he'd given up on basic self-care, likely made worse by his daughter's absence. The house itself resembled a drug den or an abandoned squat, and Henry couldn't dismiss the idea that squatters might actually have been here at some point. It was obvious George needed far more help than just warding off thugs, but Henry resolved to tackle one problem at a time.

George shuffled deeper into the hallway, toward a room that Henry assumed was the living room. His steps were heavy with age and vulnerability. As Henry followed, George spoke in a trembling voice. "They took everything worth a penny," he said. "Even my wife's jewellery. She passed away two years ago... those pieces were all I had left of her." He turned to Henry, grief shining in his cloudy eyes.

The raw pain in George's words made Henry bristle with anger. He placed a reassuring hand on the old man's shoulder. "I'm here to help, George. Tell me exactly what happened."

The living room might once have been respectable, perhaps in the 1980s. Now, torn floral wallpaper clung to the walls, and a scattering of Pendelfin ornaments occupied a row of dark wooden shelves beside an electric fire. A pungent smell of mould hung in the air, prompting Henry to wonder when the heater had last worked.

George lowered himself into a small rocking chair, its worn wooden frame creaking under his weight. It was the only piece of furniture still largely intact, though its surface was nicked and faded. The rest of the room lay in ruins, broken chairs, splintered tables, and slashed cushions spilling their foam after years of neglect and vandalism. Henry surveyed the wreckage, thinking about Lila. She had clearly been away too long, and it seemed unlikely she knew the true extent of her father's living conditions. More likely, George had hidden just how dire things had become, either out of pride or stubbornness.

George gestured for Henry to sit. Scanning the debris, Henry settled on a three-legged stool braced against the battered wall, precarious but serviceable. Perched there, he listened intently as George recounted each attack he could remember, most followed the same grim pattern. While George spoke, Henry's mind methodically mapped out a plan. He needed to set a trap that would catch these predators off guard and put a stop to their terror.

"The ring leader's the worst of the lot," George went on, his tone growing bitter. "A nasty piece of work called Tommy. He pushes the others to come at night, riding those bloody electric bikes."

Henry listened, mentally cataloguing each detail. Gangs like Tommy's might be small-time, but they could easily serve as conduits for bigger, more dangerous players, often without knowing it themselves. In his experience, street-level crime rarely stood alone; it was usually just one branch of a far more twisted tree.

"Tonight," Henry said powerfully, filling the room with bravado, in an effort to raise Georges spirits, "We'll make sure it's the last time they terrorise you, George."

A wavering smile lit George's face, and for a moment, he looked decades younger. Henry couldn't help but smile back. Part of him would have done this job for free, but he knew he couldn't afford that, his fledgling PI business was barely scraping by, and most of his post-discharge work had been mundane marital surveillance. This, at least, would demand a different skill set, something more tangible than snapping photos of an unfaithful spouse.

Henry began a thorough sweep of the house, mentally cataloguing every door and window. This place reminded him of countless other terraced homes he'd seen, and the one he'd grown up in, in his own small northern town. After finishing his interior checks, he moved on to the front and back streets, studying the stone cobbles and potholes for potential escape routes. He wasn't worried about his own exit; he wanted to know exactly where these vandals might run.

He kept a low profile as he recced the area, aware that his military bearing made true anonymity unlikely. People tended to notice him no matter what, sensing the authority in his stride. Still, he doubted the gang would roll in during broad daylight; it didn't match their established pattern, but that didn't mean he'd relax his guard. Old habits die hard, especially the ones that keep you alive.

Satisfied with his methodical, thorough checks, Knox withdrew, mentally confirming that he'd left no loose ends. Certain of his plan, he moved the Land Rover from outside George's property and parked it beneath a soot-darkened stone viaduct. He set his phone to silent and dropped it into the central cup holder, then draped a green tarp over the vehicle, retrieved from a side bin.

Knox's Land Rover was more than just transport; it was his home, his office, and his constant ally on the road. In the rear, where seats should have been, black kit bags were stacked, each stuffed with clothing, equipment and gear for whatever life or work might throw at him. Side bins held more specialised equipment, flashlights, first-aid kits, a portable stove, everything he needed to live rough if necessity demanded it. He had slept in there more nights than he cared to recall, lulled by the drum of rain against the metal roof.

Now the Land Rover was to be concealed beneath a towering 19th-century stonework that threw a deep shadow. As always, Knox parked in reverse; he'd learned long ago that backing in made for a faster getaway, a crucial advantage if trouble arose. His motto was straightforward: Prior planning and preparation prevents piss poor performances, colloquially known in the military as:

The 7 Ps

Satisfied that his prep was complete, he settled into position, well hidden, leaning on the bonnet with his elbows. Now it all became a waiting game, and Henry had patience in spades. He wasn't in a hurry; a good stakeout demanded calm and careful observation. As dusk bled into bruised purples and deep blues, he readied himself for whatever the night might bring.

CHAPTER TWO

Secreted beneath the shadow of a train track arch, Knox remained stalwart and focused. The dusk had morphed into night, the light of the short day being chased away by the dark shadows of winter. His eyes pierced the frigid air, staring from within a deep and dark recess. From his position, Henry had a perfect view of Kipling Street, where the terraced houses stood in their tired, crooked lines. The old industrial town stretched out in a stark, unrelenting grid, its streets meticulously designed to serve the insatiable hunger of the industrial machines of old. These rigid arteries converged on vast, blackened factories and smoke-belching mills, their towering chimneys dominating the skyline.

Once, these streets had thrived with life, men and women trudging to work, children darting between the shadows of progress, but now they stood largely empty, shadows of a past shaped as much by toil as by the relentless rhythm of the machines they served. The train lines and mills had been the town's lifeblood, the chimneys belching black smoke into the sky. Now, those chimneys were as lifeless as the factories they served. Most had been torn down or converted into supermarket forecourts, leaving only their ghosts to loom over the town. Everything else had decayed, including the people.

The night hummed with a nervous quiet, the kind of silence that comes before a storm. Every distant sound, a scrape of metal or a soft murmur, crackled in Henry's ears, keeping his focus razor-sharp. He could feel the street alive beneath the stillness, holding its breath.

It did not take long after the streetlights flickered to

life for the first hum of electric bikes to cut through the evening's calm, signalling the arrival of the expected gang. Knox took note of where the bikes had come from. That would be their escape route. These guys were not trained like the military; they would not know to alternate their routes to avoid setting patterns, and they would not know that they were driving into an ambush.

The gang swept into view, moving with the arrogance of predators who had never known fear, their coarse laughter breaking through the night's quiet like a mocking taunt. They moved past Knox without a flicker of awareness, their noise and bravado shielding them from his sharp eyes that tracked their every move from the darkness. They turned into the street fronting George's house, their jeering voices carrying a sinister promise, oblivious to the silent shadow that watched their arrival.

The first to dismount was a lanky teen with a shock of bleached hair. He jumped from the bike, which skidded into a parked car and shuddered to a halt before flopping on the ground. He ran straight into the door with his shoulder, and the door burst open easily. The light in the hallway of George's house breached onto the flags of the pavement in front of the door.

Three others ran in, giggling, after the blond-haired teen. All three kicked the door or the doorframe as they entered the house. A lone skinny male in his late teenage years stood guard on the bikes, but he was not doing a decent job of being a lookout. He was too busy shouting at the others and trying to pry into the house. He was laughing and pointing. Knox, like a ghost, departed his cover, taking a straight line from the train arch directly to the front door of George's terrace house. The teen, too preoccupied by how much fun the others were enjoying, failed to take notice of the dark figure that approached quickly and quietly behind him.

As Knox approached, his mind ran through the tactical considerations of striking the opponent in front of him. He knew well that his hands, while indispensable for many tasks, are poorly suited for delivering effective blows. Many inexperienced fighters rely on them, swinging wildly, hoping for impactful contact. Often, they land a punch low on the knuckles, resulting in broken metacarpals in these smaller protuberances, which bear the brunt of the impact. These bones are weak and prone to breaking under stress. Knox's own hands bore the marks of such early errors, scars and even old teeth marks from fights long past, stories of a time before Knox knew how to hit someone correctly.

In his seasoned experience, Knox preferred using parts of the body built to withstand and administer force. The heel of the hand was ideal for this purpose. It allowed for a swift, sharp jab, quick and controlled, the padding of the heel absorbing some of the shock, minimising the risk to himself while maximising the damage to his opponent. A bent elbow, too, was a formidable weapon that could deliver a devastating blow in close quarters, the power concentrated in a small, brutal impact area, although it meant you had to get close, sometimes too close to the enemy.

Additionally, the apex of the head could serve as a powerful battering ram. Though it required a precise, close engagement, the hard bone of the skull could inflict considerable damage, especially in a clinch where distance and space were limited. Knox considered these options as he prepared to neutralise the threat swiftly and efficiently, with minimal fuss and maximum effect.

Henry studied the gang member quickly. The kid was not large but knocking him out cleanly required precision. Henry's target was the subtle indentation where the skull meets the spine, an ideal spot for incapacitation without a high probability of causing too much permanent injury.

After all the calculation and permutations, Knox settled on a simple jab despite his reservations. He would just need to execute the blow with precision, which he performed perfectly delivering a well-aimed strike to the soft juncture at the base of the kid's skull. Knox's fist connected with a solid thud, the satisfying resistance of flesh and bone telling him his timing had been perfect. The force vibrated up his arm, a jolt of power that grounded him in the moment, controlled, sharp, and purposeful. He used just enough power to ensure the boy would be knocked out. The impact sent the kid stumbling forward, and as his body slackened, Henry caught him before he hit the floor. He swiftly dragged him out of sight, away from the doorway, and gently laid him down in the recovery position.

A quick pat-down revealed a flick knife in the kid's pocket. It was a basic model, about four inches long, with a cheap plastic handle designed to mimic wood. Henry quickly used the knife to disable the gang's escape route, methodically slashing the tires and brakes of the four bikes parked nearby. With the immediate threat neutralised and their transportation sabotaged, he snapped the knife's blade to prevent its reuse and dropped the remains into a road grate.

Knox silently moved forward to the side of the doorframe and peered into the barely lit hallway; it was empty. He could hear glass being smashed somewhere in the house, and there was the faint sound of a spray can being used, probably more graffiti on the walls. Henry's face was stern and focused as he stepped over the threshold for the second time that day.

Henry advanced with a predator's caution along the

wall of the dimly lit passageway. Fresh, wet streaks of red paint trailed down the opposite wall, slowly seeping downward in the bleary fluorescent glow. Henry's familiarity with the house's blueprint was now his ally. To his left was the living room door. There was no light to betray the intruder's location, but the muffled sound of metal striking metal told Henry one of the gang members was inside.

With a burst of speed, Henry surged into the room. He kept low, minimising his silhouette against the faint illumination from the hall, an instinctive tactic to prevent giving the youth any chance to react before it was too late. However, his stealth was unnecessary. The gang member was engrossed in his destructive task of kicking the electric fire free from the wall.

At the last moment, Henry's movement caught the corner of the intruder's eye, and as he turned, Henry seized the moment, using the heel of his hand. He propelled forward, targeting the spot just under the youth's chin. The impact was sharp and sure, a direct hit that sent vibrations through Henry's straight arm. The youth's body buckled under the force, collapsing as swiftly as if his strings had been cut. Henry caught the limp body before it could crumple noisily to the floor, guiding the unconscious form down with the same meticulous care as the first, the soft descent barely disturbing the air, allowing the silence to hold and his ambush to remain perfectly intact.

Henry positioned the second young man in the recovery position, carefully adjusting his limbs so he was stable yet securely incapacitated. As the youth lay motionless on the floor, as if asleep, the stillness filled the room. Henry took a moment to listen. He closed his eyes, his senses heightened, and he could almost hear the heartbeats of everyone in the house. He listened intently, focusing on the locations of the remaining gang members. One was in the kitchen, and one upstairs.

The element of surprise remained firmly on Henry's side, a tactical advantage he was not about to squander. With a couple of the gang members now neutralised, the balance of power had shifted significantly, but Henry knew that overconfidence now could prove costly. He allowed himself a small smile: two down and two to go, he thought.

The only other room downstairs was a large kitchen, which had last been updated around 1975. From the sound of the crashing Henry could hear emanating from the room, it suggested that the decor was being drastically remodelled.

Henry's entrance into the room was swift, and as he rounded the corner, he came face-to-face with a figure caught in the stage between adolescence and adulthood. The youth, no older than twenty, wore a dark tracksuit and a conspicuous thick gold chain that looked too large for him, draped around his neck. The youth's eyes widened in shock as he immediately registered the presence of an intruder. Fear spread quickly across his face, transforming into stark terror as he processed the sudden and threatening disruption to his evening.

In a fluid, instinctive motion, Henry thrust a sharp jab into the youth's midsection, aiming just below the ribs. The punch landed with a solid crunch, effectively driving the breath from the young man's lungs. Gasping for air and unable to scream or even shout, he stood frozen for a moment, clutching his stomach, the shock of the blow and the abrupt loss of oxygen rendering him momentarily helpless.

The kid doubled over, clutching his midriff, struggling to catch his breath. Knox did not hesitate. With a quick, brutal movement, he drove his elbow into the top of the youth's head, sending him crumpling to his knees, unconscious. Out of habit, Knox caught the boy's head before it could collide with the hard-tiled floor, avoiding a loud thud that would give away his position. Stealth was no longer necessary. With the majority of the gang dealt with, only Tommy remained, and Knox wanted him to know he was the last one standing.

Henry walked up the steep stairs and turned onto the landing at the top, heading toward the sound that came from the front bedroom. The light flickered brightly from the main bedchamber, as the noise of breaking pottery and glass continued. Knox stood at the entrance to the room, filling the doorway with the breadth of his shoulders, his head slightly bowed, forehead leaning forward, eyes focused on the prize. He raised his fist and knocked on the doorframe. “Ding dong,” he said with a hint of a smile. He was enjoying himself.

A tall young man with gangly arms and bleached-blond hair stood in the centre of the room. This was clearly Tommy. He spun, suddenly alert and startled, toward the door, a broken chair leg held as a makeshift weapon in hand, his eyes wild with fury and confusion. “Who the fuck are you?” He shouted wildly “Where is George? The little black twat! I wanted to say hello.”

“I'm the new landlord, Tommy. George is now under my care. He is nice and safe... unlike you.” Knox replied in monotone.

Tommy smiled, his broken, yellow-and-brown-marked teeth on display. “You know my name, old man, but do you know who I am?”

Henry shook his head. “Nope, and nor do I care. What I do know is this is the last time you come to this house. This is the last time you trouble George.”

“You and whose army?” Tommy laughed. “My dad is Ronny Marshal. I am sure you have heard of him. He will cut you open from belly to balls if you lay a finger on me."

"I will take my chances, Tommy," Henry replied flatly. "You have one chance. Leave now and never come back, or your dad can come around and take you home in an ambulance."

Tommy, blind with fury, ignored the warning and hurled himself at Knox, spewing threats. Henry moved with the grace of experience, sidestepping the reckless swing of the chair leg and then ducking effortlessly beneath the backswing. In one fluid motion, Knox struck back, his hand moving with brutality. He drove the heel of his hand upward into Tommy's jaw, and the unmistakable crunch of bone or teeth breaking filled the air. Tommy's head snapped back, his body folding as his legs buckled, sending him crashing silently to the floor. Henry moved quickly, checking his pulse before gently rolling him onto his side. A thin line of blood trickled from Tommy's mouth, but his airway was clear.

Henry quickly patted Tommy down, his hands deftly locating a mobile phone tucked away in the young man's pocket, before using Tommy's thumb to unlock the device.

Scrolling through the contacts, Henry searched for any entry labelled "Dad" or similar. His eyes narrowed as he spotted two possible numbers. One was simply listed as "Dad," but the other had a distinguishing detail, "Ronny" in brackets.

Henry called the number and pressed the phone to his ear, waiting for the call to connect, his gaze fixed on Tommy's prone form, vigilant for any signs of stirring as he prepared to confront whoever was on the other end of the line.

A couple of rings later, a gruff voice came on. "What the fuck do you want?"

Knox calmly asked, "Is this Ronny?"

"Who the fuck are you?" the voice on the other end of the phone shouted, clearly irate.

"I am waiting for you at George's house, pop down when you have five. We need to talk about how to parent your kids."

Knox ended the call, his grip loosening on the phone as he let it slip from his fingers, the device bouncing off Tommy's forehead with a muffled thud before clattering loudly on the hardwood floor.

Henry turned the room light off and moved to the large bedroom window. He stood motionless, his broad frame cloaked in the darkness of the room. His eyes locked onto the view outside the window, scanning the deserted street below. The world felt unnaturally still, the quiet broken only by the distant hum of a car passing close by and the occasional rustle of leaves stirred by the wind. Under the flickering glow of the streetlights, shadows danced across the cracked pavement below, casting eerie patterns around the discarded bikes strewn across the road, left in haphazard disarray by the youths in their rush to unleash chaos. In the blackness Knox waited for Ronny.

CHAPTER THREE

Knox's gaze remained fixed on the corner of the street where the gang had first appeared. That was where Ronny Marshal would come from; it was the only logical approach. Knox knew Marshal would not even consider deviating from his normal path, the one his gang had ritualistically followed. It also did not matter if Marshal pulled up in a sleek symbol of wealth or a battered thug-mobile. Knox had dealt with too many men like him to care.

Within minutes, the low growl of engines sliced through the night air, amplified by the concrete canyons of the terraced buildings, announcing Marshal's arrival with an arrogance that dared anyone to stand in his way. What Marshal had not foreseen, what he could not have imagined, was that the route he had meticulously carved out for his gang was now the very path that delivered him to Knox, placing him squarely in the crosshairs of danger.

The roar swelled, growing into a snarling beast that tore apart the silence. Knox caught the flicker of headlights breaking through the far corner's shadows. He leaned forward, every muscle tightening, as a heavy, expensive car barrelled into view. It tore down the street with reckless abandon, skating on the black tarmac as it slid to a sharp halt directly in front of George's house. Knox took a large and deep breath through his nose and stepped back from the window. The frayed curtains swayed slightly, enough to obscure his silhouette but not his view.

"Showtime," he muttered under his breath.

Knox's hands remained relaxed. There would be time

enough for them to tighten into fists, but there was no point in expending that energy now. Instead, he waited and watched the unfolding drama below. Ronny clearly had an eye for theatrical entrances. This was not merely an arrival; it was a show of power, an entrance meant to unsettle, to scare, to dominate. This tactic might work on the weak and the vulnerable, on frail old men cowering in their homes, but not Henry Knox. Ronny Marshal was not intimidating him. If anything, he was confirming Knox's expectations and letting him know the game was on.

The high-end BMW gleamed under the streetlights, its polished exterior an ostentatious beacon in the middle of desolation. Knox studied it carefully, its sleek frame out of place amidst the crumbling, rust-streaked vehicles that littered the street.

The doors flung open, and three large men stepped out, moving with deliberate power and deadly purpose. One swung a baseball bat casually in his hand, while another held a large machete, its blade flashing ominously in the dim light. The third man, lagging slightly behind, spoke in low, commanding tones, his calm, authoritative presence a clear indication that he was in charge.

Henry's eyes narrowed as he took in the scene unfolding before him. It was clear who Ronny was. The authoritative stance and the effortless way he commanded the situation left no doubt about his leadership role. He watched as Ronny, with a calm yet commanding presence, gestured to his associates, signalling strategic positions in front of George's house.

Inside, Henry's mind worked rapidly, years of hard-earned experience allowing him to size up the situation in an instant. He knew he needed to act with both speed and precision. The arrival of the men, wielding a baseball bat and a machete, signalled a significant escalation; they were ready for violence. The element of surprise had tipped slightly out of his favour, but Henry was not fazed. The game had shifted, but he believed he still held the winning hand.

Henry quickly ran through a series of scenarios, calculating the most effective strategies for neutralising the threat while keeping himself out of harm's way. Experience had taught him that bullies were best dealt with through swift, decisive violence, and that they needed to understand exactly who was delivering the punishment and why. There were not many options at his disposal, but Knox did not need many to finish the job.

Henry stepped away from the window and walked slowly down the stairs, along the slim hallway, to position himself squarely at the house entrance, his figure framed by the weak hallway light that spilled out onto the street. His shadow stretched long and foreboding across the pavement, an ominous silhouette that seemed to expand and darken as it extended further from his feet.

The stillness of the evening was pierced by the soft, insistent murmur of neighbourhood curiosity, a quiet hum that rippled through the air like an unspoken question. Knox noticed the subtle movements of curtains in the windows up and down the street. The neighbours, drawn by the sound of screeching tyres and loud voices, peeked out of shadowed windows to catch a glimpse of the unfolding drama. Yet, none dared to step outside. The tension in the air, coupled with the intimidating sight of the three-armed men, kept them securely behind their broken doors, their presence marked only by the occasional twitch of a curtain.

Knox, aware of the eyes watching from the safety of their homes, stood unflinching. He was a lone figure against the backdrop of a quiet suburban fear, ready to confront whatever was about to come his way. He kept his posture calm and relaxed, but in his mind, he was on alert. These men were not here just to make up numbers; they were Marshal's muscle, and they liked to dish out pain. He needed to be focused and ready. Knox waited for the men to approach him, a power play. This was his ground, and he was not about to give it up easily.

All three men appeared to be in their early to mid-forties, with large, stocky builds, the uniformity of bald heads shining under the streetlights. Their expressions were set hard, like slabs of granite. They wore crisp white tracksuits and gleaming trainers that screamed designer labels.

As Knox readied himself mentally, the largest of the trio, a brute of a man clutching a baseball bat, charged forward. His face was twisted in a grimace of unbridled fury, veins bulging at his temples as he bellowed threats. The bat, held high, sliced through the air, an extension of his rage aimed with reckless intent as he bore down on Knox. Henry could feel the weight of his anger, the sharp crack of his voice splitting the quiet of the evening, "I'm gonna fuck you up, you little shit."

Knox assessed his opponent with a cold, calculating gaze. The big man, all muscle and anger, gripped the baseball bat like a warrior wielding a broadsword. Knox knew a typical swing with such a heavy weapon would be slow, laden with momentum. Although the bat could also be jabbed forward as a poking weapon, the man's fury hinted at no such finesse; he was primed for a crushing blow.

Predicting the arc of the impending swing, Knox prepared his counter. His response was swift and lethal, a coiled spring inside him suddenly released, and he surged forward with explosive agility, closing the distance before the man could commence his swing.

Knox jumped forward and drove his crooked elbow hard into the man's forehead. The connection was solid, the impact resonant, echoing slightly in the quiet street. This time there was no attempt by Knox to ease the man's descent; he let the aggressor crumble where he stood. The bat clattered out of his grasp, hitting the pavement with a wooden thunk that cut sharply through the night air.

Stepping back smoothly into the light of the doorway, Knox reclaimed his original stance. His voice, calm and low, broke the brief silence that followed the thud of the falling body. "Next," he said quietly, as his eyes flicked to the next threat, ready to engage once more.

The two remaining men hesitated, exchanging uncertain glances as they absorbed the swift downfall of their companion. The air thickened, the moment stretching as they calculated their next move. Ronny broke the silence with a sharp command, his voice laced with frustration. He directed the man holding the machete, who up until now had been a looming figure in the background, to advance on Knox.

The machete-wielder faltered, his initial movements hesitant and jittery. Fear flickered across his face, the turmoil swirling within him. He had witnessed how decisively Knox had dealt the first attacker, and the memory of his colleague crashing to the ground haunted him. Yet, the weight of loyalty, or perhaps, even the fear of retribution from Ronny, forced him to stay and fight. He knew on which side his bread was buttered, and with a resigned sense of dread, he edged forward, compelled by his boss's stern orders.

Despite his reluctance, the machete-wielder's advance was a clear signal of compliance. His grip tightened around the handle of his weapon as he wrestled with his fear, stepping into the fray with shaky determination to fulfil the role Ronny demanded of him.

Knox stood firm, his expression unreadable as he observed the reluctant machete-wielder approach. The scene before him was painfully familiar, like a clichéd script from a worn-out action movie, one he had seen replayed countless times. Bullies like Ronny, who orchestrated violence from a distance, relying on the fear and loyalty of their underlings to enforce their will. Knox knew this game well, and he knew how it ended.

Knox again relaxed his shoulders, rolling them to drop tension from his stance, his eyes tracking every tremor of hesitation in the machete-wielding man's approach. Knox was ready, his mind and body synchronised in anticipation. He knew that for George and the rest of the street to be free of a man like Ronny Marshal, they needed more than a few broken bones and black eyes. The entire cycle of intimidation and fear had to be broken.

But first he had to deal with the machete-wielder, who was drawing closer. Knox prepared to end this scenario on his own terms, ready to dictate the conclusion of this all-too-familiar plot once again.

The second attacker had not learned from the mistakes of the first. He believed that the weapon in his hands was the deciding factor of this confrontation. He lunged with reckless aggression, the machete slicing through the air in chaotic, untrained swings. It was obvious he lacked any real finesse, but that hardly mattered. A machete did not need precision to be deadly. Its sheer weight and size could tear through flesh with ease. Yet, for all its destructive power, the weapon needed room to operate, and Knox had no intention of giving him that space. As with the baseball bat and the chair leg Tommy had brandished, the real chance lay in the split-second heartbeats between each wild swing, the moments when the attacker left himself dangerously exposed.

Henry waited for that perfect heartbeat, then struck with a flawless combination of timing and technique. He sidestepped under the wild charge, moving fluidly, sharp and quick. As the attacker barrelled past, Knox delivered a perfectly executed clothesline, using the man's own momentum to amplify the force. With a smooth, calculated step forward, Knox added his weight to the move, maximising the impact.

The forearm strike caught the assailant flush in the face, his body whipping backward from the force. Knox, maintaining control and momentum, forced the man downward, directing his fall. Knox made sure of the collapse by sweeping the attacker's feet out from beneath him, and he crashed to the ground, his head striking the tarmac with a sickening thud. The sound of soft flesh and hard skull meeting tarmac echoed in the quiet street, a grim punctuation to the swift takedown.

The man lay motionless, his body limp on the ground. Knox dropped to a kneeling position across the man's arm, the hand still tightly clutching the machete. Henry's breathing was steady, controlled. He forced the machete clear of the hand and threw it backwards toward the house, placing himself between the blade and the attacker. He raised his head to scan the scene for further threats, sensing Ronny's next move even before it happened.

Ronny had attempted to flank Henry, but his eyes, his posture, and every hint of muscle tension had telegraphed his plan to deliver a brutal kick at Knox's head. It was exactly what Knox would have done in his place: exploit any advantage to keep an opponent down.

But Knox was prepared. As Ronny's foot arced towards him, he reacted quickly and mercilessly. His left hand rose, not simply blocking but actively deflecting the kick to disrupt Ronny's flow. Simultaneously, his right hand caught the lower part of Ronny's leg, his grip firm.

Using Ronny's extended leg as leverage, Knox surged upwards to his full height, pulling Ronny off balance in one smooth, forceful move. The sudden shift left Ronny vulnerable and exposed. Seizing the moment, Knox drove his elbow, with the full weight of his body behind it, into Ronny's groin. The blow was devastating.

Ronny's body crumpled, his knees buckling as he fell to the ground, clutching himself in anguish. Knox stepped back, watching dispassionately as Ronny writhed, pain and nausea overtaking him while he vomited bile, his body curled into a foetal position.

Calmly, Knox reached down and rifled through Ronny's pockets, extracting the car keys with a swift tug. As Ronny, driven by pain and desperation, made a weak attempt to grab at Knox, Henry responded instantly. His fist connected sharply with Ronny's face, the sound of breaking bone mingling with the sickening splash of blood and vomit on the tarmac. Now, Ronny had a broken nose as well as the agony in his groin.

As Knox straightened, keys in hand, the doors of nearby terraced houses began to open cautiously. Residents, who had been long intimidated by the gang's presence, peered out. Relief flooded their faces, mixed with a sense of tentative freedom. They had been living under a shadow of fear, and now, seeing their tormentor in chief lying helpless and defeated, they felt a surge of hope.

But even as the neighbourhood began to stir from its forced silence, Knox knew the night's work was not over. The gang had been crippled, but the deeper issues that allowed such terror to thrive remained. Knox looked down at the incapacitated Ronny, a plan forming in his mind, ready to address the problem at its root. This was a small victory, but it was far from the end. Ronny would crawl back from under his rock the moment Knox was gone. Tonight, it needed to be finished, for good.

Knox used the key to unlock Ronny's BMW, a sleek machine coated in glossy black, its polished exterior an ostentatious beacon of ill-gotten gains. The luxury car was equipped with modern features, financed by the proceeds of crime. Henry slid into the smooth leather of the driver's seat, the material cool and supple beneath him. He reached out and pressed down the ignition button.

The engine responded with a low, assertive rumble, far different from the Land Rover's ignition, Knox thought. The BMW logo illuminated the dashboard display, quickly giving way to a sophisticated menu system. Knox navigated to the map application and scanned for the recent locations.

Knox exited the car and approached the incapacitated Ronny. Despite the groans and weak resistance from the beaten gang leader, Knox dragged him to the rear of the vehicle and used the key fob to pop the boot before heaving Ronny inside, ignoring his weak protests with clinical indifference. The boot slammed shut loudly, echoing down the quiet street.

Knox returned to George's house, where Tommy still lay unconscious from their earlier confrontation. Knox hoisted Tommy's limp body onto his shoulder with a grunt.

He manoeuvred down the stairs and through the narrow hallway, out to the BMW parked ominously outside. Opening the back door, he bundled Tommy into the back seat, securing him by wrapping the seat belts around him so he would not tumble during the ride. Comfort was not a priority; security was. Knox double-checked the restraints, making sure everything was tight, then closed the door with a solid thud.

Knox then settled into the driver's seat, closing the nearside door behind him. He glanced once more in the rear-view mirror, ensuring everything was as it should be, then released the handbrake with a definite click. His foot pressed firmly on the accelerator, and the BMW responded at once, gliding forward into the obscurity of the night.

As he drove, Knox skimmed the display screen, searching for the map feature. Once he found it, he scrolled through the past destinations. Locating the right one, he set it as his target, and the screen mapped out his route. Knox continued by tapping a second icon on the touchscreen, a green square with a white phone receiver, and used the keypad to dial 999. He reported the break-in at George's house and the injured gang members, making sure to cover all bases, in case the neighbours had hesitated to make the call themselves.

The drive to the destination was short and uneventful. The lock-up was a nondescript building situated just off the main road, isolated and quiet, away from prying eyes. As Knox parked, he could hear faint banging from the boot, a reminder that Ronny remained inside. He chose to ignore it for the moment, his focus on the task at hand. Knox stepped out of the car and headed toward the lock-up.

Knox pressed the button on the key fob, making the garage door of the lock-up rumble open, revealing the dark interior that soon exposed the unsavoury secrets of a criminal empire. The cramped space was filled with a trove of contraband: shelves were laden with drugs, the air thick with their chemical scent. Equipment likely stolen from countless unknown victims lay stacked haphazardly against the walls, and racks of counterfeit designer merchandise gave the place the garish look of a rogue's market.

In the midst of the chaos, a solitary box sat on a battered table, its contents spilling over with wads of cash, presumably the gang's recent spoils, hastily left as Knox's orchestrated diversion had lured them away. Knox's eyes lingered on the money for a moment before he methodically began pocketing the notes.

Turning his attention to the unconscious Tommy in the back seat, Knox gripped him by the arms, dragging him across the cold concrete floor with a resolute tug. He positioned Tommy next to a table cluttered with more incriminating evidence, including a bag of white powder perched on top. With a firm push, Knox propped Tommy against an old chair, watching as the youth's head lolled forward, lifeless in unconsciousness. As Tommy's head hit the table, a cloud of white powder erupted into the air, particles dancing in the beam of a solitary light bulb overhead, casting ghostly shadows on the walls.

Knox stepped back, surveying the scene with satisfaction. Now for the final touch.

Henry walked back to the car, his footsteps echoing slightly in the quiet of the deserted area. He pressed the button to unlock the boot, bracing himself for what might follow. As the lid swung open, he was met with a scene of unexpected chaos. Ronny had not stayed idle. The back seat was shredded by his desperation and fingernails, torn leather, wood, and foam revealing the man's frantic attempt to escape or produce a weapon.

As soon as the boot swung open, Ronny lunged forward, his fear and fury boiling over. His hands shot out, desperate to clamp around Knox's throat in a final effort to overpower him.

But Knox was ready.

He knocked the grasping hands aside and, without

hesitation, delivered a crushing blow with the heel of his hand into Ronny's face. The strike was overwhelming; if Ronny's nose had not already been broken, it certainly was now. The unmistakable crack of bone and flesh echoed through the night like a shot, the violent sound slicing through the stillness.

Ronny's momentum and the force of the punch sent him reeling backward, his body going limp as he lost consciousness mid-lunge. He collapsed back into the boot, a heap of defeated muscle and malice.

Knox gripped Ronny by the ankles, dragging the unconscious man out of the boot and across the dirt-streaked floor. His body scraped lifelessly behind him as Knox reached a large crate, its contents hidden beneath a loose tarp but obviously part of the drug cache. Knox grabbed a bungee rope coiled nearby and swiftly wrapped it around Ronny's wrists, securing him to the crate. The binding was firm, ensuring there was no chance for Ronny to escape once he woke up.

After ensuring Ronny was fully immobilised, Knox returned to the sleek interior of the BMW. He leaned over to the integrated display screen and dialled 999 once more, where he reported the sounds of gun fire at a lock up before leaving the line open so the dispatcher could hear the ambient sounds of the lock-up: distant traffic, the soft groaning of the restrained Ronny.

Using a rag from the car, Knox wiped the vehicle down, ensuring the screen, steering wheel, and any surfaces he had touched were clean. He pocketed the rag and left the car, distancing himself from the direct chaos he had orchestrated. Looking back, the lock-up glowed with security spotlights, illuminating the scene with an intensity that reminded him of Blackpool illuminations.

Finding a spot in the shadow of a narrow back street, where he felt most at ease, Knox maintained a clear view of the lock-up. A blend of satisfaction and anticipation brewed within him, knowing the police were only minutes away. He had set the scene meticulously, almost theatrically, to get exactly the attention he sought, ensuring the final act played out as he imagined.

Suddenly, the night air was punctuated by the distant wail of sirens, growing louder, the sure sign of the police's imminent arrival. Soon, the blue flashing lights of four police cars cut through the darkness, converging on the lock-up.

The officers spilled from their vehicles, moving swiftly. They approached the open garage, where Ronny lay unconscious, tethered by bungee ropes before a pile of stolen paraphernalia. Tommy was also quickly found, slumped and unresponsive, covered in white powder and surrounded by bags of drugs.

Knox could not help but smile faintly from his vantage point. The police arrival, their quick action, and the abundance of evidence laid out so clearly must have felt like a windfall for them, a criminal jackpot unwrapped in the early hours of the morning. Christmas had come early, if only by a couple of days.

Within minutes, the area was alive with more police units. It felt as though half of Greater Manchester Police had descended upon the lock-up. Officers moved in and out of the illuminated garage, faces bright with smirks as they recorded evidence and coordinated efforts, each eager to participate. They seemed aware of the massive impact their find would have.

With the scene now awash with police, Knox slipped back to where he had parked his Land Rover, concealed in the shadows. Removing the tarp that hid his vehicle, he packed it away. He opened the driver's door, feeling just how old the Land Rover was compared to the BMW, and reached into the central cup holder for his phone.

The screen lit up, displaying numerous missed calls, all from Catheryn, his estranged wife.

Puzzled, Knox hovered his finger over the callback icon, then swiped the notifications away and dialled George's number. After a few rings, George answered in a cautious but relieved voice.

"Hi George, can you meet me at your house? We're all done here," Knox said, his voice carrying quiet assurance.

Minutes later, George stepped out from a neighbour's house, his pace hesitant as he approached Knox. The front street was teeming with police officers and ambulances, chaos abounding. Yet across all that carnage, George smiled at Henry, relief and gratitude lighting his face, clearly showing that he had witnessed everything.

"Your problem is sorted," Knox greeted him briskly, sparing details. "They won't bother you again. But I'd suggest finding a safer place to stay for a while."

George glanced sadly at his home, his eyes clouding with emotion. "It was the only house we ever owned, me and my wife," he murmured, the weight of memory apparent in his tone.

Knox nodded sympathetically. "The police found the stash of stolen goods. Hopefully, your belongings are among them. It might take a while, but with luck, you'll be reunited with what they stole."

A flicker of hope lit George's eyes as he thought about possibly recovering his wife's jewellery. "Oh, my wife Gina would be pleased to have her things back. Have you seen her?" he asked, his voice laced with a mix of hope and confusion as he surveyed the street, looking for her.

Knox offered a sad, knowing smile, choosing his words carefully to avoid more painful truths. "This might come in handy," he said, handing George a stack of banknotes.

"There should be enough here for you to move to Canada and stay with your daughter for a while."

Gripping the money, George's eyes glistened with tears. "Lila would love that," he whispered, overwhelmed by the gesture and the prospect of safety.

"Stay somewhere safe tonight and enjoy the money," Knox advised, giving George a final pat on the shoulder. Then, turning, he walked back to his vehicle, leaving the night's turmoil behind him.

Knox felt his phone buzzing in his pocket. He glanced at the screen, which displayed a bright message against the darkness. "We need to talk. I'm on my way back to the U.K. today, call me back." The message was from Catheryn. His stomach lurched. She had been silent for weeks. Why was she suddenly returning to Britain? Knox puzzled over the text, before switching the screen off and sliding the phone back into his pocket. That was another problem for another day.

CHAPTER FOUR

Henry Knox sat alone in a corner booth of a greasy spoon cafe, tucked away on a slip road along a busy A road in rural Lancashire. The diner was a relic of another time, an American diner style from the 1950s set with a quintessential British edge that was resistant to time and change. The wallpaper was stained yellow from years of absorbed cigarette smoke, and the fluorescent lights above buzzed incessantly with the monotonous drone of neglect. The tables, covered in chequered red and white cloth, still held old cigarette ashtrays, even though smoking had been banned indoors for years.

The air inside was thick and heavy with the smell of burnt toast and sizzling bacon, mingling with the less appetising odour of damp that seemed to seep up through the worn floorboards. Outside, rain pattered against the windows, turning the view of the rolling hills and scattered trees into a watercolour of blurred greens and greys, all beneath a sky heavy with spitting dark clouds.

At forty-five, Henry's face told the story of his life, every line and scar carved by years of military service and the endless days spent chasing shadows as a private investigator. He rubbed his eyes, gritty with fatigue, the weight of sleepless nights settling behind them. His blue eyes, sharp and unwavering, carried the keen awareness of a man who had seen too much and forgotten nothing. Once thick with life, his chestnut brown hair had faded to a salt-and-pepper hue, retreating with time from his forehead. His hands, rough and calloused from years of hard-earned experience, traced the deep grooves etched into his skin, a record of battles fought both in distant deserts and in the quiet, relentless wars waged within his own mind.

His build was still solid, his shoulders broad and his arms muscled from a regimen that did not end when he left the British Army's police force, the Royal Military Police. He wore a dark-coloured leather jacket that had seen better days, its surface scarred and worn but more dignified for it. Underneath, a worn, dark shirt with AC/DC emblazoned on the front stretched slightly across his bulky chest.

On his wrist was a G1098 watch, a simple military-style black round-faced watch, no frills, with a Royal Military Police Corps colour wristband, a memento from his service days, one that he had conveniently forgotten to return to stores at the end of his service. A worn gold band adorned the wedding finger of his left hand.

The cafe was sparsely populated, a soft stillness hanging in the air. Behind the counter, a chef and a waitress moved lazily, their pace dictated by the quiet lull of a slow morning. In the corner, an old man sat, as he did every day, never ordering a thing. Henry suspected the old man had very little money and that he came here for dry warmth and not for food and coffee.

Henry had chosen a corner booth deliberately; he always selected a place where he could see the entire room, including all the exits. Even in such a benign environment, he wanted to be ready. His eyes, sharp and vigilant, scanned the room regularly, noting everyone present and anyone who entered. This vigilance was almost subconscious, a habit ingrained from years of military service, one that he could never quite shake.

Henry was sorting through the stack of letters and envelopes he had picked up from his P.O. box, a predictable wad of bills and a few gaudy advertisements, exactly what Knox had been expecting but with one exception: a heavier, cream-coloured envelope that stood out from the mundane collection. Using the butter knife from the neatly placed cutlery in front of him, he slit open the envelope and then placed the knife aside neatly. He then lifted the oversized mug of tea, tasting its warm sweetness that was so excessive it bordered on being as thick as treacle syrup, enough to make a spoon stand upright in it.

He placed the cup back on the table and investigated the envelope's contents by removing a thick, creamy off-white folded piece of paper. He opened the document to find a funeral invitation, printed with hard black lettering pressed deeply into the textured paper. The subdued and smartly presented design contrasted sharply with the colourful diner placemats that advertised the full English breakfast he had ordered but had left untouched in front of him. The juxtaposition was jarring, a funeral invitation amid the mundanity of cafe life, immediately dragging Henry's emotions down, his heart sinking.

The card invited him to the funeral of Mr. Michael Henley, a name that brought a flood of memories, both good and bad. Michael had been a friend, someone Henry had shared the burden of the military covenant with. They had worked together on numerous postings and operational tours. His death was unexpected.

Their friendship had waned, as was common in military circles, after their service. The last Henry had heard, Michael had fallen deep into the world of conspiracy theories: tales of government spies, artificial intelligence gone rogue, and aliens hiding in plain sight.

Knox only dealt with facts and truths, not the made-up tabloid stories that littered social media platforms and convinced those of a certain persuadable mindset that the world was out to get them. Of course, Knox knew that the world was out to get them, just maybe not in the same way they assumed.

Curious and concerned, Henry removed his laptop from a bag near his feet and flipped open the screen, its exterior surface worn but still serviceable, much like Knox. He connected to the diner's spotty Wi-Fi, the connection icon flickering uncertainty before stabilising. He began searching for any information about Michael.

Henry first checked Michael's social media pages, only to find a chaotic swirl of posts and rants that spiralled into increasing paranoia. The disjointed narrative was filled with cryptic warnings and frantic accusations, each more erratic than the last. There was no mention of illness, only a never-ending stream of posts that would have any outsider labelling him a madman, especially if they did not know him better.

Knox leaned back in his chair, which creaked under his weight, his mind piecing together the disjointed information. Michael's descent into conspiracy theories contrasted sharply with the disciplined, rational man he once knew. Henry suspected Michael had never adjusted properly to leaving the forces. Knox had been lucky in his own transition, but many were not, and maybe Michael had not been able to cope.

Knox leaned forward again, his mind now active and probing. Even if Michael was struggling, he was still too young to have passed away. The circumstances surrounding his death demanded closer scrutiny.

Switching tabs, Henry searched for Michael's local newspaper. A West Yorkshire news site popped up, and he quickly scanned the headlines until he found the brief, clinical report about Michael's death, which had been announced as a suicide. The article stated that Michael Henley, a former Royal Military Police officer, had been found dead in his vehicle, which was parked in his garage, from apparent carbon monoxide poisoning. It was the standard explanation for a tragic end, tied up neatly with a mention of PTSD, the usual go-to explanation for former soldiers who died in similar circumstances.

Knox's thoughts strayed away from Michael and instead to his wife, Catheryn. Had she heard of Michael's death? Maybe that was why she was coming back to the UK, he pondered. Once upon a time, she would have been right beside him, sharing the burden of such a loss. Now, she was little more than a shadow in his life, lingering but never reaching him.

Henry's focus shifted to his phone on the table, its screen dark yet full of unreturned calls from Catheryn. She had been trying to reach him since the day before, but he did not want another argument. He pictured Sophie, his daughter, living in Cyprus with Catheryn. They had shared many strained phone calls, and he was never sure if Sophie heard all the tension. Had Catheryn come back to the UK alone, or had she brought Sophie along? Henry wanted desperately to see his daughter, but part of him recoiled from whatever confrontation might be waiting with his wife.

Then he pushed that thought away. He doubted she was home for him or Michael and dismissed the image of his wife from his mind. He rubbed his temples, feeling the weight of the last few days. Yesterday he had been knee-deep in a gang problem; today he held a funeral invitation for a friend who deserved answers.

As the rain outside grew heavier, tapping out a relentless pattern against the roof, Henry's thoughts grew more intense. His first inclination was to return home, pack a suit, clear his schedule, and get ready for the funeral. But a nagging feeling gnawed at him, something that did not sit right. The straightforward narrative of Michael's death clashed with the man Henry had known and the complexities of his recent life.

Something about this entire situation felt wrong, and Henry felt compelled to uncover the truth, to look beyond the convenient explanations and see what lay beneath.

Henry closed his laptop with a sharp snap that reverberated in the nearly empty diner. He shoved it back into his rugged bag, edges worn and frayed from years of being slung over chairs and opened in unsavoury locations. He took one last gulp of tea, the cloying sweetness sticking to the back of his throat, then stood up.

He walked over to the counter. "Sorry, I have to rush, I have no time for breakfast," he said, placing a couple of five-pound notes on the countertop next to the till. "Give it to him," he added, jerking his thumb toward the only other occupant in the cafe, the dishevelled man in the opposite corner. The man immediately sat up straighter, eyes widening with excitement. He picked up his knife and fork in anticipation, the promise of a hot meal brightening his weary face.

Knox offered a brief nod to the waitress and turned to the door. The exchange was quick, almost perfunctory, but it left a faint sense of satisfaction amid the growing unease in his mind. The door shut behind him with a jingle of the bell, and he stood under the small wooden canopy covering the cafe entrance. He lifted the collar of his leather jacket against his neck and hunched his shoulders, bracing against the cold and the rain that whipped around him.

His Land Rover was parked in the grey stone-laden car park in front of the cafe, looking as weather-beaten as Knox felt. He reached it in a few quick strides, the rain stinging his face and hands. Inside, the wipers squeaked in protest as he turned the ignition, battling the downpour that had turned the outside world into a blur of water and grey clouds.

CHAPTER FIVE

The drive to Michael's place in West Yorkshire was a quiet one, filled only with the heavy hum and rattle of the engine and the steady beat of rain against the windscreen. The morning roads had very little traffic, which allowed Henry's mind to race away as he navigated the familiar border roads between Lancashire and Yorkshire.

Michael had always been intense, a man of action. He was certainly a bit of a loner in later years, but suicidal? It did not fit. The Michael Knox remembered was more likely to charge headfirst into a fight than surrender to his demons. The thought gnawed at him, a persistent doubt that refused to be silenced by the rhythmic thrum of the rain.

The newspaper article had mentioned Michael's home address, and Knox used his mobile phone as a navigation tool to find the exact location. Pulling up to Michael's house felt like stepping into a forgotten story, one that ended abruptly with too many questions left unanswered. The property was a secluded bungalow, tucked away behind a cluster of overgrown hedges and a rusty gate that hung slightly askew. The house itself was a mirror of Michael's recent life: wild, untamed, and unwelcoming.

A narrow tarmac drive led to a garage on the right-hand side of the property. Blue and white police tape, once pulled taut across the entrance posts, now flapped in the wind, torn and tattered. Its frayed edges fluttered in the cold, wet morning air. Knox's gaze lingered on that small garage, where the grim scene had unfolded days earlier. The image of Michael, a man once so full of life and determination, succumbing to such a tragic end was hard to accept.

Knox shook off the dark thoughts and refocused on the task at hand. He needed to get inside, to look for anything that could explain the incongruity between Michael's supposed suicide and the man Henry remembered. The answers had to be somewhere within those walls.

Henry killed the engine of his Land Rover and sat for a moment, collecting his thoughts, and planning his next steps as the rain hammered heavily on the metal roof. He steeled himself for what he might uncover.

He stepped out of the vehicle into the looming shadow of the house, its windows dark, the front door standing as a guardian to whatever secrets lay beyond. He approached the entrance cautiously, his senses sharp and alert. He tried the door; it was locked, unsurprisingly.

Henry began a slow circuit of the house, looking for any visible or invisible weak points. He scanned every corner, every crevice. One of the main windows caught his attention: the curtains had not been fully drawn, leaving a narrow gap through which he could peer inside.

Using the light from his phone, Knox illuminated the interior of the living room. The beam cut through the darkness, revealing a room that felt stale, heavy with dust and neglect. Papers and books were piled high in every corner, the walls plastered with maps and notes scribbled in a frenzied hand. The scene was chaotic, a physical manifestation of Michael's tormented mind, far removed from the disciplined soldier Knox had once known.

As he peered deeper, Henry's mind filled with questions. Something here did not add up, and he was determined to find out what it was. He angled his torch slowly through the narrow opening, taking in every detail, searching for any clue that might explain the troubling contrast between the official story and the man he remembered.

Even if the situation felt off, Knox knew he was not about to barge into his dead friend's house. Something was wrong, but Knox could not pinpoint it just yet. Breaking into the home of a recently deceased soldier would not look good, no matter his intentions. The last thing he needed was to get caught in a legal bind, especially when he was still piecing together the truth.

Reluctantly, Knox walked back to his vehicle. Just then his phone buzzed again, another missed call from Catheryn. After weeks of silence, she was suddenly reaching out, and the timing felt all wrong. Then again, nothing had felt right with Catheryn for a long time. But this? The timing felt especially off.

He opened the door of his Land Rover and sat in the driver's seat, the rain continuing its relentless assault on the roof. He shook himself free of the water that had seeped into every crevice of his clothing and reached into his laptop bag, pulling out the funeral invitation and examining it once more. "Blake Funeral Home" was printed in small, dark letters at the base of the cream card. It was worth a try. The place that now housed Michael might hold the next clue Knox needed.

Henry keyed the funeral home into his phone's web browser, and directions appeared on the screen. He placed the phone back in its cradle, which was stuck to the windscreen of the Land Rover, and it began barking orders. Knox started the vehicle again and drove the short distance to the location highlighted on the digital map.

The funeral home was a cold, stone-fronted, two-storey building. The stone looked like it was locally quarried and had been stained black from years of pollution, either from the hundreds of nearby factory chimneys or from the exhaust pipes of thousands of vehicles that had travelled the main road in front of the building. Knox did not know which.

Black window frames surrounded transparent glass panes, with net curtains peeking through, adding an unsettling touch of domesticity to the otherwise morbid facade. "Blake Funeral Home" was written in huge white script on a black background, hanging prominently above the doorframe.

Knox walked through the front entrance into the main reception room, where a frumpy woman in black attire sat behind a large, deep dark oak desk. She smiled, professional yet warm. "How may I help you?" she inquired politely.

"I am here to see Michael Henley. I am a long-time friend," Knox replied, his voice steady.

The lady patiently waited for more information.

He had used this technique many times during his years as an investigator in the Military Police. Leave silence hanging; let the awkward tension do the work. People hated a void, so they filled it, often betraying more than they intended.

The trick was simple. Stay silent, stay calm, and let the tension do the rest. Knox had seen it work repeatedly. A suspect might trip over their story or share something they did not mean to. Lies were fragile, and silence had a way of breaking them.

Knox smiled weakly. "We were in the military together," he said.

The lady, now satisfied, nodded understandingly and stood, gesturing for him to follow. She led him into an adjoining room that was dimly lit. The air was thick with the scent of incense, likely meant to mask the more unpleasant smells associated with a funeral home. The room was small but tidy, with simple grey wallpaper on the walls and a single seat in the corner. The dominant object in the room was a dark coffin, resting horizontally on a set of pine wood legs. The rest of the space was sterile, devoid of any religious iconography, adding to the sense of quiet finality.

Knox's eyes were drawn to the coffin, the reality of Michael's death hitting him with a fresh wave of sorrow.

Knox peered into the coffin, his breath catching slightly at the sight. Laid out was a thin, large-headed man whose features were unmistakably Michael's, though thinner and greyer than Henry remembered. Five medals adorned his chest, their coloured ribbons and shiny medals which looked like coins, offerings to pay Charon, the Ferryman to carry his soul across the river Styx. The medal were in order or achievement for operational tours, Kosovo, Iraq, and Afghanistan, with the last two medals considered gizzits, both being jubilee medals.

Henry's gaze moved over Michael's body, noting the clean, recently cut fingernails, the absence of abrasions on his knuckles, and no cuts to his face, no bruising. Visually, there was little wrong with Michael, apart from the glaring fact that he was dead.

For a moment, Knox considered that he was searching for something to prove his suspicion. He had seen it before, someone gets an idea that something is wrong and pursues that thought to the ends of the earth, regardless of evidence. He breathed out slowly, reconsidering his perception. Perhaps Michael had indeed taken his own life. Maybe he had become so entangled in his own conspiracies that he saw no way out. Maybe Knox should just accept it and prepare to bury his friend.

He turned from the coffin, his eyes wet but tears held back, a tightness in his chest that he tried to shrug off with a deep breath, reaching out for the door handle and leaving Michael to continue his onward journey alone.

As he left the room, his mind anywhere but where his feet were automatically guiding him, he almost collided with a young woman in her early twenties.

CHAPTER SIX

Sarah recognised Knox instantly, her mind instantaneously catapulted twenty or so years backwards. Back then, Henry was a fresh-faced young man, who had stepped into their home to babysit her and her younger sister, Jess. She remembered the thrill of his visits, he would always bring with him the latest games console and games, transforming their living room into a place of excitement and adventure. She fondly remembered the sounds of laughter and playful competition that filled the house, while her parents enjoyed the trappings of a Friday night in Northern Germany.

Henry, however, took a moment longer to place her. The years had transformed Sarah into a striking young woman, her features matured, her stature taller. The girl he remembered had grown into someone altogether different. Startled, Henry mumbled an apology, his mind momentarily disoriented from its darker contemplations. But when Sarah gave him a weak smile, the years fell away. Recognition dawned in his eyes as he saw the little girl she once was behind her grown-up facade.

Henry, taken aback, found his voice. "Sarah?" he asked, a mixture of surprise and warmth colouring his tone. He had not expected to see a familiar face here, although he mentally chided himself for not considering it at all.

The soft murmur of mourners emanated from the surrounding rooms, but the sound faded into the background as Henry and Sarah, separated by many long years, reconnected. In that brief moment, a glimmer of joy emerged amidst the sorrow, a small light cutting through the heavy, gloomy atmosphere of the funeral home.

Sarah was a slight, thin woman, standing about five feet six, although her high heels added a few extra inches to her height, a touch she enjoyed. That day, she was dressed entirely in black — a pencil skirt that draped elegantly below her knees, and a large coat still speckled with raindrops from her journey to the funeral home. She clutched a black umbrella, its wet fabric glistening under the dim lights. The attire matched her mood perfectly and reflected the heaviness in her heart.

Both Henry and Sarah simultaneously blurted out questions at each other, their words tumbling over each other in a chaotic rush.

"How are you?"

"What have you been up to?"

"How long has it been?"

Their synchronous inquiries collided, leaving both of them momentarily silenced, with a faint awkwardness settling between them. Sarah shifted on her feet, tucking a strand of hair behind her ear, her eyes darting briefly toward the polished mahogany caskets lining the walls.

Henry cleared his throat, suddenly aware of the loudness of their chatter cutting through the silence and stillness of the funeral home.

"Maybe we should talk outside?" Henry offered, his voice lowering instinctively. His tone carried a subtle edge of guilt, as though their intrusion on this solemn ground had become something profane.

Sarah nodded quickly, her face tinged with a flicker of embarrassment. She glanced at the numerous adjoining rooms, imagining a grieving family in each, disturbed by the joyful chatter outside.

"Yeah of course, let's," she said softly, her gaze

meeting Henry's.

They walked outside side by side, the air fresh with the scent of rain. Finding a wooden bench across the road from the funeral home, they sat down, their eyes naturally drifting back to the dark, sad building opposite them. The rain had ceased, and the sky, though still grey, seemed a shade brighter.

Sarah's delight upon seeing Henry was evident. He had been the brotherly figure she had longed for during her formative years, a role cruelly taken away by the sudden upheaval of a posting order that so often defined military life.

For Henry, seeing a familiar face amidst the chaos of recent events felt like a breath of normality. In a world that had shifted so much, this reunion felt like a port in a storm.

They caught up quickly, their conversation flowing effortlessly, as if the years between their last meeting had been but a fleeting moment. Yet, beneath the surface of their cheerful reunion, both were keenly aware of the elephant in the room: the reason they were on a park bench outside Blake Funeral Home, the painful occasion that had brought them back together.

Henry finally decided to grasp the nettle. With his head held low, he asked quietly, "Can you tell me what happened with your dad, please?"

Sarah stopped smiling and her gaze dropped to the wet ground. She forced a breath through her nose, grief pressing heavily on her chest. "He was different from when you knew him. He had changed from being the life and soul of a party to.... well, I don't know, someone else...." Her voice trailed off.

Knox waited patiently for Sarah to continue.

"He had started to believe in some crazy stuff. He tried talking to me about it, but often it didn't make any sense." She paused, catching her breath, "But last week," Sarah said, her voice breaking slightly, "he found something. He seemed to be back to his old self again, almost normal. I felt like I had my old dad again. He seemed reinvigorated, almost happy. He said he felt that things had finally made sense." She paused, the memory of his renewed energy clashing with the stark reality of his absence. "Then the next thing I know, he was gone."

That last sentence was spoken so softly, as if saying the words made them true, even if she already knew they were. The grief in her voice rasped, tears clawed at her eyes, a raw wound that had yet to begin healing.

"His last words to me were that he had something important a friend had given him, something that would prove he wasn't mad."

Henry sat for a while in silence, taking in Sarah's story, her truth. He did not want to voice his suspicion that Michael had lost his grip on reality, spiralling into a world of far-fetched theories. Even though Sarah had hinted at the same. He could not find the right way to say it; he could not be so blunt, not to a daughter grieving her father.

Then, Sarah inserted herself into the stony silence, "He didn't kill himself, I am sure of it. He did many outlandish things, but I don't believe he would ever do that."

Henry looked at her, seeing the determination in her eyes. She was resolute, convinced of her father's innocence in his own death. It matched the doubts swirling in Henry's own mind, giving him a strange sense of validation.

Around them, the world carried on obliviously, the sound of traffic passing by, the shuffle of feet from other mourners heading inside. Sarah straightened in her seat, the weight of memory stretching her expression into a tight mask of sorrow.

There was something about Knox's presence that made Sarah feel steady again, as if the ground had stopped shifting beneath her for the first time in weeks. It was not simply an old friendship, but familiarity, the feeling of homecoming after years adrift. The idea of Henry had once been her shield, her sword, her comfort, whether he realised it or not. She felt safe in his company and felt emboldened just knowing him. Fantasising that he would come to her rescue when things got bad.

Now, as she sat beside him again, that same comfort enveloped her, guiding her through the turmoil she could barely withstand.

For Knox, the feeling was simpler yet no less profound. Sarah was not just Michael's daughter, she was family, a younger sister in every sense that mattered. When Sarah was little, Henry had vowed to be there for her. That promise he had broken many times over the years. Now, with the world spinning in chaos, his purpose felt painfully clear. He had let Michael and Sarah down before, but this time he would honour that vow, no matter the cost. He would shield her from the coming danger, protect her, carry her if need be. Not just for her sake, but for her father's too.

Then a realisation slammed into Knox like a physical blow: Michael did not have one daughter, he had two. Sarah and Jess.

The thought blindsided Knox, slicing through him: Jess. He had not even asked about her. Guilt tore at him, memories of Jess surfaced unbidden. She had been so little the last time he saw her, barely old enough to talk, let alone leave a lasting impression on someone outside her immediate family. But she did. Sarah, loud and energetic, demanded attention, while Knox had been more than happy to give it. Jess, though, was different.

Quiet, still. She was always watching from the sidelines, wide-eyed, clutching a favourite toy. She never cried, never called out. But she was always there, a calm, steady presence Knox never appreciated enough at the time.

But Jess would not be a toddler anymore; she was an adult, with a life and struggles he had not bothered to ask about. She mattered, just as much as Sarah, just as much as Michael. And he had forgotten to even think of her.

He berated himself silently, realising he should have asked Sarah about Jess, about how the two of them had coped, what had happened since Michael's death. Instead, he had been laser-focused on himself and Michael. The words were on the tip of his tongue, half-formed in his mind: an apology, an acknowledgement of his oversight.

But before he could speak, Sarah broke the silence, her voice shaking with anger and pain.

"He found something," she blurted, anger lacing her words, before her voice turned bitter and venomous. "And they killed him for it."

Henry sighed, feeling foolish for dithering. He rubbed his head, trying to conjure the right words to reason with her. "Your dad..." he began, but his sentence trailed off in the thick gloom of grief, not wanting to be too direct, too hurtful to the daughter who might be clinging to hope.

Sarah spoke to prevent next words, "The police locked his house up after they had conducted their investigation, and I think someone has been inside since. Whatever my dad had, it must still be in there. Maybe they didn't find it the first time."

Henry nodded, "All right," he murmured, half to himself, half to her. "I'll go with you. We can look together."

A flicker of relief passed across Sarah's face as she met Henry's gaze. She was steeled, determined to find the truth. "Yes. Let's go now," she said.

Henry gave a short nod. They rose together and left the bench, the drizzle still hanging in the air, pattering lightly on the pavement. As they walked towards the Funeral Home car park, an unspoken understanding passed between them. They were embarking on a search that might provide closure, answers, or might open more questions. But it was the only path they had.

CHAPTER SEVEN

The drive to Michael's house was mercifully brief, though it did not feel that way to Sarah. The Land Rover's interior was rugged, built for function rather than comfort, and she looked distinctly out of place. Her outfit, smart and carefully chosen, seemed to clash with the vehicle's utilitarian nature. She shifted in her seat repeatedly, trying to find a position that did not dig into her or crease her clothes, her discomfort evident in every movement.

Henry could not help but feel a pang of embarrassment at the stark functionality of his life. The Land Rover, with its rough edges and practicality, seemed to reflect everything he had become efficient, stripped-down, and devoid of the finesse that once softened the edges of his world. That finesse, he realised, had been Catheryn's gift to his life, a touch of grace and elegance that had vanished the moment she walked away.

As they turned the corner onto Michael's street, Sarah sat up and looked at the building through the passenger door window. Its silent facade betrayed none of the chaos hidden inside.

To Henry, the house seemed almost diminished compared to how it had appeared that morning, as though it had withdrawn into itself, reluctant to surrender its secrets.

Still and lifeless, the house was cloaked in a tangle of overgrown greenery, the untrimmed plants reaching out like grasping fingers, giving the place an abandoned, almost haunted feel. Yet, despite the eerie stillness, Henry knew appearances were often deceiving.

Sarah, with a small silver key in her trembling hand, exited the Land Rover and walked to the front door. Knox followed her, a step or two behind. Sarah slotted the key into the keyhole and turned it, and the bolt slid into its housing with a soft, well-oiled click. The door creaked ajar, and they both stepped inside.

On the other side of the door was the living room, where the air was thick with dust and neglect, clinging to the space like a suffocating mist. The interior was a disordered mess of notebooks, newspapers, and rubbish piled high with no discernible pattern. Each step they took disturbed another thick layer of dust, sending motes swirling in the air, illuminated by a shard of light piercing through the same half-drawn curtains that Knox had peered through earlier in the day.

The light sliced through the dimness, casting jagged shadows that shifted and flickered across the cluttered room. The scene was like peering straight into Michael's mind, chaotic and overwhelming. It reflected a scattergun approach to uncover the truth, with thoughts and ideas fired off in every direction, desperate to hit a target. The sheer disorder felt suffocating.

Henry's gaze swept over the chaos, his mind racing, attempting to make sense of the scene. Somewhere in this disarray, he hoped, lay the answers they needed. Or maybe they did not, he was not sure anymore.

On the walls there seemed to be a mass of cork boards, maps, letters, and newspaper cuttings, along with black and white photos of buildings, places, vehicles, and people. Coloured string attempted to tie them together, but gravity had a way of undoing those webs.

The room reeked of age, the air thick with a musty scent that seemed to crawl into Knox's lungs. It was the dry, stale smell of dust and forgotten paper, of old documents and photographs long consigned to shadows. It carried the unmistakable weight of time, of lives lived, secrets buried, and history left to fade. It reminded him of a library deep in disrepair, or the crumbling pages of a book untouched for generations. The smell enveloped him, clinging to his skin and clothes.

The same thoughts flooded both Henry's and Sarah's minds. It was impossible to tell if anyone else had already rifled through the chaotic piles of books, magazines, and papers; the mess was so overwhelming. Yet more daunting still was the question of where to even begin. How would they find the one piece of information Michael had thought was crucial, let alone something worth killing for?

But Henry was nothing if not diligent, and he knew the only way to ensure nothing slipped past him was to check everything meticulously. Starting in the corner of the room, he cleared a small space and began working his way through the piles of rag tabloid newspapers and conspiracy magazines, each colour coded with highlighters, one by one. Sarah helped, piling new material in front of him and discarding the sifted documents into bin bags.

His training at the old RMP Training School in Chichester had taught him how to do a thorough search, and he used those skills now with great effect. He was determined not to miss a thing.

He used his mobile phone to photograph fragments of the information, even then it felt fruitless. What was written was outlandish and bizarre. Incredulous.

Most of the notepads were a scattered mess of scribbled, barely legible content but generally aligned to the newspaper stories. Aliens and conspiracy theories about the late Princess Diana dominated the pages, alongside repeated mentions of the JFK assassination and the moon landings.

After hours of sifting through outlandish theories and disjointed notes, Henry felt mentally drained. Eventually, he managed to clear the living room of its clutter. Sarah, who had been bagging the documents after they were examined and discarded, had hauled the bulging bin bags full of Michael's post-army life's work onto the tarmac drive outside.

Henry stood up, stretching his stiff back, feeling numb. He had discovered nothing of consequence, nothing of importance, nothing noteworthy, and certainly nothing worth killing over. A deep sense of deflation settled over him. Perhaps Michael had taken his own life after all. Maybe they had reached a dead end, and the idea that someone else was responsible for this horrible crime was fading in Henry's mind.

Sarah stepped back into the front room, looking just as drained and broken as Henry felt. He managed a weak attempt at a smile, but it was clear they were both thinking the same thing. With a trace of sarcasm, Sarah muttered, "There are still more to go yet..."

Henry nodded, "I'm going to check the garage." He walked toward the hall that led to the kitchen and the side door, Sarah following him. When he reached the door, his hand rested on the handle for a moment, hesitation flickering across his face. "You don't have to come with me if you'd rather not," he said softly, turning to look at her.

Sarah squared her shoulders. "I'm alright, let's go," she said, her tone resolute.

Henry opened the door and stepped into the dark, musty garage.

He fumbled for the light switch, pressing it. A fluorescent strip overhead sputtered briefly, casting jittery flashes of light before settling into a harsh, sterile glow. A low buzz filled the air, fading into the background.

At the centre of the garage sat a dark blue 1990s-era Volvo, eerily undisturbed. Medical equipment was scattered across the floor, as though dropped and forgotten. The doors of the car were dusted with white fingerprint powder, but besides that, it appeared that little crime scene work had been done. A pipe trailed from the exhaust into the car's rear window, a grim and unmistakable reminder of the reported cause of death.

In Henry's mind, the scene seemed like a textbook suicide. He dropped into a push-up position, eyes sweeping the area beneath the car, but nothing suspicious appeared. Rising to his feet, he took out a pair of latex gloves from his back pocket and slipped them on. He opened the passenger door and leaned inside.

White fingerprint dust speckled the dashboard and steering wheel, signs of the police's superficial investigation. It was the sort of half measure that suggested they had accepted the scene at face value, seeing no reason to look deeper.

The driver's seat had been pushed all the way back, the passenger seat forward. Henry checked the seat fabric, running his fingers gently over it, then slid it back and checked underneath. Unlike the disarray in the house, the car's interior was strangely clean and neat.

Knox opened the bonnet and boot, methodically checking every part of the vehicle, but uncovered nothing. He shook his head, frustrated. If the police had dusted for prints and discovered nothing, and he too could find no sign of foul play, it strongly suggested that no one else was involved.

Henry glanced over at Sarah, whose disappointment matched his own. He shrugged, raising empty hands to demonstrate he had found nothing.

Sarah shook her head, her voice edged with exasperation. "No, it's here, or someone's taken it."

Henry slipped off his gloves, rolling them up and discarding them in the bin.

While Sarah continued scanning and photographing the garage, Henry sat on a small step, staring at the car. His mind revisited the bleak scenario of Michael feeding a pipe from the exhaust, sitting behind the wheel, turning the ignition. Henry hoped at least that it had been quick and painless. But the more he thought about it, the more he accepted it. Every detail pointed to an inescapable conclusion, the same one the police had reached: Michael had killed himself.

Suddenly, metal scraped against metal, shocking Henry out of his thoughts. He turned to see Sarah opening the top drawer of a large filing cabinet with vertical suspension files. She flicked through documents with a rushed determination, the flash on her camera firing repeatedly, before slamming the drawer shut with a loud clang. She repeated the process with the next drawer, and the next, until she had checked them all.

The entire back wall was lined with filing cabinets, triggering memories for Henry of the Platoon Offices in the RMP, each one holding section casefiles, evidence, individual post, as well as stashes of coffee, tea and sugar.

"Nothing," Sarah whispered, disappointment heavy in her voice as she slammed the last drawer closed.

"Alright," Knox replied quietly. "It's time to call it a day. I need a hotel, and maybe a strong drink." He stood, giving the Volvo another quick look before heading back inside. Navigating the hallway, he paused by the bedroom. The place was equally disorganised, documents everywhere, only a thin strip of bed left uncovered. Knox noticed there was no TV or radio.

"Sarah," Knox called, his voice echoing in the silence. "Did your dad have a laptop?"

"No," she replied, stepping into view. "He thought it could be tracked, so he didn't even use a mobile."

Knox raised an eyebrow. "So how did he do all his research?" he queried.

Sarah shrugged, a small sad smile on her face. "He went to the library and used their PCs."

Knox nodded, glancing again at the unkempt bedroom. "Got it. Right, I'll clear this room, then I'm off to find a hotel, and a decent pint," he said, eyeing the piles of papers.

Sarah just nodded, looking lost in her own thoughts. Together, they cleared the last of the clutter. In far less time than the living room had taken, the floor was now visible. Sarah made the bed. The house was finally searched from top to bottom, but all they had found were conspiracy newspapers and magazines with cryptic scribblings in notebooks, and no evidence whatsoever that pointed to murder or a cover-up.

"Okay," Knox finally sighed, accepting defeat. "I'm going to find a local hotel. And I still need a suit for the funeral tomorrow."

Sarah let out a long, resigned breath, her shoulders slumping. After a moment, she nodded wordlessly, her gaze down. They left the property together, the door clicking shut behind them. Tension and unease lingered in the air.

She locked the front door, then joined Henry at the Land Rover. Passing by the mounds of black bin bags on the driveway, the debris from an exhausting day, she said quietly, "I'll get rid of these later. That feels like a bonfire and whiskey kind of night."

Knox climbed into the driver's seat, adjusting the rear-view mirror to look at himself. He caught a glimpse of his own tired eyes before he turned the key, the engine rumbling to life. Sarah slipped in beside him, giving directions softly as Knox drove the dimly lit streets.

When he dropped her off, he called up his phone to search for a nearby hotel, his mind drifting away from the day's labours. A short time later, he checked into the closest one and grabbed a small kit bag from the Land Rover's side bin, hauling it into his room. He laid out his clothes for the next day, though they were not funeral-appropriate, but they would be at least clean on, allowing him to drive and buy a suit. And he had his own toiletries.

He lay on the bed, feeling the weight of the day's search behind him, and he fell asleep within moments.

CHAPTER EIGHT

The next morning, Knox awoke early, his mind still sifting through the mountain of useless information he had gathered the day before. A night's rest had given him time to process it all, but none of it seemed important or credible enough to explain why Michael could have been murdered. Knox reached for his phone, no messages. He took a shower, but an insistent feeling tugged at him, as though something crucial had been overlooked.

Dressing in his spare clothes that he had taken from his Land Rover the night before, a pair of washed-out jeans and a grey hoodie, Knox replayed the events and the crime scene in his mind. Despite his thorough search, nothing had emerged as a clear lead. It left him with two unsettling possibilities: either it was the work of professionals who had taken what they needed, or Michael had truly done this to himself. Both outcomes bothered him and gnawed at his consciousness, casting a shadow over his thoughts as he prepared for the day ahead.

Within half an hour, Knox was seated in the hotel restaurant, finishing a breakfast that twenty-four hours earlier had eluded him. He held his cup of tea containing three large dollops of sugar, staring into it as if the answers might somehow reflect from its surface. Yet something nagged at him, a faint but persistent sense that he had missed something crucial. There was not time to dwell on it, because today was Michael's funeral, and he needed to get a suit.

His next stop was a nearby supermarket, where he purchased a black suit, a white shirt, and a tie. Knox usually packed for various situations, but a funeral had not been on his radar when loading up the Land Rover. He had briefly considered driving back to Lancashire to retrieve his suit from the dry cleaners, but the thought reminded him too starkly of what else he had left behind. His medals and beret were buried somewhere in the MFO boxes he had stored after his marriage fell apart, so he dismissed that option. A cheap suit would have to do.

After paying for the clothes, he found a discreet spot in the car park and used the side of the Land Rover for cover while he changed.

Knox pulled the suit from its hanger, his mind drifting to Catheryn. She used to fuss over his suits, making sure every detail was perfect, turning him into someone out of a magazine. That was before she moved to Cyprus, before the silence between them grew wider than the miles. Now, each suit he bought served as another reminder of how much life had changed. He doubted she even knew about Michael's death. Even if she did, he was not certain she would care.

Knox adjusted the tie around his neck, his fingers fumbling slightly as he studied his reflection in the wing mirror. The face staring back at him appeared unpolished, a man out of sync with the occasion. He tugged on his well-worn Alt Berg boots, their slightly bulled polish catching the dull light. They carried the wear and comfort of countless miles but were nothing like the pristine, patent-leather shoes other mourners would be wearing.

He straightened, taking in his reflection: a mismatched ensemble of an ill-fitting suit, no medals, no head-dress, and boots instead of dress shoes. It was hardly ideal, far from the sophisticated image he would rather portray at the funeral, but he was there, and that was enough for Knox.

Knox arrived at the cemetery and parked on a side road. Across from the cemetery gates, Blake Funeral Home stood in silent austerity. He imagined the preparations taking place inside, the undertakers and ushers working diligently to ready Michael for his final journey.

Turning into the cemetery, Knox walked slowly down the path towards the small church. The grounds were silent, each step on the pathway magnified in the stillness. It reminded him of old drill parades, the crisp, rhythmic sound of boots on parade squares, a memory etched into him. Yet now the sound felt hollow and haunting in the quiet surroundings of the cemetery.

Knox entered the stone clad church, slipping into a seat on the rearmost pew. He surveyed the mourners, dissecting the ritual with a note of bitterness. Funerals, despite all solemn pretence, were routines, meticulously timed events that did not pause for personal sorrow. A coffin arrived, a family wept, the coffin removed, and the cycle repeated. The funeral directors played their parts, polished, sombre, but Knox saw past the pageantry. He had attended too many funerals to be persuaded by the choreography. There was no real space for sentiment here, only the relentless churn of loss.

He stayed on his own, unnoticed among the crowd. The turnout surprised him, faces he recognised mingling with those he did not. All bound by their connection to Michael.

Sarah caught Knox's eye, but his attention turned to the woman beside her, Jess. She stood near the altar with quiet grace at odds with the deep grief written across her features. Her shoulders trembled slightly, and her face showed the struggle not to be overwhelmed. Knox stayed put, giving her space. Funerals were for family, and though Michael had meant a great deal to him,

Henry knew he was not truly one of them.

Then the organ's note rose, a morose tune filling the vaulted ceilings of the church. It reverberated, swelling in the air. The congregation stood as one, a choreographed motion. Knox stood as well, eyes forward, breath shallow, as if breathing too deeply might break the delicate hush.

The pallbearers came in, wearing their Number 2 dress uniforms, red peaked caps, red armbands with MP in black letters, white gloves, and belts, their faces set with solemnity. The coffin was draped with a British flag. The slow procession down the aisle felt interminable, each footstep accompanied by the organ's toneless drone.

When they reached the front, the pallbearers placed the coffin onto the plinth, and the congregation sat. The wooden pew groaned slightly under Knox's weight. He lowered himself, the cold of the polished wood seeping into his back.

The service was short, too short, finished before it had time to truly begin. Like a door slamming shut on something that had not fully arrived. The harsh, unyielding nature of funerals always left Knox uneasy. The stone floors and echoing walls of a church in December only magnified grief rather than eased it. The padre's homily was efficient, ticking boxes, but Knox sensed the man had not really known Michael. It felt impersonal, mechanical, aimed more at moving on to the next service than truly honouring the one departed.

Knox shifted, discomfort growing with each passing minute. Perhaps it was the service, perhaps his cynicism, but it felt hollow. He had attended too many funerals, laid too many friends to rest. The old, empty promises of God and forgiveness no longer soothed him.

When the service ended, mourners left the church in

a slowly, quietly offering condolences to the family before heading back to the cold December air. Knox remained in his seat, waiting for the crowd to thin. He was not ready to join their shared grief.

He studied them as they passed, scanning each face. Some bore genuine sorrow, etched into their features, while others looked detached, going through the motions. He recognised some of them from shared postings or mutual acquaintances. A loose-knit family bound by service, paying their respects to a fallen comrade.

Eventually, Knox moved to join the final line at the rear. Everywhere he looked he saw the unmistakeable marks of military tradition. Service medals glinted in the cold winter light, immaculate, and red caps stood out like splashes of blood among the black attire.

Knox felt the absence of his own medals and beret like an open wound. That void left him feeling exposed, a man out of uniform, out of place. Yet, it was all so familiar. He had walked this path countless times, burying fellow soldiers lost in the line of duty, or to the quiet battles of civilian life.

The pallbearers began to lower the coffin into the grave with taut bands. Knox recognised the movements, well-drilled. He glanced at them, seeing only young faces who had never met Michael. He gently edged away, giving Sarah and Jess the privacy to grieve as they deserved. Others stepped in to comfort them, closing the gap Henry left.

Suddenly, Henry felt a firm hand on his left shoulder. He turned quickly, heart jolting with old reflexes. He felt his posture snap upright, almost as if a drill instructor had barked an order.

It was Colonel Archibald Gray, technically retired, though he carried himself like an officer still on active duty. Precision exuded from him. His black suit looked more expensive than many cars in the car park, an overcoat cut to fit his wide shoulders. A neat line of miniature medals gleamed on his chest, and a red beret with a cloth cap badge rested in his hands. His shoes were polished to a mirror sheen, reflecting the muted morning light.

"Stand easy, Knox," Gray said, his voice measured. "I'm not your commanding officer these days."

Knox forced his shoulders to relax, realising he had snapped to attention on instinct. He felt slightly foolish. "Sir," he answered before he could stop himself.

Gray gave a detached smile that did not quite reach his eyes. "How have you been, old boy?" he asked.

"I've been better, considering, but I'm still standing," Knox said, his eyes flickering to the coffin resting on the bands.

Gray nodded, scanning the row of headstones. "Yes, life turns quickly sometimes." He paused, then added, "I heard your wife left you. Moved to Cyprus?"

Knox felt the familiar ache. His thumb rolled absently over the gold wedding band on his ring finger. "Yes. She took our daughter. There were friends there from an old posting. We speak a bit, but not much."

By now, the vicar had started the committal, voice quiet and solemn. Knox turned slightly, wanting to pay attention, but Gray stepped closer, posture radiating authority like old times.

"You never answered me about that job," Gray said, his voice low so as not to disturb the brief sermon. "I still need someone who knows how to keep things quiet. The pay is rather good. Better than the scraps you earn trailing unfaithful spouses or missing pets." There was a hint of dry humour in his eyes.

Knox looked down at the cheap suit he wore, tie thin

and shirt rough. "This isn't my usual look," he said. "I wasn't expecting a funeral."

"None of us were." Gray cast his gaze around the graveyard. "Still, I wouldn't let opportunity slip by just because of the circumstances. Cal and Rhys took me up on it. They're doing rather well. Earning enough to never worry about bills again. That's how it should be for men of our background."

Knox frowned. He remembered Cal and Rhys from the times he served, both were good operators. Cal had been Michael's friend, an unlikely duo, but military life never conformed to normality.

"I run a business," he said, half-apologetic.

Gray's polite smile held an undertone of cold calculation. "Yes, I saw your card once, Knox Investigations. That's fine, but do you really see yourself chasing lost dogs forever?" He let the question linger.

Before Knox could respond, Gray leant in, a confidential note in his tone. "You might want to think about it again. There's more in my line of work than you suspect. No end of interesting contracts. You know, we can do a lot of good for our country, if you keep an eye on the bigger picture."

Knox turned his head, focusing on the coffin. The vicar's words carried solemn finality. Sarah clung to the edge of the grave, Jess weeping at her side. Knox's heart felt heavy.

Gray's calm voice broke through again. "The pay is remarkable. Money finds its way to the right people. Let's say it falls through the cracks."

A smug hint crossed Gray's face. Knox blinked, a puzzle piece snapping into place in his mind. If Michael had hidden something, Knox now knew precisely where to look. A place easily overlooked.

Unaware of Knox's thought process, Gray continued.

"You'd be wasted in that detective service of yours." He began to say more, but Knox had already moved away, making a beeline for Sarah and Jess at the coffin.

Knox arrived beside Sarah, who looked at him with eyes red from crying. He lowered his voice, "I need the keys to Michael's place."

Sarah, without hesitation, passed him a small set of keys. He gave her arm a brief, grateful squeeze, offered Jess a sorrowful nod, then slipped away.

Behind him, Gray watched, eyes narrowing with distaste. He disliked losing control of any conversation, especially to someone he used to command. He offered a stiff nod to a mourner, then strode towards two other men: Rhys and Cal. They dipped their heads in acknowledgement. One nod from Gray, and both Rhys and Cal peeled away from the group, following Knox.

Gray exhaled softly, adjusting his gloves. The vicar concluded his prayer. Gray observed the crowd. Ex-soldiers, a few sobbing relatives, Sarah and Jess clinging to each other by the fresh grave. The vicar's final words rose in the chilly air. Gray stepped back, letting them bury their grief privately.

A flicker of impatience passed through his mind. He had no time for prolonged mourning. He had other duties, a bigger plan. He checked his watch, an item easily costing more than his first car.

Time to move.

With a curt, polite nod to one mourner who attempted a greeting, he walked towards the cemetery gates. The bleak day and biting wind did not deter him. He was already considering Knox's abrupt departure, planning how to ensure it posed no threat to his plan.

He left the graveside without another glance at the coffin or the grieving women. In his view, it was only another box ticked, another show of respect for form's sake. His mind was set on larger ambitions, Britain's Glory and the fortunes waiting for a man cunning enough to grab them. A man like him.

CHAPTER NINE

The Land Rover thundered through the thin winding Yorkshire streets, its engine snarling as Knox pushed the vehicle hard into each corner. The heavy, non-power-assisted steering wheel fought him with every twist, resisting each turn like a dead weight. The Land Rover shook with the speed, the rattling felt like a spaceship re-entering Earth's atmosphere, the vibrations so intense.

Knox threw his entire body into it, muscles straining as he forced the Land Rover to do his bidding. Every corner required a full-body effort, but he pushed through, rattling and wrestling with the steering wheel every step of the way. He kept the gears low, revs high, forcing the tyres to grip the road with the tenacity of animal claws. Parked cars, pedestrians, and street signs all blurred past, mere smudges at the edge of his vision as he focused on the road ahead.

It brought a surge of memories from his time in Germany, tearing through narrow roads during blue light runs, where balancing saving lives and making an arrest depended entirely on his skill and split-second decisions. The adrenaline, the urgency, the weight of what was at stake, all returned sharper and more vivid with every mile he covered.

Knox's mind turned to Michael and the thought that his old friend might have left a trail for him, something hidden and meant only for certain eyes. It spurred him on, his foot pressing harder on the pedal. Michael had always been clever, cunning in his own way, with a mischievous streak. A wry smile flickered across Knox's lips, fleeting but sharp. It was just like Michael to leave a puzzle behind, a breadcrumb trail for the right person to follow, perhaps even expecting Knox to be that person.

Knox swung hard into a sharp turn, the Land Rover's tyres screaming as he accelerated out of the bend, pushing the vehicle to its limits. He could not afford to waste a second. He had left the funeral early, slipping out as subtly as possible, although he had not gone unnoticed. Murmurs and curious looks had followed him, but he ignored them. Michael would have understood, and so would Sarah and Jess, if he was right.

At that moment, none of it mattered. Knox's only priority was arriving first, finding whatever Michael had hidden before anyone else touched it, if indeed it was still there.

The bungalow came into view suddenly, squat and solid in a sprawl of overgrown vegetation. Black bin bags lined the driveway, guarding the entry to the property. Knox slammed on the brakes, barely letting the Land Rover stop before he jumped out, slamming the door behind him and leaving the vehicle idling in the centre of the road. He sprinted up to the front door, jammed the key into the lock, and felt the crisp click.

Inside, silence wrapped around him, thick and heavy. Only the day before, he had stood in this space with Sarah, cluttered with the fragments of Michael's life: newspapers, magazines, notepads and scattered memories lying around like debris. Now, stepping into the dim interior, the house felt oddly tidy.

Long shadows, cast by the overgrown trees in the garden, seemed to dance along the walls, hinting that Michael himself might still be there, seated on a worn sofa, waiting for his daughters. But Knox knew differently. Michael was gone, and whatever he had left behind, Knox intended to find.

Knox moved quickly through the house, heading

directly for the garage. There, aligned in front of him, were the filing cabinets, precise and straight, like soldiers at attention. A faint smile touched his mouth; it was typical of Michael to keep those in neat order, when the rest of the house was a jumble of chaos. The stark contrast felt very much like Michael.

When he served in the RMP, there was a common trick: if a case file needed to disappear, maybe the investigation lacked enough work or had too many loose ends, the best hiding spot was often behind the filing cabinets. Before everything went digital, each case was a physical folder, numbered, labelled, shelved. And if one was too much trouble, it vanished behind a drawer, where no one else would think to look.

Knox knew the tactic intimately. He had done it himself, sliding certain cases behind cabinets, sealing them in silence, at least until the RSM discovered they were missing. If Michael had hidden something here, it would be precisely where he expected it, waiting for the right eyes to find it.

Knox shoved the first cabinet aside, the metal screeching against the concrete. His movements became more frantic as the search expanded. He dragged another cabinet out, and another, leaving them scattered like debris from a wreck. His frustration flared, and he gave one a swift kick, sending it wobbling precariously. Then he paused, eyes narrowing at a sudden realisation.

He tipped over the cabinet. It crashed down with a clatter of metal. He continued, toppling them one by one.

Then he saw it: a single light-brown pen drive, secured with tape to the underside of a cabinet.

Anticipation crackled through Knox's veins. He tore the memory stick free, its robust, reinforced casing solid in his grip. It felt weighty, not merely physically but in what it might hold. The design was unmistakably British Army issue, a rugged, no-frills device made to withstand the chaos of hasty transport. Knox had encountered these devices before, in a life of rifles and DPM. They were used for passing classified data between locations and Headquarters, protected from interception.

This was not the kind of item one simply stumbled across. It was not for sale in regular electronics shops, nor was it readily available on the internet. Its existence was not exactly top secret, but its movement was tightly controlled, always tracked and logged. Typically, it would be locked away in RHQ safes, released under strict oversight, only to officers with the clearance and the need.

Knox turned it over in his hand, the smooth surface cold against his skin, his mind flooding with possibilities. If Michael had one of these devices, it was not by chance. It was deliberate. Intentional. Michael had somehow acquired a tightly controlled piece of military hardware, and Knox knew if Michael possessed it, he was not just storing family photos. Henry's pulse quickened, a steady, demanding beat, as a single thought rooted itself in his mind.

Whatever was on this memory stick might have been the reason Michael was dead.

Knox continued to roll the elongated device between his fingers, weighing the possibilities. One thing was certain: Michael had deliberately kept this secret. This memory stick was either the key to unravelling the turmoil that had consumed him or the bait that had drawn him to a fatal end.

His thoughts churned, scenarios spiralling, but the conclusion was clear. The decision had been made long ago. No turning back. That had never been an option. The only path lay forward, to uncover whatever secrets the device held, whether they were truths or delusions, salvation or ruin. There was nothing else left to do. He had exhausted every other angle, this was the only remaining thread. And he knew he had to pull it.

CHAPTER TEN

Knox slipped the memory stick into his pocket and pivoted sharply, heading into the living room. Instinct took over, driving him to a shadowed corner where he could secure a vantage point. From there, he positioned the laptop, so that he would be able to work and still have a clear line of sight to the front door and down the corridor leading to the garage, both were critical points of ingress from the outside.

He powered the machine on, its faint hum filled the room, a sound so soft it might have been comforting if not for the storm raging within Knox's mind.

Methodically he then moved to secure the room, sealing the garage door, checking the front door was locked. He drew the curtains with a sharp tug, snuffing out the last grey remnants of the day. The world outside faded into darkness, the distant hum of traffic, the rustling of wind in the trees, gone.

Satisfied that the living room was secure, Knox sat heavily in the corner of the room, hidden in shadow, with his back pressed against the wall. His legs were crossed wide as he lifted the laptop onto his lap. His fingers hovered over the keyboard, ready to uncover the secrets held within the stick.

Two hours later, Knox looked like a different man, a dishevelled shadow of the one who had started with such optimism and focus. His jacket lay abandoned across the arm of a nearby chair, his shirt untucked and creased, the top button undone as if it had given up and snapped under the pressure. His cheap black tie was long gone, discarded with the jacket in frustration. He knelt on the floor, his face bathed in the cold blue light emanating from the laptop. The glow painted sharp angles on his face, highlighting the deep wrinkles and crags of his face along with the determined furrow in his brow as he focused, fingers gliding over the trackpad.

The stick had been a right ball ache.

He had wrestled with the laptop and the memory stick for what felt like an eternity, two hours, maybe more, and had lost every single battle. The military level encryption held firm, its secrets buried behind layers of impenetrable, digital fortifications.

After two hours of dead clicks, of forced reboots, and muttered curses, the memory stick stubbornly defied him, almost as if it carried the same unyielding spirit as the man who had once owned it.

Henry ran a hand over his face, his fingers dragging through his short, dishevelled hair as he exhaled slowly, frustrated. The device seemed to mock him, sitting snugly in the port, its small green light blinking rhythmically, taunting him with its quiet defiance.

It was a minor victory, he supposed. For an hour, the laptop hadn't even acknowledged the device's existence. Now, at least, a small icon glowed faintly on the home screen, a silent, indifferent acknowledgment that it was present. No fanfare, no revelations. Just an acceptance that refused to deliver.

He had removed and reinserted the device so many times he'd lost count. Occasionally, the laptop gave a glimmer of hope, a soft chime signalling the device had been removed, only for that hope to be crushed moments later when the USB drive failed to appear on the list of connected devices, despite the green light blinking on stubbornly.

Knox narrowed his eyes at the screen, frustration

simmering beneath the surface. Defeat tugged at him, but he wasn't ready to give in. Whatever secrets lay buried within this stubborn, unyielding piece of hardware, they wouldn't stay hidden for long. One way or another, he would unearth them.

Then, his concentration was shattered. A faint, sharp click echoed through the house. The front door handle shifted, the elongated bar trembling slightly, as if straining against the confines of the door, desperate to break free. Knox froze, his eyes narrowed, his breath stilled. Someone was here. And they weren't invited.

He dropped the screen, closing the laptop, and slid silently to the side of the door.

A key was thrust into the lock and turned with a sharp click, shattering the oppressive silence of the room. The lock turned slowly, the metallic clicks reverberating through the empty house. Knox stilled himself, his instincts honed to override the impulse to flee, driving him instead to confront danger head-on.

He shifted his weight soundlessly, adjusting his stance, ready for whatever, or whoever, was about to come through that door.

His hands flattened into blades, poised for both offence and defence, and he waited.

The handle finally moved freely, turning 45 degrees to the 6 o'clock position and the door creaked open, the sound of the cold evening air rushed into the house and dim light spilled into the room, framing two figures in shadow.

Knox didn't breathe. He was tracking and calculating every detail, the height, the gait, the lack of urgency. His mind raced through possibilities, filing and discarding threats as his hands hovered at the ready, no wasted motion, no unnecessary thought. Then, as the shadows stepped fully into the light, their features resolved into familiarity.

Sarah. Jess.

Knox exhaled silently, his body easing out of its coiled state without a flicker of outward weakness. His hands lowered, the faintest whisper of tension leaving his shoulders.

Sarah and Jess stood in the doorway, motionless, their faces etched with emotions that diverged sharply. Jess's expression was a mixture of disbelief and nostalgia, her gaze sweeping over the empty room with its faded wallpaper and worn carpet, both looking like they had been untouched for years. The absence of clutter, the missing notebooks, newspaper cuttings and magazines, she had half-expected to find, struck her harder than she had anticipated.

For Jess, the emptiness was almost worse than the chaos she'd encountered countless times before, when her father was alive. It was like staring into a hollow shell where their father's obsessions had once breathed life into the walls.

Sarah, by contrast, had been here only the day before. The empty room was no surprise to her. She had seen it in this state, had even helped to strip the room of its contents, but she still felt the weight of its silence, and the hollow feeling of loss that came with it. But standing here now, alongside her sister, it felt different. Heavier. More final. Her eyes went straight to the closed laptop on the floor, the only object that seemed out of place.

Jess finally stepped forward, hesitating as if the air itself might give way. "It looks strange with it all ... gone," she murmured, her voice a whisper, equal parts sadness and confusion.

Sarah glanced at her, swallowing hard. "I know, it feels empty, without him and his batshit crazy stuff," she replied quietly, her gaze focused on the laptop, which faintly hummed in the quiet of the room.

Knox moved from his position at the side of the door, and both women jumped, before reclaiming their composure.

"Jesus, Henry," Sarah spoke sharply, as though trying to steady herself through sheer will. Her hand pressed over her chest, as though trying to contain a heart that was threatening to leap free. She exhaled slowly, her eyes darting to the laptop and lingering there before they returned to Knox.

"I'm hoping you found something?" she asked, tilting her head slightly, her words wrapped in a fragile layer of restraint, but the tone was undeniable, potent a mix of hope and fear.

Knox let out a low grunt, "Yeah," he said, his voice rough. "I found something."

His words lingered in the charged silence, and Sarah held her breath, waiting for more.

Knox's eyes drifted to the laptop, a faint shadow of weariness etched into his features. He rubbed the back of his neck absently, his voice low and resigned. "Feels like I've been chasing a white rabbit through wonderland," he muttered, as though speaking more to the room than to her. "Just hoping this trail doesn't lead to a dead-end."

Knox moved towards the laptop, "But like everything Michael left behind, there are more questions than answers."

He paused, catching a look from Jess, her quiet gaze intense in a way that felt oddly familiar.

"Hi, Henry," she said softly, her voice calm and serene, a contrast to her sister's urgency. Jess looked younger than Sarah, her complexion clear and untouched by grief. She was smaller, more delicate, yet her resemblance to Sarah was striking.

Jess was dressed in black from head to toe. A long black overcoat, too thin to fend off the biting Yorkshire wind, hung loose around her slender frame. Beneath it, she wore a simple black blouse and skirt, the polished sheen of her high-gloss shoes.

Standing side by side, Sarah and Jess looked like two versions of the same person, reflections separated by years and experience, each carrying a part of Michael in their expressions.

Henry drew in a steady breath. "Hi Jess," he said quietly, "I'm very sorry for your loss."

She offered him a sad, fleeting smile, a shadow of warmth that couldn't quite conceal the grief in her eyes. "Looks like you missed the wake," she murmured, glancing at Sarah, who was already on her knees, opening the laptop with a determined focus.

Knox felt a brief flicker of embarrassment but pushed it aside, overwhelmed by a sense of relief. Leaving the funeral early might have seemed disrespectful to some, but Michael was gone and he wasn't about to lecture Henry about etiquette from beyond the grave. The best way to honour him wasn't with hollow rituals but by uncovering the truth and catching whoever had taken him from this world.

The connection between Jess and Henry was delicate, more of a thread spun from Sarah's stories rather than something tangible. Back when Knox had been part of their lives, Jess had been a toddler, a bundle of watchful contemplation confined to a highchair. Her world then had been small and safe, her memories of Knox non-existent. Everything she knew of him came from Sarah, who spoke of him with reverence, intertwining his name with their father's legacy in tales that carried the weight of heroes.

Now, standing in his shadow, Jess felt the gap

between Sarah's myth and Knox's reality. His face bore the marks of time, lines cut deep from years lived hard. He moved with a strong authority, his presence still commanding, but there was something unspoken in his restraint. He wasn't the invincible figure Sarah had described; he was just a man carrying the burden of his own internal battles.

And yet, Jess couldn't ignore the way how Sarah had visibly changed when he was near. The tension in her shoulders and face, which had been present for years, relaxed and eased. Around Knox, her sister seemed less on edge, less ready to fight the world. That was enough for Jess. She didn't know him, not truly, but she didn't need to, not when Sarah's faith in him was so clear. Sometimes, trust didn't need shared history. It just needed a reason.

"Michael left this for someone to find, someone he trusted," Henry said, his voice steady as he broke Jess's train of thought. He nodded toward the memory stick protruding from the laptop, where Sarah was tapping away with focused determination. "I think he'd understand why I left the funeral early."

Jess cast a wary glance at the computer with a blue screen that was trying to run a command task, her expression clouded with doubt. "Are you sure this is wise, Sis?" she asked softly, her voice barely above a whisper. "Whatever is on this device... It killed Dad. I don't want you pulled into it."

Sarah, still kneeling in front of the computer, looked at her sister, her face stern, eyes steady. "I know," she replied forcefully. "But if it mattered to Dad, and to whoever did this, then it should matter to us as well."

Knox broke the stalemate, his tone calm, yet firm. "How about I go over what I know so far?" he suggested. "Then I'll take it from here, and you both can head home.

I'll keep you updated regularly and tell you when the time is right."

Sarah regarded him for a moment, then rose, brushing dust from her knees. "Alright." Her voice softened after her previous harsh words. Beside her, Jess nodded, the tension easing visibly from her stance.

"Okay," Knox said. He pulled the USB stick from the laptop and sat in Michael's armchair with a sad smile, trying to relieve some of the tension between the sisters. Sarah and Jess took their seats on the sofa, shoulders close, their expressions a blend of determination and apprehension as they braced themselves for what Knox was about to reveal.

Knox took a steadying breath. "Your dad was a bit of a conspiracy theorist, which I'm sure you already know," he began, his voice steady and direct. "But your dad had something he shouldn't have had. It is a British Army issue memory stick. Normally, this sort of thing doesn't get out of the RHQ, never mind into the hands of a civilian, not even a former soldier. These memory cards usually hold classified data and information. I doubt many people would recognise it as military issue, but I did." Henry held the stick between his thumb and forefinger, showing the device. "I'm intrigued by what might be on it, and if this is the reason for everything that has happened. Right now, it's the only thing that makes any sense."

Sarah leaned forward towards Knox, her eyes narrowed as she looked at the tan coloured USB stick. Jess, unconvinced, blinked steadily.

"You think... you think this is what got him killed?" Jess asked, her voice trembling slightly, the weight of the question hanging between them. Her eyes flicked to the small metal rectangle in Henry's hand, then back to his face, searching for answers. "What were these people after?"

Knox paused and let the USB stick drop from his fingers into his other palm, his grip closing around it as though trying to contain the enormity of what it might reveal. "I do not know for sure. Not yet anyway. But it is a lead, even if it is a spurious one. I have nothing else to go on, nothing else is even close to being a lead, unless you think aliens have taken over the UK government."

He paused again, weighing up his next words carefully. "The fact that this is a British Army memory stick, used for classified material, suggests that your dad was given this by someone who knows what is going on, or it was stolen. I do not think Michael just stumbled across this lightly. My hunch is that someone was feeding him pieces of something big. Maybe they wanted him to blow the whistle."

Jess looked at him for a long moment. "You sound like my dad. He always believed there was something going on behind the scenes, but it was all just outlandish conspiracies. Are you sure you are not getting caught up in this?"

Knox turned the USB stick in his hand. The dull, desert coloured metal casing caught what little light the room offered. For a moment, he stared at it as though sheer force of will, could penetrate its secrets, unlocking the layers of data it held.

"This," he said, his voice low and steady, his eyes never leaving the stick, "is evidence, Jess. And I work with evidence. It doesn't belong here. Your dad should never have had it. The fact that he did raises all kinds of questions. Questions I need to find the answers to."

He continued turning the stick over between his fingers. "Whatever is on this," he continued, his tone darkening, "I'm betting it is not something trivial. It's encrypted, very heavily. My guess is military grade. I don't have the tools to crack it." He paused, lowering the stick and finally meeting Jess's gaze. "But if I can get it to someone who does, someone I trust, we might be able to dig through the protected layers and see what your dad was onto. Maybe then we'll understand why someone wanted him gone."

Jess glanced nervously between Knox and her sister. She felt torn between what was real and what was conjecture. Then she broke. Her heart sank, and realisation hit her all at once: her dad was dead, his house empty, and someone could have killed him.

How did it come to this? Jess's mind screamed at her as she sat frozen in the stark, empty room. If only she could rewind time, pull her father back from the brink, stop him from spiralling into the abyss that now stared back at her with cruel indifference. The ache of regret swelled in her chest, sharp and unforgiving. She covered her face with trembling hands, her quiet sobs breaking the oppressive stillness.

Knox and Sarah exchanged a glance, unspoken understanding passing between them. They both shuffled closer to Jess in unison and placed a hand on her shoulder as she quaked under the heavy burden of loss. Jess did not look up, but the warmth of their presence seeped into the cracks of her despair.

The room fell silent again, save for Jess's muffled whimpers, the fragile sound echoing against the cold walls.

No one spoke. There were no words that could cut through the fog of grief that enveloped them. They sat together, an unsteady trio united by shared sorrow.

Sensing the need for a reprieve, to take her sister's thoughts away from her loss, Sarah looked up, her voice soft but slightly too bright. "How have you been, Henry?" she asked, a small smile lifting her lips. "It's been years since we last saw you. What have you been up to?"

Knox managed a faint smile, understanding what Sarah was trying to do. "Well, I left the army and thought I would try being a private investigator." He gave a slight shrug. "It's very different from the army. No rules, no policies, but also no backup. Leaving felt like stepping off a cliff. Some days, I'm still not sure I landed."

Sarah nodded in understanding. Jess looked up, her face streaked with tears, but listening now, the shift in focus allowed her to think about something other than her loss. "I heard you got married!" Sarah said, glancing at the simple gold band on his left hand. "I wouldn't have believed it, but there it is."

Knox followed her gaze, looking down at the ring, feeling its weight in a way he had not felt in a long time.

"Yeah, I did that," he said, his voice carrying a sadness he could not quite hide.

Jess, calmer now and intrigued, leaned in. "Are you still married? What's her name?"

Knox looked at her, at the open curiosity in her expression, and it struck him just how young she was, how much hope she still held. She had been drawn into a nightmare, but part of her remained untouched, still naive. He almost envied that.

"Catheryn, and she left me," he admitted sadly. "The PI work is a hard life. At first, there wasn't much of it. There still isn't, if I am honest. Catheryn didn't like me being home all the time. She preferred it when I was away." He paused. "I was ready to settle down, to be around more after the army, but she didn't want that."

His voice trailed off, leaving the room cloaked in further silence, a silence thicker and heavier than before. Sarah reached over and rested a gentle hand on his arm, then broke the stillness. "Do you have children?"

Knox nodded, a faint spark lighting his tired eyes.

"Yes, I do! A little girl. She's about the same age you were when I first met you, Sarah." For the first time in days, a genuine smile lifted the weariness from his face, a glimmer of warmth untouched by the darkness surrounding them.

Jess and Sarah shared the smile, the three of them briefly held in memories of better times, of hope.

Then Jess straightened, her tone hardening. "All the more reason to find these people and stop them," she said, determination clear in her voice. "We should take this to the police," she added, pointing at the USB stick.

Knox shook his head, his lip lifting at the corner in a grimace as he spoke. "There's no point, Jess. Not yet anyway. The stick is, at the very least classified material; they would hand it straight back to the MOD without even looking at what's inside. Nothing would come of this unless we find out what is on it."

He twirled the small memory stick in his hand. "But there's a reason this was in your dad's possession. There was a reason it was sellotaped to the base of the cabinet. Whatever's on here, I bet it's worth hiding. Once we crack it, maybe we will have something real to take to the police."

He tried to sound confident, to reassure them, but he could feel the doubt in his own voice. He slipped the memory stick into his trouser pocket, letting his hand rest there for a moment, giving it an unconscious pat.

Suddenly, both Sarah and Jess jumped to their feet, determination blazing in their eyes. "Well, we can't just sit here, Henry," Sarah said, urgency sharpening her tone. "There must be more, something else hidden away. Where did you find the stick?"

Knox used an open hand to gesture towards the garage. "It was taped under one of the filing cabinets, but I'm fairly sure that was the only thing there." His voice faded, as Sarah and Jess were already moving towards the garage. Jess led the way. "Well, if we do not look, we won't find anything," she called over her shoulder, her tone leaving no room for argument.

A faint, genuine smile rose on Knox's face. Like father, like daughters, he thought. The apple does not fall far from the tree. Michael's stubborn streak had not skipped a generation; it had multiplied.

Moments later, the house reverberated with the unmistakable sound of metal scraping against concrete. From behind the garage door came a series of heavy thuds as lockers crashed to the ground, the sisters moving with relentless determination.

Knox lingered in the living room, arms crossed, watching as they dismantled Michael's garage piece by piece. He let them work, knowing better than to get in their way.

Henry walked over to pick up the laptop and unplugged the cable from the electrical socket when a faint smell reached him. It was subtle at first, almost masked by the dust and stale air, but then unmistakable, sharp, chemical. His instincts switched on as recognition hit. Gas.

He turned suddenly towards the hallway leading to the garage, alarm surging through him. He opened his mouth to shout, but there was no time, no chance to call out. Before he could move any further, a deafening explosion tore through the house. A wave of heat and force slammed into him, ripping through walls and swallowing everything in a heartbeat.

In that instant, the world dissolved into darkness.

CHAPTER ELEVEN

Gray left the cemetery, his shoulders set against a December wind that felt like needles against his skin. He barely noticed the chill. He was thinking too fast, like pieces on a board each moving closer to the moment he had been arranging for months.

The sky hung low and grey, promising rain that stubbornly stayed in the clouds. He crossed the uneven car park.

He glanced at the funeral home across the road, where Michael's daughters would soon be heading after the funeral. Gray felt only a flicker of annoyance at the memory of them. Collateral. That was how he preferred to see anyone who got in his way.

It was for the greater good.

Approaching his black Range Rover Sport, he pressed the key fob. Indicators flashed in polite response, a show of quiet wealth and well-crafted engineering. He paused by the driver's door and scanned the vehicles left in the car park. Knox's Land Rover was gone. He had left the funeral in a rush, a man with a purpose.

Gray considered Cal and Rhys, who had been commanded to go after him. He had given them a single nod, a silent order to follow Knox and tie off loose ends. He trusted Rhys's merciless approach and Cal's sense of discipline. But Cal's compliance had needed some gentle encouragement, Gray held Cal's family somewhere quiet, safe, out of reach. Cal had so far done as instructed.

He slid in behind the wheel and felt the leather grip him, tight and expensive, then hit the ignition button.

The engine came alive, purring. It was soothing, a reminder of what he had gained since leaving the Army: comfort, influence, power. But that was only half the story. Anger still churned inside him, anger at what his adopted country had become. What it had failed to do.

He had grown up in Canada, looking at Britain from a distance. He liked what he saw. He liked the sense of honour, the centuries old traditions. The moment he was old enough, he signed on the dotted line and joined the British Army. He thought he was stepping into something solid, something true.

But Iraq and Afghanistan tore away the illusions. The politicians sent them to fight without the right gear, without a real plan. They seemed more worried about headlines and polls than about giving the troops a fighting chance. The nation had gone soft. Bloated. Weak.

That reality sank in deep. It got worse when he saw soldiers from the Northern Ireland conflict dragged to court, while IRA killers walked free with money in their pockets. The final blow came after Special Forces took down IRA gunmen who had attacked a police station with a DShK heavy machine gun. A brutal assault, yet the court ruled the soldiers' action unlawful.

Defence spending fell to two percent of GDP, while adversaries poured money into their armies. Successive governments shrugged. Soldiers who once risked everything got left out in the cold, literally on the streets. Homeless, ignored, forgotten.

Meanwhile, NATO let the Americans shoulder the load, leaving Europe's security in someone else's hands. No one stepped up, not really. A world of dangerous corners, leaving the Brits with chipped gear, half measures, and hollow promises. That was the sorry truth. And it left everyone a little less safe.

Gray had seen too many politicians smiling at funerals, shaking hands, and pretending to care. They hadn't marched patrols in boots that melted beneath the merciless desert sun. Hadn't sweated inside battered Northern Ireland Snatch Land Rovers hastily painted desert-tan, with air-conditioning units bolted on as afterthoughts. Hadn't worn ECBA vests, useless slabs of nylon and foam with a laughable five-inch square of Kevlar that wouldn't even slow the round that killed you. Politicians didn't get it because they'd never had to. But Gray had. He remembered every failure, every betrayal, every coffin draped in a flag.

Gray had, and he remembered every betrayal.

That was it for him. His anger had gone nuclear. If Britain wanted to slouch toward mediocrity, fine. But he had a plan to show them just how strong they could still be, if the right incident lit the fuse. For that, he needed cash. He needed men like Normanov to fund his vision.

Normally, Normanov was the sort of man Gray would steer clear of.

He was a Russian oligarch, deep pockets and deeper secrets, always looking for an edge. Exactly the kind of contact you avoided if you had any sense. But Gray needed resources, real dangerous things no one else could source, and Normanov had them.

So, Gray had swallowed his misgivings. Hated every second. Hated watching Normanov strut around like he was king. But the truth was simple: Normanov's money and influence meant Gray could pull off what no one else could. And if the Russian had his own angle, so be it. Gray was ready to pay that price.

For now, anyway.

He reached for the centre console and tapped through a list of contacts. Normanov's name gleamed on the screen. He selected it and the screen changed colour.

It rang once before Normanov's deep voice came through. "Grei," the Russian said, rolling the single syllable in a mild accent. "Have you solved your problem Colonel?"

Gray bridled at the question. "Knox is still a nuisance, but I have people on him. He will not interfere with our schedule."

Normanov gave a low, knowing chuckle. "Do not let him slip away. You assured me everything was in place. No delays, no danger."

Gray eased back in the seat, one hand on the steering wheel. "Everything is ready," he said. "The drones, the airfield. Once the cargo lands, we move. The military grade equipment I acquired will handle dispersal. By the time anyone realises what happened, it will be too late."

Normanov paused, then spoke with pleasure. "Ten kilograms, yes? A neat sum, enough to make a real statement."

Gray felt a heaviness in his stomach at the size of the lethal delivery. Death, lots of death, but necessary. "Yes. Ten. The payment will follow our usual channels."

"When this is done," he said, "we meet on the yacht. I will have concluded my end of things here, and you can do what you like with your other plans."

Normanov gave another laugh, heavier this time. "Britain will be made strong again, you said, or so you claim."

Gray drummed his fingers on the wheel, a faint smile curving his lips. "It just needs a push," he said. "A sudden catastrophe blamed on foreigners. Gives the government no choice but to hit back. I am just setting the stage."

He knew it was a dangerous game. Normanov had his own angles, his own motives for handing over this lethal payload. But Gray believed the ends justified the means. A 9/11 on British soil would shake the world, show them the old girl still had fight in her, remind everyone of Britain's glory.

Force Britain to stand up to her bullies. Face down her enemies and become the guiding light for the world, which was blindly following America into hate and the abyss. Britain had once had the greatest empire the world had ever seen and could be a force for good in the world, again.

She would have to suffer first though.

But through that suffering, pain and grief, she would emerge strong and powerful again. Willing to take the hard choices and bring peace and order to chaos.

And if that meant that Normanov fancied himself the puppet master of Western politics. Let him believe it.

Russia was ripe to be manipulated, into war, into conflict.

Gray knew the West could hit back and hit hard. Russia had failed to take Ukraine, Britain didn't need to fear a nation that had failed to annex a country of farmers.

But also, opportunity presented itself to Gray, Action met reaction, which was the rule. War would create fear, and fear would drive private security contracts. Gray would be right there to reap the benefits. Britain would stand tall again, and he would grow rich making it happen, a perfect loop of power and profit.

It would be a win, win situation.

Normanov's voice dropped. "Your man Cal. Is he dependable?"

Gray's eyes narrowed. "Dependable enough. His family are in a property I control. He would not dream of stepping out of line. If he does, I remind him that I decide where they sleep, what they eat, who they speak to."

He felt no remorse at that, only a sense of satisfaction. It had been easy to corral Cal. The man had moral scruples but love for his family made him pliable. Gray needed obedient pawns.

Normanov gave a thoughtful hum. "Then I will leave it in your hands. See that you do not fail."

Without waiting for a farewell, Gray ended the call. By pressing the red logo on the screen. Normanov was a snake, but a useful one, at least until the final stage. Gray had never cared about forging alliances. If Normanov became a liability, Gray would drop him like any other expendable ally.

Gray's knee bounced in rapid rhythm, a relentless piston pumping up and down, his heel never quite reaching the Range Rover's floor. The vibration echoed through his bones, each twitch betraying a truth he refused to accept. He was losing control.

The conversation with Normanov replayed endlessly in his head, like a tape stuck in a loop. He hated dealing with the Russian, hated the oily certainty in the man's voice, but Normanov was a necessary evil. Gray had sat across tables from enemies before, breaking bread with the Mahdi Army in Basra, smiling at men he'd gladly shoot in other circumstances. He'd watched those same negotiations destroy good men, hardened soldiers crumbling under the weight of their duplicity. It was the hidden cost of war, moral corrosion that rotted from within.

But not him.

He wouldn't break. He was stronger, smarter, better. Those other men were weak; they hadn't understood what he knew so clearly. Wars weren't won by honour; they were won by knowing exactly how far to bend without breaking. Gray's knee bounced again, harder, sharper, but his resolve held firm. He'd come too far to lose now.

He put the Range Rover into gear, rolling out of the

cemetery car park onto the main road. The windscreen wipers flicked on automatically as droplets started to fall. His mind returned to Cal, to Rhys, to Knox's sudden exit from the funeral. Loose ends. He had to be sure none of them derailed his carefully laid plan.

Traffic was light on the way back to the motorway. Gray allowed himself the briefest moment of reflection. He had been a soldier who believed in the Union Flag and the pride of a regiment. He still did, but the world was at a precipice, and it needed to be tipped one way or the other. He saw the cracks in the system, and in those cracks, he had discovered opportunities. Men like Normanov were simply stepping stones to wealth and power.

He guided the Range Rover onto the dual carriageway, pressing the accelerator. Trees blurred past, the steady drone of tyres on wet tarmac filling the cabin. He remembered the last time he had visited Cal's family, how the child had asked when her father would be home. Gray had smiled politely, given her a chocolate, and promised Cal would be back soon if he completed his work. It was all a matter of leverage.

CHAPTER TWELVE

Catheryn sat at the small dressing table of a luxury room in a Hilton Hotel, just outside York's city walls, brushing her dark hair in long, slow strokes while her mind raced far ahead. She had landed in the UK hours ago, stepping out of the warmth of Cyprus into the cold sting of an English winter. The difference in temperature felt like a rude awakening, or perhaps a reminder that she had left one life behind for another.

The hotel room offered neat lines and artificial comfort: crisp white linen on the bed, plush chairs, warm lights trying too hard to be welcoming. It did not feel like home. She glanced at Sophie, sprawled asleep across the bed, a tangle of blankets half covering her small frame. The child was worn out from the flight and the sudden change of surroundings. Catheryn wished she could rest as easily.

Catheryn was tall, a living force, a woman you'd spot in any crowd. Deep green eyes, sharp as knives, could cut clean through the noise and pin you in place. Her face was unforgettable, the kind you'd recall weeks later without trying. Strength radiated off her, raw and confident. She moved with a subtle command that made people step aside, uncertain whether they were entranced or terrified.

She set the brush down, reaching for her phone. She had tried Henry twice already that day, and both calls had gone to voicemail. She told herself it was to be expected.

He always did this. He never liked facing real conflict with those he loved, he never challenged her or pushed beyond the safe boundaries in a relationship. He wanted a dull civilian life after years of military service, but she didn't. Yet a part of her still felt stung. If he had any inkling of what had driven her back to the U.K. so suddenly, perhaps he would have picked up. Maybe he would have tried to talk her out of it. Then again, that was wishful thinking.

She stepped over to the window, pressing a palm to the cold glass. York's old Roman walls were visible in the distance, half lost in an early evening gloom. The city lights blinked sporadically through the winter haze. Behind her, the low buzz of the room's heater sounded hollow, like white noise in an empty space.

The phone vibrated in her hand. She looked down, pulse quickening. Archie's name shone on the caller ID. She hesitated before answering, her heart giving a small leap that she both welcomed and despised.

She kept her voice soft, mindful of Sophie. "Archie," she said, stepping away from the bed.

"Did you arrive safely?" Archie asked, his voice calm and steady, hiding the impatience Catheryn always heard beneath it. "Britain waits for no one, least of all, us."

"I am here," she said, keeping her tone brisk. "I tried calling Henry, but no luck."

Archie let out a low sound that might have been a thoughtful hum. "I see. Are you sure you should bother with him? He was never a big picture sort of guy."

Catheryn felt a twist of annoyance at the truth behind Archie's words. "He still deserves to know we have landed," she said. "At least for Sophie's sake. I want

Sophie well away from all of this, and he will do that for me. For her."

A pause. "Yes, for Sophie," Archie said, his voice gentling. "We can talk about everything else later. Get some rest tonight. You will need it."

Catheryn nodded, forgetting for a moment that he could not see her. She ended the call and placed the phone on the bedside table. She stared at the black screen, feeling the pull of something she both craved and feared. Archie had a way of making her feel part of something bigger. He spoke about the world in broad strokes, about power and influence. She had never heard Henry talk like that, not once in all their years of marriage.

She caught a glimpse of herself in the mirror next to the bed. Her face looked tired. The flight had been long, and she had spent too many recent nights staring at documents and screens, reading about the bigger picture, global conflicts, and political movement. Archie had pointed her to articles on false flags and historical tipping points, claiming these were moments that reshaped nations. He had a knack for pulling her deeper without ever being too direct. She needed to know more if her plans were to become reality.

Archie had explained at length about how defence expenditure had been cut and cut and cut, reliance on old thought processes, on mismanagement, on poor governance by shady politicians eager for their own slice on expensive military contracts. Feathering their own bed.

This offered her opportunities to move up the ladder, to become important on a world stage.

She needed to know more than Archie, more any those she wanted to shape.

She would let Archie think it was his plan. He enjoyed control, savoured it, but Catheryn knew control was about knowing when to surrender it, just enough to keep him hooked.

Sophie stirred on the bed, rolling over, a small sigh escaping her lips. Catheryn's chest tightened. She had uprooted her daughter, brought her halfway across Europe for reasons she could not explain, neither to Sophie nor to Henry. So, she told herself it was a fresh start. She told herself the opportunities would be worth it.

She tried Henry again. Three rings, then voicemail. She hung up. She did not know why she expected anything different. Even in the Army, he had never chased promotion or pushed to rub shoulders with senior officers. Though he had attained rank, he remained a soldier in his mind. Catheryn used to host dinner parties, hoping he would network and sweet talk the right people. He had always preferred honesty rather than the platitudes that officers craved. He was too honest and too direct, and people in power did not like that. She had grown frustrated, wanting him to reach higher. He never did, because he could not temper his righteousness.

She laid down on the bed and shut her eyes. She could almost hear Archie's voice in her head, urging her to focus, not to waste energy on Henry. Yet she remembered the days when Henry had been the steady rock she leaned on, before it all drifted apart, because she wanted more that what he was offering.

She could not sleep. Perhaps she was excited about tomorrow. After all, it had been her idea, and she smiled at the thought that her voice would soon be heard around the world. She would finally have access to power.

She opened her eyes, lifting herself slowly off the bed to avoid waking Sophie and softly padded a few steps to the kettle that sat on a desk under a huge mirror. She contemplated making a cup of tea, but the thought brought memories of Henry and his massive mug with too much sugar. Everything she did reminded her of him. Why? She was getting what she wanted, what she craved, what Henry could not give her, yet she still thought of him and his simple outlook on life. She sighed, placing both hands on the desk, her eyes locked on her reflection. It was too late now, she told herself.

Her attention was drawn by the news channel on the TV, which rambled on about a drug bust in Manchester where a local gang had been smashed by police and a large number of stolen goods and drugs had been recovered.

Catheryn flicked the TV to standby, killing the chatter in one swift motion. Enough. Sophie needed rest, and so did she, if her mind would let her. She sat at the edge of the bed, brushed her hand over the duvet where Sophie's small foot stuck out, half in a sock. Then she switched off the bedside lamp and lay beside her daughter, letting the darkness have the room. Outside, faint city lights filtered through the curtains. Her phone lay silent. No call from Henry. She registered a flicker of disappointment, tried to ignore it. Henry had made his choices. She was making hers. No backing down now.

Eventually, her eyelids grew heavy. She drifted into a restless sleep, one arm draped protectively over Sophie.

Catheryn awoke with a jolt, her heart hammering. She could have sworn she heard a scream, sharp and piercing, slicing through the stillness. The room was pitch black, and instinctively she reached towards the opposite side of the bed, but her hand found only cold, empty sheets. Sophie was gone.

Fear gripped her chest like a vice. She scrambled out of bed, her pulse racing as she frantically searched the room. Under the bed, nothing. The bathroom was empty. She hurried onto the small balcony, the biting cold winter air cutting into her skin, but Sophie was not there either. Her little suitcase still sat by the dresser, untouched, the clothes inside neatly packed just as they had been when they arrived.

Panic consumed her, her breath coming in shallow, frantic gasps. Where was Sophie? Where had she gone?

Then, suddenly, the electronic door latch clicked and light from the hallway spilled into the room, harsh and jarring in the darkness.

Sophie burst into the room, grinning, holding a cone with a massive scoop of ice cream that dripped onto her hand. Relief crashed over Catheryn so hard she fell to her knees, arms wide open. Sophie ran into her embrace, her small, warm body pressing against Catheryn's trembling form.

Catheryn buried her face in Sophie's hair, breathing in her scent as the sharp edge of panic slowly dulled. But just as she was about to let out a shaky breath, her heart stopped. A figure stood in the doorway, casting a large, unmoving shadow across the room.

"Hi, Catheryn," said a familiar voice that she recognised immediately. "I have some really bad news about Henry."

CHAPTER THIRTEEN

Neon blue lights cut through the dark skies over the small Yorkshire town as Amy Thornton's unmarked police car rolled to a stop. She took in the scene, where three or maybe four marked police cars, their lights flashing, blended with the steady red glow of two fire engines, casting jagged shadows over the street. A crowd had gathered, restless, murmuring, caught somewhere between fear and fascination. The flames devoured what remained of the house, competing with the blue lights in a twisted battle for the night sky.

Amy was small in stature but fierce. At only five foot two, she made up for a lack of height with sharp intelligence and unbreakable determination. She had spent years pushing against the limitations of her slight frame, a challenge that might have defeated others. She was forged in the military. Her father had served before her, and she had attended the Royal Military Academy Sandhurst, where she bore the same weight as any man. For Amy, every challenge was half mental. If she set her mind to it, nothing could stop her.

She took pride in her appearance, a trait ingrained during her harsh military training. Whether in a tailored suit or a military uniform, Amy commanded respect, moving just as confidently in smart, low-heeled shoes as she once had in boots. Her military career had taken her across the world, into landscapes and situations only the British Army could provide. She continuously sought to test her limits and, when the opportunity arose to join West Yorkshire Police, she seized it without hesitation.

The transition was seamless. While based at 150 Provost Company in Catterick, she had worked closely with the civilian police, even sharing offices in the same building. Swapping her MTP uniform for police blues felt like a natural step. With three years of Royal Military Police casework and tours in Iraq and Afghanistan, she had handled several high profile, serious crimes with the Special Investigation Branch, from murder to intelligence leaks.

This experience made her an asset to Yorkshire Police, who saw not just potential in her but the refined skills of a seasoned investigator. Recognising her abilities, they fast tracked her into an Inspector role as a direct entry, bypassing a few years in the lower ranks. Her sharp suits matched her sharper mind, earning respect from those below her and trust from those above.

Amy was dressed in a suit blazer and trousers, she straightened her jacket, smoothed her blouse, and fixed her eyes on the illuminated wreckage of a building. What had once been a small, unassuming bungalow was now a charred skeleton of twisted metal and brick. Dispatch had briefed her enroute about a house explosion at the site of a suspected suicide involving a former soldier, which had occurred the previous week.

She had known the former soldier, Michael, back when she was a fresh faced Second Lieutenant in the Royal Military Police, straight out of Sandhurst and still learning the ropes. He had been a seasoned Staff Sergeant, the steady hand and experienced guide who helped her navigate the complexities of military life during her early, uncertain postings. At the time, he had been more than a mentor. He had been a friend, but that felt like another lifetime now.

Yet here she was. The initial suicide theory did not add up, and perhaps it never had. Michael did not strike her as someone who would take his own life, though the evidence at the time had suggested otherwise.

She moved toward the blue tape closing off the driveway. Black bags of newspapers and half burned magazines were scattered about, curling and smouldering in the winter air. A uniformed officer raised a hand to stop her. She pulled out her ID, flashed it with a nod, and stepped into the heart of the crime scene. The air was thick with smoke and the acrid bite of melted plastic, mingling with something else she could not name but felt in her gut. This was not just a house fire.

As Amy made her way up the driveway, a firefighter strode toward her, his face and hands streaked with soot. "We've got the blaze under control," he said briskly, his tone as formal as his stance. "Once we get the all clear, we'll hand the scene over to you."

He did not introduce himself, and Amy raised an eyebrow. "Hi, I'm Inspector Thornton," she replied, her voice edged with sarcasm. "Nice to meet you too."

The firefighter's brows furrowed in brief confusion before he gave a curt shake of his head, muttering something as he turned back to the fire engine.

Exasperated, Amy scanned the scene, her gaze landing on a young Constable standing by the tape. She strode over, her low heels clicking on the uneven drive. "I want CSI to examine these bin bags," she said firmly. "There's blood on one of them that wasn't there a week ago. Get another officer to go door to door, find out what the neighbours saw, ask if anything suspicious has happened in the last few days, or if anyone was hanging around. Once the fire team clears the house, I want a second CSI unit inside. Examine every inch. I want to know what happened here."

The PC nodded, scribbling notes as quickly as he could under her steady gaze.

"Don't you want the fire team to look for the cause?" he asked, his voice tinged with hesitation.

"Not really," Amy replied, her tone resolute. "I already suspect arson. They can establish the point of ignition, but I don't want them trampling over my evidence like last time."

This was the same tug of war every time, balancing the fire brigade's need for a cause against the Crime Scene Investigators' precision. The fire crew was vital, but they often prioritised speed over meticulous procedure, and Amy did not want to risk contamination. She saw no reason to think this was anything other than deliberate, so every clue mattered.

She looked back at the house, its blackened skeleton silhouetted against the night sky. There was no room for mistakes, not with this case.

The blaze had barely been put out when the call came through: two bodies had been found inside, charred, small, and slight. Amy's stomach twisted. They appeared to be female, likely in their early twenties. This was exactly what she had feared. There had been no reports of gas leaks, no known electrical faults. The house had been searched only days ago, with nothing found that might suggest an accidental fire. Amy's instincts told her this was no accident. It was murder.

Amy relayed the news to her command via her Airwave radio handset, maintaining a calm, controlled tone that conveyed the gravity of the situation. Within minutes, a senior investigator would be assigned to the case, someone from higher up who could handle the political fallout and the magnitude of the event. Until that person arrived, Amy retained full command of the scene.

Wearing white Tyvek suits, face masks, and hoods over their hair, the forensic team moved in, carefully collecting evidence. They photographed everything in place, bagged even the tiniest fragments, and recorded any significant areas for further analysis. Samples were taken to test for accelerants, and any blood traces or evidence near the bin bags were logged. Each step followed strict protocol, minimising contamination. Only after the forensic team finished could the investigators enter, disturbing as little as possible.

By the time Amy gained access, the sun had started to rise, casting a feeble light over the devastation. She stepped into the burnt-out shell of the house, imagining the horror that had unfolded here. Walking slowly, her footsteps crunching through ash, she pieced the scene together in her mind.

Based on preliminary CSI findings and input from the Fire Investigation Officer, the fire was almost certainly deliberate, with the ignition point located just outside the property. A gas main had been punctured, flooding the house with flammable gas. The garage doors had been barricaded from the outside, preventing escape.

Accelerants, probably petrol, had been poured around the barricade and the exits, fuelling the rapid spread of the flames. Near the garage doors were remnants of propane cylinders, apparently rigged to generate the explosion that destroyed the house and ensure the fire spread quickly and brutally.

The two bodies had been discovered in the garage, slumped near each other. Early indications suggested they had died from the explosion's impact rather than from the flames, which was a small mercy, if any mercy could be found here.

There was evidence that a third person had been at the scene. In a bin within the garage, forensic technicians found a pair of discarded rubber gloves. They had been sealed and sent off for DNA testing.

Outside, a trail of blood led from the living room down the drive, stopping abruptly at the main street. This prompted officers to push the police cordon further, securing a larger perimeter. The injured person had either been hurt or involved in a struggle before escaping.

The use of propane in the explosion, a slower and heavier gas than methane, might have been the reason the third person survived. Unlike lighter gases, propane does not detonate instantly. It stays close to the ground, spreading lethally but without the explosive force that would have killed everyone in an instant. Its slower burn rate provided an extra few seconds, enough time for the individual to flee.

Witness statements from neighbours provided a few details. Several residents recalled a stocky man in a black suit, likely in his mid to late forties, visiting the property twice in the past twenty-four hours. He had drawn attention, particularly during his last visit, when he arrived in a battered old Land Rover that sat idling outside while he went in.

Most telling was one neighbour's account of seeing the same man leaving the house just after the explosion, barely visible through the smoke.

Amy did not need the witness accounts to tell her more. She knew the identities of the two victims before the forensic results would confirm it. She already knew who the man was, the one fleeing after the blast. She had seen all three of them just the day before, standing sombrely among the mourners at Michael Henley's funeral.

Amy reached into her pocket and retrieved her phone, scrolling through her contacts for the name. Henry Knox.

CHAPTER FOURTEEN

Knox's vision blurred as he struggled to right himself, his world reeling from the blast's impact. The garage was gone, obliterated in a violent flash of heat and sound that left his ears ringing and his chest heaving. He had been thrown back, slamming into a wall that drove the breath from his lungs, leaving him dazed, his mind caught in a fog of muscle memory and instinct. It felt like a mortar attack, the kind he had suffered on countless operational tours, but this time the explosion had struck painfully close to home.

Henry was covered from head to toe in dust and rubble, with grime and streaks of blood smeared across his face. His white shirt was torn, stained with droplets of blood. His trousers were shredded, frayed at the knees and flecked with red, barely holding together. He looked like a wreck, dishevelled and battered, but he was alive, and for now that was enough.

Flashes of memory slammed into Knox, sharp and brutal. A blinding eruption of light. The crushing black that followed. The roar of the explosion that seemed to tear the earth apart beneath him, throwing him like a ragdoll into chaos. The heat felt alive, seething and clawing at his skin with greedy fingers. The air was thick and unbreathable, choked with the acrid stench of fire, dust, and charred wood. It was suffocating and unrelenting.

His memory returned swiftly, and he looked around for Sarah and Jess. There was no movement, only the large remnants of what used to be a bungalow. He knew he needed to reach the garage. That thought consumed him, rising above the haze of pain and panic that swirled in his mind. His thoughts were a fractured blur, tangled in the grim reality that the fire was devouring everything, and potentially everyone, inside.

He lurched forward, each step sending pain through his body like a knife. The blast had left him battered and bruised, every muscle and joint screaming for relief. Yet the thought of Sarah and Jess drove him on, overriding the agony. Desperation clawed at his chest, fierce and unrelenting. This was not how it was supposed to end. He refused to accept it.

The internal garage door was now a fortress of destruction, with an enormous roof timber sprawled across the entrance, splintered and burnt, while bricks from the collapsed wall had formed a jagged, unyielding barricade. Sarah and Jess were inside, buried under that.

He stumbled forward, each step a grinding battle against his body's protests. Pain lanced through his legs, shoulders, and chest, every joint and nerve battered by the blast. His head throbbed with every heartbeat, yet he kept moving. He had to. The desperate need to reach them burned hotter than the flames, scorching away any hesitation.

Knox made his way through the gaping hole where the front door had once stood. It now hung precariously from a single hinge, swaying in the heat and smoke. He turned towards the external garage door, his eyes narrowed against the chaos. What had once been a sturdy metal safeguard, bolted and solid, was now a warped and twisted shell, barely recognisable. The surrounding brickwork had crumbled with it, collapsing inwards to bury the contents beneath a suffocating weight of rubble and debris. The entire structure was nearly flat, with only the faint outline of its original shape hinting at what it had been.

Knox's heart sank, but his resolve did not falter. The sight of the wreckage, imposing and seemingly final, should have stopped him cold, yet his body moved forward as if propelled by sheer will. Each step felt heavier, each inch closer a new test of endurance. Stopping was not an option.

Instinct took over. He reached the mangled ruin of twisted metal from the garage shutter and gripped it tightly. Its jagged edges cut into his hands, but he did not care. He heaved, his body shuddering with the effort, muscles screaming in defiance. The debris did not move at first, sitting like an immovable wall of despair. Knox refused to quit. He pulled again, each attempt tearing at his hands, his strength powered by desperation.

Eventually, the wreckage began to shift, slowly, painfully, inch by agonising inch. Knox clawed at the rubble, brick by brick, splinter by splinter.

His breath caught when he saw the streaks of blood, dark and glistening, smeared across the rubble. It was thick, almost black in the dim light, dripping between the jagged remains of bricks and charred wood like a macabre message left behind by the chaos.

For a moment, he thought it was his. He knew he was bleeding, feeling the sting in his leg, the mix of sweat and blood sliding into his eyes. But no, it was not his blood. It could not be.

There was too much of it.

He paused, his hands hovering over the debris, his body trembling with exhaustion and a deep dread. He realised that the more he dug, the closer he came to tearing away the final threads of hope he clung to.

Schrödinger's cat flickered through his mind, a fleeting, absurd thought yet painfully apt. Right now, Sarah and Jess were both alive and dead, existing in that terrible space between possibility and certainty. The moment he moved one more brick, the illusion would shatter, and fate would hand down its merciless judgment.

Sirens rose in the distance, a mournful wail slicing through the night, their cold blue lights faintly touching the horizon. Knox plunged his hands back into the rubble, his heart pounding.

A brick fell away in his hand.

He had found them.

Sarah and Jess lay lifeless, draped in a shroud of dust and blood. Their faces, once so full of life, were hidden beneath the violence of the blast, leaving only shadows of who they had been. Knox stared at them, his chest constricting as the world around him slipped into an oppressive silence.

He reached for their necks, his hands shaking, searching desperately for a pulse, for any sign of hope.

There was none.

And he had known it all along. From the first thunderous wave of the explosion, from the moment he started digging, he had known. Still, the truth crashed over him like a hammer, brutal and inescapable.

For a long moment, Knox knelt in the wreckage, his eyes never leaving their still, lifeless forms. The edges of the world blurred, collapsing into the numb quiet around them. The weight of his failure pressed down on him. He had failed them, failed Michael, failed everyone who trusted him to set things right.

It was now obvious that Michael's death was not suicide, someone had killed him, and now they had taken Sarah and Jess as well.

That realisation burned in Knox's chest, transforming grief into a fierce resolve. He could not bring them back, but he would make whoever did this pay. He rose slowly, his eyes locked on the two broken bodies, his blood and dust covered hands hanging at his sides. Then he patted his pocket, feeling the reassuring shape of the memory stick. It was still there, his only lead. He had to find out what was on it before more people died.

Knox knew what staying meant. The police would flood the scene, arrest him, and drag him in for endless questioning about his involvement. He would be locked away with questions he could not answer, leaving the real killer free to vanish. It went against all his instincts to abandon Sarah and Jess, but he had no choice. Potentially more lives hung in the balance, and the trail would soon go cold.

Slowly he realised he was the perfect suspect. Running or not, he had handed them everything. The funeral, his rushed departure, the explosion, every detail aligned too neatly. He had opportunity and the means, all pointing to him with damning precision. He had no alibi, no airtight explanation. His DNA was all over the house, left there in the hours he had spent moving newspapers and walking from room to room. If anyone looked closely, they would see he had the know-how to set up a blast like this. His military background was now working against him.

The witnesses at the funeral would remember him leaving early, slipping out with a focus that would now look suspiciously like premeditation. Every detail painted him guilty, a neat narrative even if he had not done it. He could practically see the headlines, feel the cuffs locking around his wrists.

He scrambled to his Land Rover, which was still ticking over with its engine running, slamming the door and revving the engine. Without a second thought, he shot down the narrow road, his eyes flicking between the wing mirrors and the road ahead. He had a rough destination in mind, the A1, and then heading north, but before he could take that route, he needed to put some distance between himself and the destruction he had left behind. He knew the risks; he was leaving a trail that could lead the police straight to him. If he wanted any chance of staying free and catching those responsible, he would have to shake them off and create some space.

As he pressed the clutch to change gears, a sharp, searing pain shot through his leg, so intense it blurred his vision. He glanced down, struggling to process the sight of a large shard of glass embedded in his thigh, blood soaking the fabric around it. The pain was brutal, white hot, but he forced it to the back of his mind. He needed somewhere safe to pull over, somewhere to patch himself up before things grew worse.

Gripping the wheel, he focused on the road ahead, the throbbing in his leg a reminder that he was running out of time in more ways than one.

Knox finally cleared the village edge, the Land Rover rattling onto a winding B road that cut through open pastures. His leg continued to throb as he used the gears to hold speed and control on the twisting route.

He knew the night ahead would be relentless. He would have to abandon the Lanny, clean up, then head north on foot. About fifteen miles lay between him and his goal, perhaps a difficult five-hour trek across rough terrain. If he could push himself, maybe four hours, but the injured leg would slow him.

He passed the A1 turn off, scanning for the service stations he had pictured in his mind. He avoided the first, adding a few more miles between himself and his last location. At last, the second station appeared, isolated and dimly lit, just what he needed. Leaving the Land Rover here would widen the search radius, forcing the police to consider various routes north, south, and east.

He pulled into the darkest corner of the service station car park, switching off the headlights by using the huge dial set into the centre dashboard and guided the vehicle into a shadowed spot near an old brick wall, before killing the engine.

First, he had to tend to his wounds. His leg was the worst of it, and if he ignored it, matters would only get worse. Reaching under the passenger seat, Knox pulled out his Team Medic first aid kit, fingers moving swiftly through its familiar contents: super glue, elastic bandages, antibacterial wipes, gauze pads. He grabbed a bottle of water from a box on the rear compartment footwell and flipped open his Gerber multi tool, selecting the pliers.

He widened the tear in his trousers around the wound and braced himself, jaw clenched, before pushing the pliers into his leg, gripping the glass shard lodged deep in the muscle. With a sharp yank, he dragged it free, the jagged edge pulling through his flesh. Blood welled up, dark and quick, gathering around the injury. He poured water over it, letting the cold sting his nerves.

Knox cleaned the wound thoroughly, wiping away blood and debris with gauze and searching carefully in the dim light for any remaining glass fragments. Satisfied he had removed everything he could see, he pressed the torn edges together. He uncapped a small tube of super glue and, squinting in the dark of the Land Rover's cabin, applied a thin line along the lips of the wound, ensuring the glue did not seep inside the gash itself.

A sharp sting flared, but he held firm, keeping the wound closed until the glue set, sealing his skin as well as possible. Once he felt it was secure, he pressed a clean gauze pad over it and wrapped it tightly with an elastic field dressing, winding until the pressure felt sufficient.

Knox knew it was a temporary fix. The wound was deep, and the glue might fail before morning, but the gauze would absorb further bleeding, and he could reapply the glue if needed. He had miles to cover and no time to lose.

Stripping off his filthy clothes, he winced as he peeled the material away from bruised, tender skin. He poured the last of the water over his head, letting it trickle down his face and clear away layers of sweat, blood, and grime. Using a packet of wet wipes, he scrubbed himself, wincing each time he uncovered fresh cuts or scrapes. He disinfected the worst of them with antibacterial wipes, covering what needed dressing with plasters or gauze.

He reached into a black tour grip bag in the rear compartment of the Land Rover, which was packed with cold weather gear, and pulled out some spare clothing. He put on black walking trousers with zip pockets, ensuring they fitted comfortably over his bandaged thigh. Next came a green thermal undershirt, followed by a fleece lined Norwegian roll neck jumper. The thick fabric enveloped him in warmth.

Any fool can be cold, someone once told him, a lifetime ago.

He pulled on thick socks and laced up his well-worn Alt-Berg boots, scuffed and battered from the blast but still serviceable. Next, he shrugged into his old DPM field jacket, a roomy, windproof layer with large pockets. He stuffed Haribo sweets into one pocket, knowing he would need the energy soon. The hood was rolled at the collar, and a clear plastic compass hung from a button on the left side of his chest.

In the other large pocket, he tucked away a racing spoon, a SureFire torch, and a boil in the bag meal pack, hoping he had grabbed the all-day breakfast option from a rat pack in the dark. He thought of adding a sleeping bag and roll mat but dismissed the idea at once. He was not planning to be out long, and sleep was not on the agenda. Instead, he took a space blanket, folded tight in a slim plastic pouch, saving weight and bulk, but knowing it would provide warmth if needed.

He added two water bottles, secured alongside a battlefield first aid kit. Packing everything into a compact MTP daysack, he carefully arranged the weight. Finally, he slipped the pack onto his shoulders, tugging the straps until it felt secure.

Knox slid the Gerber tool into a pouch on his belt, a small yet dependable trusted companion.

He retrieved a small plastic container of cam-cream from his pocket, unclipping the lid and smoothing thick green, black, and brown streaks onto his face, down his neck, and over his ears and hands. The cold cream felt sticky, and he had always disliked it, but he knew it was essential. This was not about Hollywood style stripes; it was about breaking up reflections, eliminating the chance that a glint of light might give him away. He pulled on a black woollen hat, tucking his greying hair underneath. Then came his tan combat gloves, the rigid plastic across the knuckles fitting neatly. He resembled a shadow.

Everything was ready, he felt like himself again, this was who he was: fully prepared, every detail checked. He looked at his watch, the faint glow of the dial showing it was zero two hundred hours.

Henry took out his phone, noticing another batch of missed calls from Catheryn. Her name hovered on the screen, and he felt a pang of regret for not answering. He could feel the weight of the wedding band on his finger, but there was nothing he could do now. It was too late. He powered down the phone, wrapped it tightly in tin foil, folding the edges until satisfied, then tucked it into a Faraday bag, ensuring it was completely blocked from sending or receiving signals. No signal, no connection, no trace, he assured himself, slipping it into his jacket pocket.

Knox did a final, thorough check of his gear, patting each pouch and strap. He had taped the straps into small, tight bundles to stop them flapping around. Everything was secure and accessible. His fingers lingered on the day sack's edge, double checking his first aid kit and water. It all seemed right, but a restless sense of unease gnawed at him.

He raised his eyes to the night sky above, the emptiness stretching out, stars piercing the blackness like distant sparks of hope. The cold bit into him, an icy wind that found its way through layers of fabric. His breath turned to faint clouds in the still air. He paused, wondering if he had misjudged the chill, it would certainly be a cold night, but brushed the doubt aside. He did not plan on stopping for long. Constant movement would keep him warm, and resting was not an option.

Taking a steady breath, he turned to the Land Rover and did one final sweep. He crouched near the front bumper, wedging the key into the hollow of the metal bumper. It was not perfect, but it would have to do. If everything went reasonably well, the vehicle might still be there when he returned.

Ready to move.

Henry checked the pocket with the memory stick.

Move.

He slipped into the undergrowth, letting the darkness wrap around him like a cloak.

CHAPTER FIFTEEN

Trekking through the dark woods was no easy task, but Knox was in his element. Moving without a torch, he relied on the natural cover of trees and undergrowth, staying well clear of pathways and bridleways. The foliage pressed close, shadows stretching deep, yet he found comfort in their embrace. This was familiar territory. Years of patrolling dense forests in Britain and Northern Europe had prepared him to navigate difficult terrain in near darkness, with only the faint glint of moonlight to guide him.

The distance, however, posed a challenge. Fifteen miles north lay his destination, a course over rugged ground that he aimed to complete before dawn. The long, chilly winter night worked to his advantage, but the route demanded all his stamina. He would need to maintain a brisk, unyielding pace. Convinced that nobody could predict his exact route or goal, he felt relatively safe from any immediate ambush. Still, his solitude brought unwelcome reflection on the chaos he had left behind, and above all, on Sarah and Jess.

Knox's heart sank as he replayed the scene: the garage flattened to a heap of stone and scorched debris, Sarah and Jess lying in their cold, dusty grave. He tried to convince himself that he had had no choice but to leave.

Yet guilt clawed at him. Sarah and Jess had not needed to be there. He had involved them, drawing them directly into danger. If he had warned them away, convinced them there was nothing to find, they might still be alive. He could almost see their faces in the dark, shadows toying with his vision.

He forced himself to push the thoughts aside. Regret served no purpose; he could not turn back time, regardless of his wishes.

There had been a fleeting hope that the emergency services might have saved them, but Knox dismissed it almost instantly. He had checked their pulses, felt the cold stillness beneath his trembling fingers. Their bodies had been crushed, twisted in such a way that allowed no doubt. The blood, thick and dark, pooling around them, had proven there was no chance of survival.

He turned his mind to the underlying cause, forcing away the gnawing guilt. This had not been an accident; he was certain of that. It was deliberate, but hurried and messy, as though whoever was responsible had been rushed or panicked. Michael's death, on the other hand, had been clean, calculated, and left no lingering questions.

The authorities had not investigated any deeper than necessary, content to accept the appearance of suicide. The evidence had been neatly arranged to fit that narrative. Yet this explosion was different. Its scale, the destruction, would spark inquiries. The police could hardly file it away. Alarms would ring, and a thorough investigation would begin.

Knox knew exactly where that investigation would start. He had been at the scene, his DNA scattered all over the house. Proving motive might be more difficult, but that concern would come second, and if they linked it to Michael's death, Knox would need his alibi. He kept meticulous records for work and expenses, tracking his hours precisely. He could establish his whereabouts during Michael's so-called suicide, he had been on a job in Lancashire. However, that would take time.

Nobody would consider separate, unconnected

killers. Even the civilian police would look for one suspect.

The only way to honour Sarah, Jess, and Michael was to locate those behind these murders and deliver the consequences they deserved. That, Knox realised, was his only remaining option.

He continued onward, aware that his pace was slowing. The throbbing pain in his leg felt severe, and he sensed blood soaking his bandage, warm and sticky against his skin. He needed to move faster, but the wound held him back. Gritting his teeth, he dropped to one knee beside a wide tree, shrugged off his pack, and dug through it until he retrieved his first aid kit. Inside lay a field dressing and a packet of Celox powder, which he hoped would act as effectively as the military grade version he had once used. Celox formed a gel-like clot upon contact with blood, one of the few reliable ways to stem heavy bleeding outside of a hospital setting.

His mother's words echoed in his mind as he inspected the wound: "Beggars cannot be choosers." A scar was the least of his worries.

Knox tugged down his walking trousers and peeled away the existing gauze, wincing at the sight of the raw, angry tear. The dressing had performed about as well as he had expected, which was not enough. The glue had given out, leaving the wound gaping. He tore open the Celox packet with his teeth, sprinkling the granules directly into the wound.

A fierce pain tore through his leg, as though the gash itself was resisting the powder. Knox inhaled sharply, as the Celox reacted with his blood, becoming a sticky clot. Clenching his leg, he watched the powder seal the wound more firmly than before.

He placed a fresh field dressing over it, larger than the original, ensuring it spanned the wound and caught any new blood seeping through. It pressed heavily against his thigh, but he needed it secure to prevent further bleeding.

He rinsed some of the blood from his trousers using a small amount of water before zipping them again. Then, slumping against the rough bark of the tree, hidden in undergrowth, he allowed himself a few moments of rest. Ten minutes only, he decided. He pictured his path: heading northwest until he heard the drone of the A1(M), then tracking north with the motorway on his left, following it until he reached the village road that led to his destination.

With a final deep breath, Knox stowed his first aid kit, took a slow drink of water, and resettled his day sack on his shoulders. Testing his leg, he felt the pain persist, but the dressing held. Satisfied, he got to his feet, steeled himself, and pressed on. He knew he had to walk faster, pushing aside his body's complaints. Time was not on his side, and he had already lost too much of it.

It was not long before the noise of the motorway reached him. In the quiet night, he heard the steady drone of lorries and cars speeding along the A1, a low and constant rumble, like distant thunder. Headlights cut through the darkness in swift patterns, bright beams crossing each other with unwavering urgency.

Knox watched warily for any sign of blue police lights or a set of headlights that lingered unnaturally. By now, the police would certainly be searching for him. Patrols would be scouring the roads, officers briefed and on the lookout. Remaining this close to the motorway was a necessary risk, though it set his nerves on edge.

His greater fear, however, came from above.

He heard the helicopter before he saw it, at first only a faint thumping in the night. The sound steadily grew, transforming into the unmistakeable chop of blades cleaving the sky. In a former life, that noise had often meant rescue, the approach of a Chinook or a Merlin to airlift wounded men. He had helped load casualties onto such flights countless times, battered stretchers lined up in desperation. The rotor wash, thick with dust and heat, had once meant hope.

Not tonight. Now it was the hunter, and Knox was the target. He concentrated, knowing the helicopter would be equipped with thermal imaging, capable of detecting even a small heat signature against the cold ground. He needed to conceal himself immediately.

The muddy earth underfoot offered one possibility, but he dismissed any image of smearing himself like an action film parody. Scanning the immediate area, he spotted a dense clump of trees carpeted with fallen leaves, piled in thick drifts that might, with luck, hide him from above.

He pulled out the space blanket from his daysack, the reflective material crinkling in the darkness. Working rapidly, he wrapped it around himself, ignoring the clinging chill of the metal surface. Then he scooped handfuls of damp earth and smeared it over the blanket, dulling its shine. The mud was cold and gritty against his hands, but he pushed on, determined.

He curled into a ball, drawing his limbs in tightly, and shuffled beneath the heaps of leaves. The scent of decay filled his nose as he slipped into the mouldering pile. It was not perfect, but if it masked his heat signature from the helicopter's camera, it might be enough.

The chopper roared overhead, blades beating the air, sending a flurry of dry leaves scattering through the canopy. Knox lay motionless, his lungs burning as he tried to breathe as shallowly as possible, his muscles locked in tense stillness. Even the smallest movement might betray him.

It could not end here. If they caught him, the investigation would swallow him whole, his testimony lost in bureaucratic delay, while the real killers vanished into the shadows. He had witnessed too many lives destroyed by hesitation, by losing the right lead at the wrong time. Should he fall now, innocent people would die.

The space blanket, smeared with mud, concealed his body heat, while layers of rotting leaves and undergrowth hid the metallic glint. Above him, the helicopter hovered, rotors beating like a drum across the night sky. Knox held his breath, every part of him straining to remain invisible.

Seconds stretched into agonising minutes, the helicopter's blades thudding overhead in a relentless sweep of the woods. Knox lay completely still, pressed against the cold earth, willing himself invisible beneath the undergrowth. The raw smell of soil and damp leaves filled his nostrils, which felt strangely comforting. He had spent far too many nights like this, lying motionless, heart pounding, muscles tight with anticipation. Places like these had trained him well, and they felt like old allies in a familiar battleground.

Sleep teased him, tugging at the edges of his mind, whispering that he could let his vigilance slip for a moment. The chopper's noise became a lull, almost hypnotic. Sarah and Jess drifted into his thoughts, their faces bright with laughter, their smiles easy and unguarded, now replaced by grey and lifeless expressions. They had been sisters he never knew he needed, a family he had not realised he wanted. The memory of their warmth cut through him more sharply than expected, leaving a raw ache behind.

At last, the helicopter moved away, its sound receding to the north as the woods reclaimed their stillness. Knox stayed motionless a moment longer, testing the silence to be sure it was real. Once he was convinced, he eased himself from the leaves, cleaned the space blanket, folded it, and replaced it in his daysack. A quick glance at his compass, a small adjustment, and he pressed on, pushing through thick undergrowth. A look at his watch told him he was running late, but dawn had yet to break. If he increased his pace, he could still arrive at the village when he intended.

He headed north, skirting the edge of the motorway, where multiple roads branched away from the A1 like crooked fingers. One of these roads would lead him to the village, so he had to cross each one until he reached the correct route. He crouched in the undergrowth, listening and watching for any sound, any glimmer of headlights. Only when he was certain it was safe did he move, quick and silent, running across the tarmac before vanishing back into the darkness on the far side.

He repeated this tactic, crossing road after road as he travelled further north. Then he spotted what he had been searching for, a worn sign looming in the shadows, its letters faint in the weak light before dawn. Ravensfield, 2 miles.

Reassured that he was near his goal, Knox quickened his strides, pushing harder until he reached the outskirts of the village shortly before zero seven hundred hours. The sun had not yet appeared, but a pale grey light was beginning to seep over the rolling green fields, throwing the land into dim relief. His leg continued to pulse with a steady ache, yet it had held together, and the bleeding had stopped. Small victories, he told himself.

He circled around the village, moving through the freezing mist that clung to the small hamlet before pausing on a low hillside overlooking a farmhouse hidden in a thick stand of trees. It appeared to be a converted barn, with white framed windows set into large, rugged stone blocks, rising from the ground with a blunt, square shape as though it had been carved from solid rock.

Frost glittered across the barn's roof, clinging like a brittle, pale shell. It glowed faintly where heat from the interior pushed through the brick and tiles, leaving small pockets of steam to curl upward and disperse in the morning chill.

Thin tendrils of smoke drifted from a chimney, the wisps catching the day's first rays of light as they rose, then vanished into the crisp air.

Knox settled into the icy undergrowth, lying prone and watchful for over an hour. No police cars came, no other vehicles. He had taken care to arrive unseen, but it appeared unnecessary. The occupant seemed to be alone.

His gaze moved over the farmhouse and its yard, noticing the numerous cameras positioned around the property. Each camera was set to cover a different angle, creating a technological ring of watchful eyes. Several cameras focused on the gravel drive in front of the building, ready to record any person or vehicle. Others were mounted at the corners of the house, leaving no obvious blind spots.

He knew that the moment he left his hiding place, he would appear on these cameras, and there was no realistic way to approach the house undetected. Being seen was inevitable, and Knox had made peace with that.

He moved in, staying low until he reached the rear outer wall, then followed it along until he arrived at the oversized barn door. After checking the corners to be sure the occupant was indeed alone, he knocked sharply on the door. Moments later, it creaked open, revealing a short, round man with a shaved head. Bits of breakfast clung to his stained dressing gown, which hung open to show a dirty grey T-shirt and track bottoms streaked with dirt and grease. He wore tartan slippers on his feet. His eyes grew wide, a mixture of shock and dread.

Knox smiled and gave a mock salute. “Morning, wanker. Get the kettle on.”

CHAPTER SIXTEEN

The man moved with directness and purpose, his figure striking against the neat, almost surreal setting of the Theme Park's entrance, where an inflatable Hippo drifted in the morning air. Beneath his feet, a path of interlocking bricks wound through rows of trees towards the park gates and a huge sign with the name HippoLand emblazoned on it. The scene could have come straight from The Wizard of Oz if Oz had traded its golden yellow brick road for a bleak, winter grey path snaking through skeletal trees. Instead of a gleaming Emerald City, a twelve-foot fence loomed in the distance, its black metal glinting in the pale light.

He was big, stocky, and solid, a genuine presence. He stood over six foot four tall, with broad shoulders that brushed low hanging branches as he walked. His black hair was cropped close, each line neat and meticulous. He sported a huge, thick, well-groomed black tache that seemed to define and shadow his face. A black bomber jacket stretched snugly across his frame, zipped tight, lending him the appearance of a man who belonged nowhere yet fit in anywhere. His jeans were scuffed and stone washed, and his gleaming white trainers looked fresh out of the box.

A nondescript, medium sized black rucksack hung over one shoulder, but in his right hand, he held a small digital camera. He lifted it from time to time, snapping a photo here and another there, documenting, collecting, enjoying the scenery.

He reached the entrance and scanned his paper ticket at the electronic barrier, which clicked smoothly, unlocking with a soft metallic note. He pushed through the turnstile, offering a friendly nod to the security guard.

The man studied the guard quickly, assessing him with a well-trained eye. The guard was older, his paunch straining against a too tight uniform shirt, his thinning hair slicked back as though trying to reclaim lost authority. He looked tired, disinterested, like a man on minimum wage who would barely manage more than a token glance at the bag, if he bothered at all.

Modern technology has streamlined most entry points, from rail stations to theme parks, making this part of the job easy. Automated systems rarely detected what mattered.

"Good morning, sir," the guard greeted, polite but uninterested.

"Good morning." The man's response was smooth, his Russian accent thick and deliberate. He added with a wry grin, "I am here to enjoy the rides and your famous British summer."

The guard chuckled, giving him a quick once over. "I think you mean winter, sir. May I look in your bag?"

"Of course," the man answered, his accent curling around each word. "This winter feels like summer to me. I am from Ukraine. Our winters are much colder. Here, see in my bag."

He swung the rucksack off his shoulder, unzipping it slowly, carefully, holding it open just wide enough for the guard to peer inside. A plastic food container, a large packet of crisps, a bottle of cola, a bobble hat, and a pair of thick gloves lay neatly packed.

"My lunch," he said with a small smile. "Britain is expensive."

The guard gave a brief nod, his gaze skimming over the contents with routine disinterest. “Thank you, and enjoy your day,” he said, already leaning back against the wall, settling in for another long shift that would blur into the background.

The man returned the nod, his smile still in place as he zipped up the bag and slung it over his shoulder. The moment he turned away, his expression shifted, and he slipped seamlessly into the mass of people. The Christmas holiday crowd surged through the theme park, children and teenagers chattering with excitement as they hurried between towering rides and winter stalls. Voices and laughter merged with the roar of roller coasters echoing off steel frameworks. The man blended in, walking into the throng of people until he vanished from sight.

CHAPTER SEVENTEEN

James Webster and Henry Knox embraced on the farmstead doorstep, clapping each other firmly on the back in a way that suggested a long-standing friendship. As they pulled apart, Knox observed the deeply etched lines in his friend's face, a reminder of how many years had passed since they had last met.

"It's about time you showed up," James said, his grin genuine, his voice warm and welcoming. "I thought you'd keep posting me laptops forever. Welcome to my humble abode."

He stepped back, taking in Henry's dishevelled appearance. "And you stink, mate. You need a shower."

Henry looked down, noticing the mud caking his clothes and the smudged camouflage cream on his gloves. His boots, once polished, were now scuffed and clotted with mud and leaves. He managed a grin, his white teeth in stark contrast to the grime and cam cream.

"I've been in worse states," he replied with a hint of pride. "But yes, a brew wouldn't go amiss."

James smirked, raising an eyebrow. "I'd ask you to take your boots off, but I suppose this isn't a social call," he said, amusement colouring his tone as he pushed the door open wider for Knox to enter.

Knox entered the house and set his day sack just inside the door before following James into the kitchen, which was surprisingly spacious and welcoming for a man who lived alone. It was open-plan and warm, merging modern design with a comfortable, lived-in charm. The black granite worktops gleamed in some places, while in others they were cluttered with signs of James's everyday life, plates piled by the sink, a half-empty coffee mug on the edge of a chopping board, stray utensils left mid-use.

Weak winter sunlight spilled through the white plastic-framed windows. The kitchen featured two pine-coloured wooden doors, their grain smooth and warm in the soft light. One door stood ajar, revealing a dimly lit corridor beyond, perhaps the living room or a stairway leading upstairs, while the second was firmly shut, offering no clues to what lay behind. The air was thick with the scent of fresh toast and strong coffee, aromas that hit Knox like a freight train, reminding him how long it had been since he had eaten.

"Did I catch you at a bad time, mate?" he asked, surveying the room.

James gestured towards a plate of thick toast on the counter. "Help yourself," he said, still looking Knox up and down, adjusting to the sight of him in his kitchen.

Knox did not hesitate, grabbing a slice and biting into it, savouring the warmth and simplicity of well-buttered toast. James chuckled, leaning against the counter to watch him. "Easy, Ox, leave some for me, will you? Haven't you eaten this week?"

Knox shrugged, a wry smile on his face as he reached for another slice. "Let's just say it has been a long night."

"I know," Webster said, his voice dropping to a careful tone. "You're all over the news, mate. Every channel is talking about it. I've had people messaging me, asking if you're alright. The press... they're saying you snapped, PTSD or some such bullshit, then went on a killing spree." His eyes narrowed. "They're saying you killed Michael and his daughters."

Knox froze with the toast halfway to his mouth, crumbs falling from his fingers. Slowly, he put the slice down, locking eyes with Webster, feeling a flicker of hurt and indignation. “Are you serious, Webby? Do you think I’d force march my way through half the night to your doorstep if I’d done that?”

Webster’s expression softened, and the tension broke with a crooked smile. “I didn’t really think so, mate. But you know, I had to ask. Didn’t want you murdering me for burning your toast.”

Then James realised the joke about burning was probably too close to home, and was definitely too soon, so he distracted himself by picking up his phone and scrolling through a series of messages, the strain in his voice easing. “So, what exactly brings you here, Ox?”

Knox inhaled slowly, letting the comfortable atmosphere of the kitchen calm him. His mind turned to the long history he shared with James Webster. They had started out as fresh-faced Junior Non-Commissioned Officers at Colchester, those early days spent doing exercises and police work that built the foundation of their careers. Eventually, both moved, for different reasons, to the Service Police Crime Bureau, known as SPCB, an analytical policing unit where numbers and data held greater sway than brute force.

James’s knack for detail led him to the Special Investigation Branch, the SIB. Outsiders saw the SIB as the Army’s elite investigators, but Knox understood that it was only an eight-week course, yes it was intensive, but it was more of a gatekeeper than true special training.

The SIB had always felt like a closed shop to Knox. He possessed the intuition, ambition, and experience, but he lacked the political finesse needed to survive in that environment. He aimed straight for the heart of a matter, leaving little room for diplomacy or ego-stroking. In the SIB, treading carefully was a necessary skill, knowing how to handle people smoothly, placate superiors, and polish rough edges. Knox had no time for any of it.

Where others observed strategy, he saw time wasted on self-preservation, preventing the truth from surfacing. For him, loyalty was key, staying alert to the small details that others missed. If that approach left him an outsider, then so be it. It was how he worked and always would be.

Then there was SP3C, the Service Police Cyber Crime Centre, a division that Knox did admire, the specialists who focused on encrypted drives, devices, and digital footprints. The SP3C experts were skilled at extracting and interpreting evidence from laptops and phones. Many of their cases involved child pornography, a high-priority focus, yet their remit covered the entire range of devices and data relevant to crimes across the Armed Forces.

That was precisely why he was here. James had once been one of SP3C's best operators. Back when they worked together, James had proved himself relentless, meticulous, and razor-sharp in his investigative approach. If anyone could find out why Michael died, it would be him. After last night, Knox knew he could accept nothing less than the best.

Knox reached into his pocket and pulled out the small British Army-issue memory stick, lifting it to eye level. "This. I believe this is the reason Michael was killed. I need to know what's on it."

Webster glanced up from his phone, fixing his gaze on the stick. Curiosity shifted to a darker, more knowledgeable stare. "Is that what I think it is?"

Henry nodded.

James tensed. "And why, exactly, do you expect me to help you with it?"

Henry gave a faint grin. "You're the best investigator SP3C had. If anyone can crack this, it's you."

James let out a quiet laugh and raised his eyebrows. "Seems like you've come to the right place." Stepping away from the kitchen counter, James motioned for Knox to follow him towards the pine door that was firmly closed. The smell of toast and coffee fell behind as they entered the next room, which had an earthier tang embedded in the old stone walls. Knox scanned the room out of habit, registering just two possible exits: the door they had come through and another open doorway at the far side, where a window let in natural light.

In contrast to the high ceilings in the kitchen, the roof here was lower, implying rooms above. LED lights threw a steady glow, clashing with the natural daylight elsewhere in the house. No windows punctuated these walls; everything was solid and secure.

The room was small, practical, and intentionally clear of clutter, only around a quarter of the size of the kitchen. Metal shelving lined the walls, crammed with humming machinery that emitted tiny LED glimmers. They may have been computers, servers, or heavy-duty modems, stacked with care in the corners. The air felt cooler, laced with the sterile tang of electronics and static, a faint vibration humming in the background.

Webster eased his bulk into a reinforced office chair positioned before a multi-screen console that seemed to pulse with energy. Knox counted five screens, each wired to a colossal tower that whirred with liquid cooling. It resembled a command centre more than a farmhouse office.

"Not bad, mate. Must have cost you a fortune," Knox remarked, inspecting the assembly.

"I used my medical discharge money," James replied, settling in. "Keeps me occupied, for the most part," he added with a grin, whilst patting his knee.

Knox stepped closer, offering the memory stick.

"Alright, this will have military encryption, so I'll start by firing up a sandboxed virtual machine to check for malware. Then I'll do a bit-by-bit forensic copy before dissecting the encryption in a controlled environment. If it's a hoax, it could be loaded with viruses. Decrypting it won't be quick; there could be multiple layers."

He slotted the stick into the reader, his fingers already flying across the keyboard. "Now, Ox, if you've got anything else, now's the time to spill. I'll need everything you can give me to crack this."

Knox shrugged. "The USB stick is obviously military issue. I found it sellotaped to the base of a cabinet in Michael's house, a house that had been ransacked, probably by someone searching for it. Whoever turned that place over later killed Sarah and Jess, and they tried to kill me too. They probably killed Michael as well. There's something on that stick, something important enough to kill for, and whoever wants it has not given up. That is all I know."

"The old 'hide the casefile behind the filing cabinet' trick," James laughed, "very old school."

Knox fixed James with a steady gaze. "Everything else in that house was conspiracy theories. Nothing I saw felt like it was real. Michael had newspapers and notebooks scattered everywhere, like some kind of obsessive nutjob. I took pictures of some of before we cleared it out. I can show you on my phone if you want, but I didn't find anything useful at the time. Still, I suppose something in that mess might be connected to whatever is on the drive."

Knox pulled out his mobile phone, still tightly wrapped in a Faraday bag and multiple layers of tinfoil. He held it up for emphasis, the crinkled foil catching the light. "If I show you what is on this," he said dryly, "the police will be here faster than a tramp on chips."

James glanced at the phone. "All right, I want to see what is on this phone, so let us do it carefully. I will put it on a local Wi-Fi network, mask the IP address, and keep our location off the grid. Then you can show me."

Knox nodded, watching as the virtual machine loaded. James carefully unwrapped the phone, peeling away the foil and sliding it out of the Faraday bag. He held it up, giving Knox a sideways look. "Double wrapped in foil and a Faraday bag? You didn't leave anything to chance, did you, Knoxy?"

Knox produced a small, genuine smile. "I learned from the best, mate."

James regarded Henry curiously. "Why did you never join the SIB? They could have used someone like you. You would have aced the course, no doubt."

Knox held his gaze. "Because the SIB were full of snakes, mate, present company excluded. They always looked down on us muppets, acting as though we were worthless. I liked the investigative work, but they only turned up if we had already done half of it. They would not touch a scene outside working hours. Besides, I would not have played nicely, and I doubt I would have lasted 22 years. I would have been booted out in no time."

James's laugh filled the room, deep and hearty. "You never pulled your punches, as always. You would have been a riot with the Feds. They would have hated you, but I would have paid good money to watch." He turned back to his task, still chuckling as he unwrapped the phone and plugged into his PC.

A companionable silence settled between them, built on years of trust. Knox watched, aware he had passed over every lead he possessed. In James's hands lay the only chance of uncovering what really happened to Michael, Sarah, and Jess.

"All set, IP and GPS spoofed," James said, handing the phone back with a satisfied grin. "As far as anyone tracking you is concerned, you are somewhere in Serbia."

Knox switched on the phone, and messages began pouring in, notifications lighting the screen. Some were from Catheryn, others from unknown numbers, but one made him freeze: Amy Thornton. His gut churned. Amy worked with West Yorkshire Police, she had been a great Lieutenant during her time in the Royal Military Police, and she was probably an excellent officer now. Knox immediately drew the conclusion that she must have been at the scene last night, sifting through the rubble of the explosion.

Before he could decide how to respond, the phone vibrated in his hand. Amy's name appeared on the display.

Knox looked over at James, alarmed. "I thought you said they couldn't trace where I am."

James shrugged. "They can't. The call is just connecting like any normal call. It is a phone, mate, that's what phones do."

Feeling some relief, Knox took a deep breath, thumb hovering over the screen before he swiped to answer and lifted the phone to his ear.

"Knox," he said, his tone crisp, almost formal.

James looked at Knox confused.

"Good morning, Henry. This is Amy Thornton. How are you?" Her voice was steady and calm, carrying a quiet authority. Amy had always been that kind of officer, holding control without ever having to raise her voice.

Knox's instincts responded. "Ma'am," he said automatically, slipping back into military protocol as though he had never left.

A brief silence followed. Then Amy spoke again, "I'd like you to come in, Henry. We have some questions that need answers. Can you tell me where you are?"

He hesitated, glancing at James, who was watching him closely. "I'm sorry, Amy. It is not that I don't want to tell you, but I can't right now. I know you'll have plenty of questions, and I do want to explain, but it has to wait." He softened his tone. "By the way, congratulations on joining the civilian police. It suits you."

James raised an eyebrow, his expression a mix of curiosity and exasperation as Knox ended the call.

"Why answer?" he asked, folding his arms. "Seems like it could complicate matters."

Knox shrugged. "I needed to open some dialogue, let her know I am still me, that I have not lost the plot. She'll be useful soon enough, one way or the other."

James nodded, trusting his friend. Knox knew the fuse he was burning would eventually run short, but to resolve this, he needed allies, even if they were uncertain whose side they were on.

"Jesus Christ, mate," James murmured, shaking his head. "What a nightmare. Poor Sarah and Jess. And Michael... the whole thing is tragic. I'm sorry I couldn't make the funeral. Since..." He gestured to his knee.

Knox nodded gently. "No apology needed. I know you would have been there if you could."

His thoughts churned, dragging him back to the bungalow, to the dreadful image of Jess and Sarah among the wreckage, the blood, the stillness, the crushing absence of life. The grief clawed at him, a raw impulse to break down, but he stifled it. Tears would not bring them back. All that mattered now was retribution, justice, making the people who did this answer for their crimes.

He focused on the differences between the two incidents. "When they took out Michael, it was clinical and professional. Everything about it was precise, the work of people who knew exactly what they were doing. But Jess and Sarah?" His voice caught, the pain slipping through before he pushed it aside. "That was a disaster. Rushed, full of errors. Sloppy."

His mind whirled, trying to form a coherent picture. "Either they messed it up badly, or it was not the same group. We might be looking at more than one team. One is professional and efficient, the other is reckless, maybe desperate. It could be two different agendas, or else they are rushed for time."

His voice sharpened. "The police will not take long to see the difference. They will notice the contrast in how it was done, which raises the question, why now? Why take such huge risks? Unless they are cowboys, whatever they are planning must be imminent. They would not risk a fiasco like this unless time was running out."

"Or perhaps they are professionals who have got careless. Either way, we do not have much time." James added as he turned back to the computer screen. "Let's see what's actually on this drive."

The decryption process ran, the screen flashing with progress bars until, at last, files opened, clear and legible. He hovered the mouse over an icon and clicked.

The screen took on a muted pink hue as a document loaded. Knox leaned forward, nerves strung tight while the text appeared.

James read through the document, his expression growing tense. He jerked his head back, letting out a sharp breath.

Henry shifted his attention from James's pale, shaken face to the screen, where the signature block glared back at him: Gray. A surge of alarm shot through him as the implications hit. "Gray? Colonel Gray? What is his name doing on here?"

James's hand quivered as he scrolled through the text, taking in the words with growing alarm. "Henry... there are several emails on here from Gray. It is addressed to a guy called Normanov. I'm guessing he is Russian or at least eastern European. It's about a Russian sleeper cell working in the UK." His voice shook slightly as he went on. "It outlines plans for an attack on a theme park in Yorkshire, today."

He looked up, his face ashen and etched with shock, as though the revelation had punched him. "This can't be real."

Knox scoffed, adrenaline spiking. "Does it say which Theme Park?"

James continued to scroll. And click into other files.

Knox shook his head, "Gray has always been a snake, mate. Do you remember what he pulled at the Regimental Dinner, that business with Chief Clerk's wife?" The bitterness in his voice betrayed old resentments.

James hardly seemed to hear him. "No, Henry, you don't understand. Gray texted me last night, asking if I'd heard from you. When you arrived this morning, I told him you were here, that you were safe." He swallowed, his complexion turning grey. "That's who I was messaging earlier!"

Knox felt as if he had been knocked sideways. The atmosphere in the room closed in, alive with a dark sense of anticipation. The silence became suffocating, his own heart pounding in his ears, until a new, unmistakable sound shattered it.

Pop, pop, pop.

A controlled volley of gunfire cracked through the air, undoubtedly from a Heckler and Koch MP5 submachine gun. The sound reverberated off the walls, so close Knox felt it pounding in his chest.

Someone was here and they weren't friendly forces.

CHAPTER EIGHTEEN

Rhodri Aldridge and Callum MacLeod sat in their matt black Range Rover Sport. The vehicle's dull finish caught fleeting glimpses of the overcast sky as it stood poised at the edge of a roundabout overlooking the A1 motorway. Its position had been chosen with care, giving them the kind of tactical flexibility that Cal and Rhys had lived by all their lives. A single turn of the wheel and they could head north, south, east, or west, all roads and avenues open to them. A variety of options.

Henry Knox was their quarry at this moment, but the day held more importance than just one man. Just a few miles away lay another reason for all of this, the so-called "main event", as Colonel Gray had called it. That task demanded they remain nearby. Yet the threat posed by Knox could not be ignored. Their location neatly balanced both goals.

Rhys and Cal had lived the life required for this kind of waiting game during their service in the forces. It felt innate, ingrained by their many years of military training.

Hurry up and wait.

The sudden rush of movement, followed by hours of inactivity, then another scramble. It had been the rhythm of their old lives, the constant shift between urgency and stillness.

Both men had spent years on black and green tours with the Royal Military Police Close Protection teams, refining their patience and preparedness. Black tours were the coveted assignments, perilous yet lucrative, escorting ambassadors through hotspots like Algiers or

Bogotá, travelling in convoys of white armoured SUVs. It was a risky life but with high rewards. The routine was always the same: race to secure an area, wait while the diplomats conducted their affairs, then escort them back. Controlled chaos interspersed with long periods of waiting.

Green tours were less glamorous, offering lower pay, fewer benefits, and ever-present danger. These operational deployments, carried out alongside larger military campaigns, involved swapping sleek armoured embassy vehicles for battered military Land Rovers that shook on every pothole. The risks were tangible, but the pattern remained: hurry up and wait. Over time, that rhythm became as natural to them as breathing.

Now, in the plush leather interior of the Range Rover, the waiting felt almost luxurious. Gone were the sticky plastic seats, the stifling heat in flimsy vehicles, and the constant fear of ambush. Soldiers needed routine, routine meant control, and in a world on the brink of chaos, control was everything.

Rhodri Aldridge stood a fraction under six feet four inches tall, his wiry frame a deceptive source of raw, unwavering strength. Lean and sinewy, he was built for function over aesthetics, a physique sculpted by years of surviving challenges that stripped a man to his bare essentials. His blond hair was cut close to his scalp, practical and straightforward, while deep lines in his weathered face spoke of many years lived in harsh conditions. Although he was only 34, he looked older, and his cold grey eyes were the most unsettling feature, appearing to see straight through a person, uncovering truths they had not realised they were hiding.

His clothing was as functional as his demeanour. A black tactical jacket fitted snugly, but with enough give for movement, paired with dark, scuffed jeans and black boots that were shined for practicality rather than show. A thick black digital watch wrapped around his wrist. His sharp facial features were emphasised by the permanent sneer on his lips, and his thick Welsh accent, tinged with disdain, lent an extra bite to every word.

Twelve years of military service, countless black tours, and unending danger had hardened him inside and out. When Colonel Gray offered him a way out, promising three to five times his usual pay without having to travel abroad, he made the obvious choice. Loyalty came second to opportunity, and Rhys Aldridge was always prepared to seize his chance.

Callum MacLeod differed from Rhys in many respects. He was a man who wore his years of experience like a badge of honour. At five feet eleven inches, he was not particularly tall, but his solid frame and understated authority gave him a presence that felt larger than life. His barrel chest, thick arms, and sturdy build proclaimed a life of continuous action, someone who had carried out labour and combat duties without rest, leading others through multiple tours.

His wide, round face showed few signs of age or hardship. A square jaw was perpetually rough with stubble, suggesting he had no desire or time for a clean shave. His greying hair, clipped close to his head, receded slightly at the temples, forming a widow's peak that only added to his seasoned look. His Glaswegian accent, abrupt and firm, carried a sense of authority.

Cal wore a dark grey tactical jacket, shaped to fit his bulk, was snug and reinforced at the elbows and shoulders. It hugged his wide torso, fitted with several pockets set in practical positions. His khaki cargo trousers, faded from wear, held the tools of his trade, such as field dressings, a multi-tool, and other precisely chosen items. Each pocket was systematically arranged, with everything in its rightful place.

On his wrist, he wore a heavy silver banded limited-edition Close Protection Unit watch, its bright face bearing the well-known CPU logo: a medieval knight's armour and helmet, complete with a raised sword held by invisible hands. Underneath, a scroll bore the unit's Latin motto, PROTEGIMUS, meaning We Protect.

Cal had reached the peak of his career as the Regimental Sergeant Major of the Close Protection Unit of the Royal Military Police, a role that cemented his standing as a tactical expert and a leader capable of holding the military's chaos together.

After leaving the forces, Cal joined Gray at a Close Protection firm called Capuchin Security, a tongue in cheek nod to the RMP being called Monkeys, or more specifically the red fess wearing monkey of organ grinder fame, mocking the RMP red caps.

Initially, it felt like a natural progression of his military career, providing a way to use his skills for lucrative, worthwhile goals. Yet, over time, the organisation turned into something he scarcely recognised, not at all what he had first signed up for.

Gray had systematically shut Cal out, removing him from significant operations and key decisions. His authority, once substantial, was quietly chipped away. What had once been a tightly disciplined enterprise, built on professionalism and order, turned sloppy and complacent. Gray grew the company's foreign contracts, filling the ranks with untested hires who lacked the skills for vital, high-risk assignments. The flaws were obvious, but Gray showed either ignorance or apathy. To Cal, Capuchin Security no longer represented a source of pride. It had become a hollow shell.

That was not the worst part. Cal's strained relationship with Gray had led to personal repercussions. Their arguments, heated and frequent, made Gray vengeful. Cal's family was drawn into Gray's orbit in unsettling ways. His wife and child were relocated, supposedly for their safety, but Cal knew better. Gray kept them at just the right distance, near enough to hold as leverage yet far enough to keep Cal under control. His wife's calls felt distant, her tone guarded, and her messages read as if someone else had drafted them. Gray's grip on them was tangible, a type of manipulation Cal could not ignore.

Cal longed to escape. Every sense told him to run, to resist, but Gray made it impossible. As long as his family was within Gray's grasp, he could not walk away.

Now Gray was demanding even more from him, tasks that gnawed at his conscience and contradicted every principle he had held throughout his service. Each new assignment tore at his morals, leaving him torn between the urge to do what was right and the fear that angering Gray would endanger his family further. He could not risk it, not with Gray looming over every aspect of their lives.

So Cal sat rigidly in the passenger seat of the Range Rover, his face a mask of barely contained rage that glinted faintly in the frost-touched window. He had seen enough in his career to break the toughest souls, and he had carried out orders that haunted him. Yet this was different, a line he could not bear to cross.

Rhys lounged behind the wheel, a picture of icy detachment. His pale grey eyes flicked towards Cal with a look bordering on amusement, which only heightened Cal's anger. "You need to relax, Cal," he said, his voice cutting like a scalpel. "This is the job."

Cal spun round, fury burning in his eyes. "At no bloody point did I sign up for murder," he hissed, his voice kept low. His finger stabbed the air in Rhys's direction. "How can you be comfortable with what we did? Michael? Sarah? Jess? They were innocents, Rhys. Innocents, and you killed them."

Rhys remained impassive, as though they were chatting about the weather instead of murder. His words came out deliberate and cold. "Collateral," he said in a quiet Welsh accent, laced with menace. "Michael is just another dead veteran. Nobody cares. They are ten a penny these days. And his daughters?" He inclined his head a fraction, a cruel gleam in his eye. "They got involved. That's how it goes, and you know it."

Cal stared at him in disgust. "Collateral? You jumped the gun, you fucking prick. You made a fucking mess, and now two women are dead. Innocent women, Rhys. And what about Knox? He's still out there. We have the police asking questions. It's a fucking circus."

Rhys leaned back, a slight, dismissive smirk tugging at his lips. "Everyone believes it was Knox. The news says so, blaming him for everything, including Michael's death. Gray told us to do whatever was necessary, and we did."

He allowed his smirk to spread, as though revelling in Cal's fury, his grey eyes glittering with grim pleasure. "They brought it on themselves," he went on, voice quiet and mocking. "That was their choice. All we need to do now is eliminate Knox, finish it off, and let him take the fall. Another soldier breaks under strain or has PTSD issues, it is an easy sell."

Cal let out a harsh breath, shaking his head as though trying to rid himself of the rising nausea. "You have no clue, do you, Rhys? We murdered innocent people. Innocent women. You did, when you jumped ahead."

Rhys's smile wavered, his expression hardening. His voice dropped a notch. "We agreed on what needed doing. I heard noise in the garage and seized the chance. How was I supposed to know it was not Knox?"

Cal turned sharply, his anger coming to the boil. His fists clenched, his voice sharp and accusatory. "You fucking check, Rhys. That's the job. You make certain. You don't guess. You don't fuck it up. But now, two innocent women are dead, Knox has disappeared, and the police are all over us. This isn't just a mess, it is a full-blown fucking disaster. And don't try to talk your way out of it."

Rhys's posture stiffened, but he stayed silent. The tension between them was suffocating, thick with anger and rage. Frost continued creeping across the windows, the chill outside reflecting the icy hostility within.

Cal pressed on, his voice low but lethal. "If I wanted amateurs, I would have brought one of the toms along. At least they would have had the sense to follow the plan."

Rhys leaned back, his grin slow and provoking, his neck tilting until the crack of his vertebrae echoed in the enclosed space. His tone sounded lazy, dripping with misplaced confidence. "We're still ahead of the police, simple as that. The boss has contacts everywhere. Once we get Knox's location, we'll deal with him, and the job is done. All of this will be wrapped up before the main event even starts."

Cal's stare was sharp enough to slice through Rhys's self-assurance. "You don't know that," he replied, his voice cold and cutting. "You're just guessing Rhys. You're a fucking cowboy."

Rhys gave a defiant smile, one that made Cal's blood boil. "You should calm down, Cal," he said in a mocking tone, his words brimming with condescension. "I'm sure your wife and kids would feel much safer if you just got on board."

Dark anger flared in Cal's eyes. He leaned forward, his voice dropping to a furious hiss. "Keep my family's name out of your fucking mouth," he spat, his rage so raw it hung in the air like a threat.

The dashboard screen flickered to life, its pale light illuminating the dim interior. Gray's name glowed ominously on the display, instantly changing the mood.

Rhys did not skip a beat. He tapped the green button without hesitation, his expression shifting to one of easy calm. "Morning, boss," he said lightly.

Gray's voice crackled through the speakers, low and commanding. "Morning, lads. Here is the update. Knox is at James Webster's place. He has been there for about half an hour. The location is in Ravensfield, just off the A1, north of you. I will send the address. Ten minutes should be enough. Sort it out and call me when you are done."

The line went dead, the screen fading to standby. Rhys, wordless, started the engine as Cal fastened his seat belt.

Moments later, the dashboard chimed, a text from Gray lighting the screen. Cal keyed in the address, the route illuminating the map with a path winding through the countryside. The engine roared as they accelerated onto the motorway.

The journey north was mercifully brief, Cal stared out of the frosted window, anger radiating from him in waves. Each second spent together in the tight space seemed to inflame his simmering resentment.

Rhys, in contrast, sat casually behind the wheel, his posture exuding detachment. The smirk playing on his lips served as an unspoken taunt, a deliberate push at Cal's nerves. Neither man spoke.

They turned off the motorway onto a narrow B-road that wove through open farmland, barely wide enough for the bulky Range Rover. Each car coming from the other direction forced Rhys to steer onto the verge, the tyres grinding against gravel and frozen grass as they squeezed past.

The air here felt colder, weighed down by the damp of surrounding fields and the stark silhouettes of bare trees lining the road. The Range Rover's headlights cut through the early morning fog, revealing stone walls and hedgerows that hinted at an old-world village ahead.

Upon entering the village, it was like stepping back in time. The short row of cottages, painted white, stood side by side, each one crowned with a frosty slate roof. A tiny post office with a scarlet door and a solitary fuel pump that was clearly for show sat at the village's centre, a relic from more uncomplicated days. Smoke curled from a few chimneys, emphasising the stillness of the scene.

The sat nav guided them on, its android voice providing directions. The village quickly fell behind them, a handful of houses fading into the distance until they reached the outskirts. The sat nav instructed them to turn right.

Rhys guided the car onto a gravel lane, that was hemmed in by towering trees, their intertwining branches forming a canopy of bones overhead. The further they travelled, the dimmer the light became, nature closing in on both sides.

At last, the space between the trees widened, allowing them to glimpse a clearing. The barn came into view, appearing as though it rose directly from the earth, its time-worn bricks standing firm against the pale morning sky. White-framed windows dotted the front.

As the Range Rover rolled to a stop in the yard, Cal scanned the surroundings. His gaze caught sight of cameras, the structure, and subtle signs of occupancy. At first glance, it might appear a quiet farmhouse, but Cal recognised the hallmarks of a militarised property hidden under domestic trappings.

Rhys turned the Range Rover in a way that gave Cal a clear line of sight towards the house and beyond.

Rhys frowned, searching the deserted yard. “Knox’s car isn’t here,” he said bluntly, his voice sharp with annoyance.

Cal simply grunted, his mouth set in a hard line. It was no surprise to him. Knox was too smart to park right at the target. Dumping his vehicle was exactly the kind of move Cal would expect, shrewd, efficient, and maddeningly evasive.

“You thought he would drive up to the front door, Rhys?” Cal remarked incredulously, his words clipped, underlining his frustration.

Rhys flicked an irritated glance in Cal’s direction.

“Anyway,” Cal continued, lowering his voice, “they know we’re here now.”

Rhys did not even look at him, his disdain palpable. “It won’t matter in about five minutes.”

Cal exhaled, his tone all business. “We go in loud, a bit of shock and awe. They won’t be armed. We can fire off a couple of rounds, scare them senseless, and they’ll give up in no time. Then we can go home for tea and biscuits.”

Rhys leaned back in his seat, considering the plan. “You’re assume they will fold. We need to be smarter. First, we cut the power, kill their lights, alarms, and comms. I’ll handle the power while you watch the front door.”

Cal felt his temper flare again, his voice rising. “We are not the SAS, Rhys, and this is not the Iranian Embassy siege. There’re two blokes inside, one is a cripple and the other has likely been awake all night. They don’t need their power cut to be overwhelmed, plus that wasn't a tactic that you employed last night."

Rhys refused to relent. "Fuck you Cal. Do it how you want to, but I am not leaving the backdoor unguarded. If they flee, everything goes wrong. Knox won't slip away from me again. You hold the front, I'll block the back. We keep it neat and tidy."

The tension between them hovered, a clash of wills and experience. At last, Cal grudgingly agreed. "Fine. But don't fuck this up."

Rhys smirked. "You too, old man," he retorted with mocking amusement.

Calmly, Rhys twisted round, pulling back a fleece blanket on the back seat. Beneath it lay a Heckler and Koch MP5, its black metal form coiled like a viper. He lifted it a touch, his fingertips trailing over its matte finish.

The weapon felt like an extension of his arm, cold metal reassuring him. He checked the magazine, giving it a little wiggle to ensure it was seated firmly, before pulling back the bolt just enough to glance into the chamber. A single round glinted back, precisely as it should.

Old instincts made him confirm everything, the residue of relying on the frequently finicky SA80 hammered into his memory.

Rhys slid the bolt home, hearing the crisp metal-on-metal click. He allowed himself a second of satisfaction. Then he tapped the forward assist, more from routine than necessity. Opposite him, Cal did the same. Matching every step.

They donned the rifle slings, keeping the weapons tight and close to their bodies. Then they slipped out of the vehicle without a word. Cal started to walk in a straight line towards the house, standing tall as if it posed no threat at all. Rhys dropped low, scuttling behind the engine block for cover.

"What are you doing?" Rhys hissed, his annoyance obvious.

Cal only half turned, looking unimpressed. "Treat people like idiots and they will act like idiots, you bastard," he replied curtly.

Without another word, Cal raised his MP5 to his shoulder, holding it securely, and switched off the safety catch. The first burst of three rounds tore through the crisp morning air, slamming into the barn door, splinters of wood flying in all directions.

Rhys shook his head, a slow grin creeping across his lips. "Subtle as a fucking sledgehammer," he muttered, sounding both exasperated and faintly amused.

CHAPTER NINETEEN

The first burst of gunfire tore through the morning calm. Knox dropped to the floor instantly, reacting on instinct. His body hit the cold, unyielding surface beneath him. His eyes roamed the room looking for cover out of sheer habit.

Contact, wait out.

James did not flinch, remaining seated and watching Henry with his arms folded. The corners of his mouth twitched with something close to amusement. "This is a reinforced safe room," James said, his voice calm, as though he was talking about the weather.

"It would take more than an MP5 to chew through these walls, Oxy." He gestured towards the thick stone lining the barn. "Relax."

Knox exhaled slowly and pushed himself upright, brushing the dust off his knees. A sheepish grin tugged at his lips. "Built like Fort Knox, huh?"

James levelled a flat look at him. "Do not give up your day job," he said, tone dry but with a condescending smirk. Then grin faded from his face, and his voice dropped, any hint of humour draining away. "Jokes aside, we need to move. Quickly."

Knox offered a slight nod, knowing that whatever was coming would not end at the front door.

James turned his chair back to the computer, his fingers hovering over the keyboard before clicking away. The screen flickered, switching from a cluttered desktop to live feeds of the courtyard. Camera views blinked into place one after another, covering the monitor with overlapping shots of the yard outside. Although shadows swam across the grainy images, the layout was unmistakable. It was all there, every corner, every approach. James leaned closer, eyes narrowed as he studied the feeds.

A sleek black Land Rover stood idle in the centre, its matt finish reflecting dully in the early morning light. Two figures were visible, positioned on either side, their dark outlines blending with the shadows beneath the chassis.

The first man stood tall, the stubby barrel of his firearm raised high against his chest, aiming at the front entrance of the barn. He took no cover, showing no sign of urgency. It was as though he wanted to be noticed.

The second figure showed a different approach, more cautious. He crouched low behind the engine block, appearing ready to provide covering fire while the first man moved. Knox recognised that discipline at once.

James squinted at the monitor. "A two-man team. One arrogant, one sensible."

Knox let out a slow breath, his stomach knotting. He spoke in a voice laced with disbelief. "Rhys and Cal," he said. "Christ, they are working for Gray?"

James did not look away from the screen. "So, it would seem."

Knox's mind was already racing, trying to piece together the threads of a plan. "Alright," he said, voice steadier now. "This is what we will do. I am going out. I will handle those two. You lock this room down." He looked at James. "How long can you hold out?"

James gave a short, confident shrug, leaning back in his chair as it creaked under his weight. "Weeks," he answered, throwing a glance at the camera feeds. "I don't think they brought enough dems to break through these walls." His gaze rested on the men outside. The self-assurance on his face slipped away. "But that's not how this is going to play out. You and me will settle this. They don't get to walk into my house and shoot the place up for free."

Knox met James's eyes, probing for any sign of hesitation but finding none.

"They'll pay plenty," Knox said, voice rough. "But I need you here, pulling whatever you can off that drive. That all that matters mate. I can't risk you out there limping around. Your knees are shot."

James snorted, waving him off. "It's just one knee, dickhead. I'll be fine. These CP wallers won't know what hit them." His grin widened, as though enjoying the challenge.

Knox lowered his voice. "I can't afford to lose you, mate. Stay on the phone. Get whatever you can to Amy. We need to find enough to bring Gray down."

He did not wait for a response. Knox grabbed the Faraday bag and the tinfoil from the table, wrapping his phone in tightly layered foil until it vanished from any signal. He pushed the sealed device into his pocket, tapping it once, a small gesture of habit.

James watched quietly, arms still crossed. He nodded, but a flicker of defiance flashed in his eyes. Without speaking, James opened a drawer by his side, pulling out a battered old Nokia 3310 phone and a loose SIM card, which he dropped into Knox's hand.

"When you're finished," James murmured, his voice softer, "I'll give you a call. Now go."

James and Henry both nodded at each other and then Knox was gone, slipping through the doorway like a phantom, keeping his posture low as he moved. His head stayed low, his profile as small as possible, remaining out of sight.

Head down, chin up.

He did not head towards the main door where the shots had come from, the route leading to the kitchen. That would be suicide. That was where they would expect him, the obvious path, squarely in their firing lines. Knox would not oblige.

Instead, he veered in the other direction, through the second door that opened up in a living room, which was filled with subdued light coming from the windows at the front and back of the house. Cal and Rhys were concentrated on the front door of the barn, so if Henry circled around and hit them from the flank, he might stand a chance.

Flanking was not much of a plan, but Knox had managed with less in the past.

Knox pressed forward, his muddy boots squelching on the wooden boards, the faint creak underfoot overpowered by the pounding of his heart. He moved to the window, crouching below the white frame. Outside, he heard footsteps crunching on the gravel courtyard, quiet and methodical.

Knox lifted his head just enough to see and directed his gaze to the shadowy figure behind the engine block of the Range Rover. Rhys. His rifle was raised, offering overwatch while Cal advanced. It was textbook procedure, Cal and Rhys had always been top-tier operatives. Yet seeing them here, hunting him, turned Knox's stomach.

He had worked with both men, fought alongside them. Now they stood against him, implicated in Michael's death, and in Sarah and Jess's murders too. The betrayal bit deep, colder even than the morning air seeping in through the cracks of the barn.

Cal moved towards the main door slowly, his silhouette stark on the pale gravel. Knox observed him intently. Cal had been the best of them, a Regimental

Sergeant Major. The Senior Soldier. Knox had once aspired to that role, but life had a way of knocking people off course. He had ended up on the sidelines while Cal ascended.

Cal was the man others tried to emulate, someone Knox used to admire. Now he was here, acting on Gray's orders.

He could have left the Army with honour, with a pension in his pocket, maybe even gained a commission. Instead, he was out here carrying a rifle, a hired gun in everything but name.

Why?

Knox struggled with the thought. What led a man to fall so far?

Rhys, on the other hand, had always had a mercenary streak. Knox noticed it early on. Plenty of sergeants carried that same attitude, chasing the money. Black tours, high stakes, high pay. Rhys had volunteered for them all, first in line if the cash outweighed the risk.

Close Protection was a natural step for someone like Rhys. The world grew uglier every year, with more threats and more high-profile clients willing to pay for protection. Skilled CP operators such as Rhys found themselves in demand, and he exploited that fully. The money was good, and loyalty was flexible at the right price.

It did not surprise Knox that Rhys had ended up under Gray's control, following a path well worn by men who preferred not to ask too many questions.

Knox doubted Rhys had thought much about it. Men like him did not trouble themselves with politics or morality. It was just another job, another pay cheque. Life moved quickly in their line of work. One day you were guarding a politician in Kabul, the next you were pointing a rifle at an old comrade outside a barn in Yorkshire.

And here he was. Knox's stomach churned. Rhys had chosen his side, and Knox knew exactly how this would end.

Knox could not reconcile it. Men like Gray had worn the same uniform, sworn the same oaths. They knew what duty cost, what loyalty demanded. Knox had spent his life in uniform. There was no price high enough to make him betray that. So why had Gray done it? Why Cal? Why Rhys?

Knox shook his head a little. Survive this first. Solve the reasons later.

Knox reached to his belt and pulled out his Gerber, flicking out the blade and wrapping his hand around the handle. He suddenly felt alarmingly exposed. His day sack was still in the kitchen, left where he had dropped it. It might as well have been on the moon. He ran through its contents in his mind, but nothing in there would help him now.

A sense of vulnerability wrapped around him, cold and unsettling. No rifle, no handgun, no body armour. Just a Gerber and whatever he could adapt from the surroundings.

Adapt and overcome.

Those words drifted through his mind. This was not the worst predicament he had ever faced. You manage with what you have. You push on.

Knox's eyes tracked Cal and Rhys carefully, his pulse steady despite the adrenaline coursing through his veins. Both Cal and Rhys were excellent operators with considerable experience, each one lethal on his own, far more dangerous together. Observing them was like seeing a well-oiled machine, seamlessly working in tandem. Yet this was not their usual kind of mission.

Close Protection specialists were trained for extraction, not direct assault. Their instinct was to remove their principal from danger, not charge into harm. Fighting retreats, controlled evacuations, that was their core skill set. Entering a building, clearing corners, flushing out defenders, which was infantry work, requiring a different mindset, different training.

This was where Knox held the upper hand. Most RMP had gone into the thick of strike operations, shoulder to shoulder with the infantry, kicking down doors. Knox had done it countless times before.

Still, confidence only went so far. He was alone, facing two skilled operators. That worried him.

He studied them, and then they did something he had not anticipated. To his surprise, they separated. He had been running through plans in his head, trying to find a way to break them apart, thinking how best to exploit any gap between them. Now they had done it themselves.

Cal advanced deliberately towards the house, like a hunter zeroing in on its prey. Rhys did not follow as expected. Instead, he moved off, sliding along the side of the car under cover, heading for the rear of the vehicle. It was almost a gift, something Knox had not dared to hope for. The split was risky, ill-advised even, and it played straight into Knox's hands.

Divide and conquer.

The old saying had rarely felt so apt.

Knox dropped lower beneath the window, his mind assembling the next steps. Let them separate. Let them open up a chance.

It might be the only opportunity he would get.

Knox eased himself away from the window and turned to look at the living room. The contrast was sharp. Where the kitchen was cluttered and full of signs of life, and the computer room clinical and utilitarian, this room was immaculate. No cushion out of place, no scuff on the polished floor, except for Henry's muddy footprints. It felt staged, like a show home that nobody actually lived in.

It was obvious James did not use this space much.

Knox scanned for an exit. He recalled noticing a door from the outside. His boots squelched softly as he crossed the room, his focus on a large wooden barn door set into one corner, old but solid. A thick bolt spanned the frame.

Knox gripped the cold metal bolt, lifting it gently and sliding it free with a muted scrape. He cracked the door open just enough to slip through.

The cold air struck him at once, sharp against his skin, and the early morning was still and quiet. He stepped out and let the door settle behind him.

He paused, crouching low as his eyes adjusted to the grey light. In front lay the same slope and treeline he had used that morning to watch the farmhouse. A clear escape route lay right there. He was sure he could navigate the woods, he knew where the narrow path led. He could vanish before Rhys or Cal even noticed.

He could run. Right now. Disappear into the landscape.

But to what end?

There would be no justice for Michael, Sarah, or Jess in running. Their faces flickered through his mind, Michael, Sarah and Jess. Walking away meant letting them stay in the shadows where their lives had ended.

And James... James would be left to handle this alone. Knox had dragged him into this trouble, and he pictured him now, walled in the safe room, smirking behind his screens. Tough as nails, but fortified walls would not hold men like Cal and Rhys forever.

Knox took a huge breath and exhaled, vapour curling in the cold morning air. The choice was not a choice at all.

He had to stay and fight.

CHAPTER TWENTY

James's fingers flew across the keyboard. There was no time to think, only to react. Seconds. That was all he had.

The main screen flickered as he initiated the shutdown command. One by one, modems and hard drives powered down, the hum of electronics fading as small puffs of smoke hissed from overloaded circuits. Heat and pressure vented, a standard failsafe.

James had foreseen this possibility and prepared for it, though he had hoped it would remain hypothetical. Destroying the hard drives was a last resort measure of his own design, one he had dreaded using.

The room grew darker with each passing moment, blinking lights going out like stars obscured by thick clouds.

He did not watch; he did not need to. His hands acted on their own, pulling a laptop from its cables and sliding it into a worn leather laptop bag. Two mobile phones followed, along with several SIM cards scattered at the bottom like loose coins.

His gaze fell on the memory stick sticking out of the water-cooled tower. He snatched it, pinching it firmly between his thumb and forefinger. It was of no use to him now, the encryption unbreakable without the proper equipment, and the laptop did not have the capacity to crack it. Yet he could not let Cal and Rhys obtain it either.

James stood up from the chair with a grunt, shifting his weight as he picked up the laptop bag and zipped it shut, then slung it over his shoulder.

He moved towards the same door Henry had exited through minutes earlier, while the room behind him continued slipping into darkness and silence, the remaining lights blinking stubbornly before fading out.

He opened the door, allowing a rush of cold air that swirled around him, rustling the edges of his dressing gown like a banner caught in a draught. He paused in the doorway, light from the adjacent room highlighting his tall silhouette.

The house felt still, unnaturally quiet. Only the distant creak of wood and the faint hum of dying electronics disturbed the silence.

Without shifting his gaze from the doorway, James held his mobile phone in his hand, his thumb hovering over his screen. The faint glow of an electronic command glimmered beneath his fingertip, his final line of defence, waiting for his touch.

CHAPTER TWENTY-ONE

Cal moved towards the main front door of the building in slow, wide steps, his breathing steady and his grip firm on the hand grips of the black HK MP5 snug against his right shoulder. The weapon's extended stock was locked into the socket between his pectoral muscle and shoulder. Too low, and the sights became useless. Too high, and the lack of support turned every fired round into guesswork. Balance was everything.

A standard issue EOTech XPS2-0 holographic sight was mounted on the rail, reliable and fast, built for precision. However, Cal would not need to rely heavily on precise aimed shots today. In close quarters, the iron sights would work well enough.

His finger rested outside the trigger guard, close enough but never actually on the trigger. Films always got that detail wrong: a finger on the trigger might look dramatic on screen, but in reality, it was poor practice. A single twitch or slip could cause a negligent discharge and, in a place like this, that could mean dead bystanders or, worse, dead teammates.

Cal was never sloppy. He never had been. His movements were fluid, under control. The weapon rose and fell with each measured step, the barrel pointing ahead as he approached the door, his gaze locked forward. Whatever lay beyond that door, he felt ready.

Reaching the door, Cal shifted to one side, his left hand moving to test the handle, rapping it lightly. It gave without resistance, the mechanism clicking softly. He eased the handle down and the door creaked open.

Pressing his left palm against the wood, he nudged it wider while keeping his body clear of the doorway. The MP5 remained tight against his shoulder, the barrel guiding his line of sight, sweeping over each inch of the widening gap. Everything his eyes focused on, the weapon also covered, almost an extension of his vision.

Satisfied the space ahead was clear, Cal slid his left hand back to the forward grip, bracing the weapon. It was instinct and muscle memory, supporting the firearm, keeping it agile. In close quarters, control was paramount. Short, precise arcs, no wasted motion.

Through the opening, the kitchen lay illuminated by the pale morning light streaming in through the windows. It was cluttered, full of signs of daily life. Dirty dishes teetered in the sink, and plates were scattered across the counter.

Cal wished he had a flashbang to flood the room with light and noise, to seize the advantage by forcing anyone inside into disorientation. But he had none, so he would have to rely on shock in other ways.

He charged through the doorway instead, force and momentum on his side. The MP5 stayed high, aimed forward, and he let his voice ring out, loud and sharp, cutting through the silence. Sometimes noise alone could shift the balance.

"Knoxy! Webby! Come out" He shouted.

Nothing.

Cal continued to progress through the kitchen, "Come out, and we'll sort this mess. No need for anyone to get hurt."

His words echoed through the space, but nothing answered. The kitchen was empty, carrying only the stale smell of eggs and burnt toast, remnants of James's breakfast.

Cal scanned the area, noticing two doors: one opened onto a brightly lit corridor, the other onto a darker room. Both stood wide open.

He reminded himself that neither Knox nor James should have access to weapons. Still, his training kept him close to the wall, using angles and cover instinctively. Habit and muscle memory guided him.

A faint scraping noise came from the unlit room. Cal adjusted his grip and stepped forward, moving steadily.

"Come on, lads," he called, voice lower but still carrying authority.

"Let's not make this harder than it needs to be."

CHAPTER TWENTY-TWO

Rhys watched Cal vanish inside the converted barn, his focus shifting instantly in the opposite direction. The courtyard stretched ahead, open, and exposed. He swung around, using the Range Rover as cover between him and the house.

The vehicle's doors were left wide open, standard procedure for rapid entry and exit, but now they felt like an obstacle. It wasn't a major problem, only an inconvenience. Rhys crept along the edge, moving around the open driver's door, his steps measured and light.

He paused at the rear of the Range Rover, leaning out just far enough to survey the area. The MP5 remained raised, snug against his shoulder, the barrel tracing his line of sight. His finger lay along the edge of the trigger guard, primed.

Then he moved decisively, a swift rush from the vehicle in a low run, his lean physique crossing the open ground in a fluid stride. There was nothing forced about it. Rhys made every movement appear natural. He pressed his back to the outside wall of the barn, narrowing his eyes as he slid along the brick, edging closer to the corner.

Within the building, Cal's voice echoed faintly, raised and authoritative, but the silence that followed set Rhys on edge. There was no response, no sign of movement.

A knot tightened in his gut.

If they had gone out the back, Webster might be an easy grab, heavier and slower, never built for speed. But Knox? Knox was entirely different.

Rhys exhaled, pressing on.

He would not let Knox slip away again.

Rhys kept his weapon pointed low, the barrel angled slightly forward, aiming at the ground a few yards ahead. He hugged the wall, his shoulder never losing contact with the rough brick surface that steadied him.

At the corner, he dipped into a crouch, raising the MP5 in a careful sweep as he peered around. His eyes and muzzle scanned left, then right, then centre.

Nothing.

Behind the house, the land sloped upward to a small hill thick with trees. Windows lined the building's side, gazing back at him unbroken and still. No door. It had to be on the far side, Rhys thought grimly, typical luck.

He edged forward again, following the same drills he had practised a thousand times, but this time he risked a glance through the windows as he moved. Inside, a living room looked back, neat and unlived in.

There were three doors: one firmly shut, two standing open. One opened into a room of shadows, the other was ajar at the far end, light spilling through into the space.

Rhys's stomach dropped. They had gone. Damn it.

Henry and James had slipped away, exploiting the brief pause to outmanoeuvre them.

Cal's idiotic theatrics had given them fair warning and extra time, dismantling Rhys's entire plan to corner Knox. A surge of anger churned beneath Rhys's calm veneer as the realisation dawned on him. His strategy to ambush Knox was unravelling. Cal's slip would have repercussions, and Rhys thought bitterly of how Cal's family might suffer for his ineptitude.

Increasing his pace, Rhys left cover, speeding along the wall and aiming for the far side of the building. The exit had to be there, and Rhys was determined to stop them before they vanished among the trees.

He advanced with less caution now, scanning the treeline in every direction.

He rounded the corner too quickly. Then, in a burst of clarity, he realised where Knox had gone, because Knox was kneeling in front of him.

CHAPTER TWENTY-THREE

James stood still in the doorway, outlined by the faint glow of light from the room behind him. His eyes stayed fixed through the dim space of the panic room, locked on the far door. He waited, calm and steady.

Cal's voice erupted like a hammer, breaking the silence as he burst into the computer room, heavy footfalls and a bark designed to unsettle. He pushed hard against the door, expecting it to yield, but it barely moved, grinding open by only an inch before stopping. It was far too heavy.

A subtle smile tugged at James's lips.

Without speaking, he stepped back, slipping behind the far door just as Cal surged forward, forcing his way into the darkened computer room. James's thumb pressed down on the screen.

With a quiet hiss, the reinforced door behind him slid shut, as Cal raced forward into what was now an empty room.

Cal saw the door closing and lunged, missing it by mere inches. His momentum drove him forward, slamming his shoulder hard into the steel, expecting it to give way.

But it did not move at all. Nothing.

The door refused to shift, a solid slab of reinforced metal anchored firmly in its frame. Cal stepped back, anger flaring, then hurled his full weight at it again. His shoulder struck the unyielding surface with a sickening thud, but it held firm. It felt like ramming into a wall of concrete.

The force of the impact knocked him off balance, his feet sliding on the darkened floor. He toppled backward, landing heavily in the pitch-black space behind him. The darkness engulfed him, the echo of his fall reverberating through the confined room.

A muted clunk behind him told him all he needed to know. The entrance door, the same one he had used to barge in, was now sealed shut, imprisoning him inside.

Darkness swallowed him completely.

Cal's breathing steadied as he adapted to the sudden void, but the silence was not absolute. He detected the faint smell of smouldering electronics hanging in the air. Then, from somewhere above, a vent rattled into life, followed by the constant hum of a fan. The sound ran in a ceaseless loop, the only noise in the chamber.

He lifted the MP5 to his shoulder and squeezed the trigger, sending a burst of gunfire at the door. Muzzle flashes pierced the darkness in a rapid, violent sequence, like strobe lights. The rounds pounded into steel, each impact dull and flat. None broke through.

No light came in.

Cal emptied the magazine, the smoky tang of gunpowder filling his lungs. Still no effect.

He exhaled, stepping forward to the door, his palms gliding over the surface. Cold, smooth, and seamless. His fingers traced the edges, but there were no joints to pry open, no hinges to exploit.

Steel on all sides.

Gradually, he realised he was in a panic room, a vault, and he was trapped there.

On the other side, James stood safely, just outside the sealed door. He allowed himself a brief smile, listening to the mechanism's quiet click into place, a satisfying confirmation of the trap snapping shut.

Cal was inside, and he was not getting out soon.

James knew the design intimately, every weld, every bolt, each layer of reinforced steel. He had paid a fortune for it, not out of paranoia but as a prudent measure. The world was unpredictable, and James had always believed in preparing for the worst.

This was not precisely the scenario he had envisaged when commissioning it, yet it made no difference. It had worked flawlessly.

James ran his hand across the steel frame, fingertips brushing the cold surface. Not even Cal could break through it.

"Worth every penny," he murmured to himself, turning away.

He glanced at his phone, the security feed displaying nothing but darkness where Cal was now confined. No images, no sounds, save the low hum of the ventilation.

James gave a quiet chuckle.

"Enjoy your stay," he muttered, placing the phone into his pocket.

CHAPTER TWENTY-FOUR

Rhys froze, taken aback by Knox's sudden appearance. He had not expected Knox to remain in position, let alone stage an ambush. For an instant, his confidence wavered, replaced by the shock of being outmanoeuvred.

Knox erupted upwards from his crouched stance, a burst of energy shattering the stillness as surely as a gunshot. His left hand shot out and gripped the handguard of Rhys's MP5. In one smooth movement, Knox yanked hard, hauling the barrel off target and away from his body. The weapon twisted to the right, its line of fire skimming harmlessly past the building.

In Knox's other hand, the Gerber knife flashed, curving in a quick, lethal slash.

Rhys squeezed the trigger on reflex, firing a short burst of three rounds into nothingness as the barrel veered off course. His pulse thundered at the sight of the blade swiping so close.

The sling strapped across his chest immediately became a problem. It tied him to the weapon, dragging him closer to Knox and that rising knife. Far too close, and far too quickly.

Yet Knox did not try to drive the blade into Rhys. Instead, he sliced clean through the sling, severing it with a firm pull.

Rhys still gripped the weapon in both hands, the cut sling swinging uselessly against his chest. He wrenched to the side, trying to bring the MP5 back in line with Knox, but he realised his midsection was exposed. One wrong move and Knox's blade would be waiting to finish what it had started.

Rhys jerked backwards, desperate to pull away and gain some distance. Knox followed him, closing in and refusing to yield an inch.

Rhys's thoughts spun, recalculating. The MP5 had become a liability, dead weight in a struggle moving too fast. He let go of it, letting it hang limply between them. The stock dropped vertically, supported only by Knox's grip on the barrel.

Rhys's hand snapped to his belt, fingers wrapping around the handle of his Sig Sauer, still in its holster at his hip.

Knox anticipated the move. As Rhys abandoned the MP5, Knox released the Gerber and the rifle, letting both clatter to the ground and freeing his hands.

Knox threw his shoulder into Rhys, driving him off balance and trapping his hand against his side before the pistol could clear the holster.

Rhys twisted sharply, attempting to fling his jacket wide to access the holster.

But Knox was not falling for it.

He recognised the move at once, knowing Rhy was going for his sidearm. As soon as Rhys shifted his weight, Knox pivoted, using the slight gap to his advantage. He stepped in firmly, hooking Rhys's leg out from underneath him. The world canted, and Rhys went down hard, his back slamming onto the gravel with a pained gasp.

Without pausing, Knox scooped up the discarded MP5, the movement smooth and seamless. In one fluid motion, he raised it to his shoulder, the grip settling into his hands.

The EOTech sight blinked awake, its red dot fixed squarely between Rhys's eyes.

Knox's finger hovered over the trigger, aware that a round was chambered and the safety off.

He let out a slow breath, letting the weapon level at its target, the barrel immovable. Rhys lay still, his chest heaving, eyes locked on the cold muzzle staring back at him.

Knox was prepared to fire but hoped it would not come to that. Rhys was on the ground, his weapon holstered, while Knox stood over him with a loaded nine-millimetre firearm. "Leave it alone," Knox shouted at Rhys, conscious that the bursts of gunfire could still draw Cal round the corner at any moment.

Rhys ignored him, his hand darting towards his pistol, partially dragging it from the quick release holster. Knox had no choice. He fired two shots, a double tap straight to the head.

Crows exploded from the treetops in a frantic swirl, their cries cutting through the heavy morning air as the sharp crack of the shots faded. The echoes hung briefly in the air, followed by an oppressive silence.

Rhys sprawled on the gravel, blood pooling darkly beneath him, his grey eyes staring at the empty sky.

Knox exhaled, lowering the MP5's muzzle slightly but keeping a firm hold. The fight was done, yet the adrenaline still burned, refusing to subside. His heart thumped painfully against his ribs.

Then came a sound behind him, soft steps on the gravel. Knox reacted instantly, dropping to one side and rolling into a kneeling position, the weapon brought into the should tight and firm, pointing towards the targets' centre of mass. He braced himself for Cal.

But it was not Cal.

James limped around the corner, breathing a little heavily, grinning from ear to ear.

Knox sighed, letting the MP5's barrel point towards the ground. "Jesus, Webby… I nearly shot you."

James smirked, flicking some dust from his dressing gown. "I'd have got you first, Oxy."

Knox shook his head, breath still uneven as he looked back at Rhys's body, lying still at his feet. The blood trickled continuously from the wounds in the back of his skull.

James followed his gaze, taking a sharp intake of breath. "Bloody hell, mate…"

Knox got to his feet. "What the fuck are you doing here? I said to stay in the damn room. Cal's still out here."

James's grin widened, pride in his eyes. "Not anymore. I handled Cal. CPU RSM? I've shit 'em."

Knox frowned. "You… took Cal down?" The disbelief in his voice was clear.

James shrugged. "He won't be bothering us for a while and I didn't have to kill him to manage it."

CHAPTER TWENTY-FIVE

James walked back in to the spotless living room along with Henry, its once immaculate condition now tarnished by a trail of muddy footprints smeared across the polished floor.

"Sorry for the mess," Henry muttered, his tone ambiguous. He was not certain if he was apologising for Rhys's body, still lying lifeless outside, or for the dirt he had tracked across the previously pristine room.

His thoughts lingered on Rhys. Another life cut short. Another name added to the growing list: Michael, Sarah, Jess. Now Rhys. All because of a thumb drive, and whatever bullshit Gray was pursuing.

Henry lowered himself onto the edge of the sofa, the plush fabric sinking slightly beneath his weight. He sat rigid, hands clamped between his knees, his knuckles white. The guilt gnawed at him.

His shoulders rose and fell as he tried to relax, then emotions overwhelmed him, not as tears, but as violent tremors that shook him to his core. His body betrayed him, convulsing with all the tension he had buried for the last twelve hours, since Sarah, since Jess.

James remained where he was, leaning casually against the doorframe, arms loosely crossed over his chest. He said nothing and made no attempt to fix the situation. He had seen this before: soldiers breaking under burdens that grew too heavy to carry. He had been the one to listen while young men confessed their darkest deeds, things that no civilised person should face. The Army was full of broken men like Knox, men who drowned their grief in alcohol and regret, either burying it deep or letting it destroy them.

Knox was trapped in that same pit James had seen devour others. A place nobody spoke of, but every soldier knew, dug not by one's own hand but by circumstances and choices made by others, leaving Knox to pick up the pieces. To protect others, Knox had done things he would never reveal. Some men could shoulder that load beneath thick mental armour. Others were not so fortunate.

Knox was falling apart in front of him, and James understood better than to interfere. Some wounds needed to bleed out.

Knox had held it together until now, but James saw the cracks spreading. Today, they had burst wide open.

James remained silent, allowing Knox's grief to pass through him like a storm that needed to run its course. There was no speeding up this sort of pain. You could not patch it like a physical wound or reason with it like an angry drunk at last orders. It had to wear itself out, and James knew not to stand in its way.

Yet time was against them. The ticking clock hammered in James's thoughts.

At last, James moved away from the doorframe and cleared his throat softly. Enough to cut through the moment without destroying it entirely. He offered no comforting words, no empty sentiments to prop Knox up.

"I'll get changed," he said quietly, his voice low, almost apologetic. "I can't exactly storm a theme park in this." He gestured to his dressing gown, letting the faint attempt at humour hang there.

Knox did not reply.

James lingered a moment, then slipped out of the room, leaving Knox alone with his thoughts.

Henry's gaze had trailed James's exit, the gentle creak of the floor fading with every step. Now by himself, Knox remained on the sofa, shoulders weighted by regret.

He knew they had no time to waste. Gray's plan would not halt to let him recover. There was no pause button, no chance to reset. If he failed to pull himself together, more names would join the tally. More bodies would lie in his wake.

James had granted him a reprieve of a few minutes, but Knox knew it was a short one at best.

Leaning forward, elbows on his knees, he ran both hands through his hair, tugging lightly as though the motion might unravel the tangled thoughts in his head. A tingle on his scalp reminded him that he was alive, dragging him back from the dark recesses of his mind.

This was not his first time taking a life. Far from it. But it felt different.

Rhys had not been a nameless figure through a SUSAT scope, nor an unknown threat in the chaos of battle. He was someone Knox had known well, someone he had trained and joked with. He recalled shared drinks in the mess. And now Rhys lay dead, his blood spilt by Knox's own hand.

It felt wrong.

He drew a shaky breath through his nostrils, blinking hard to clear his vision. The tearful moisture mingled with mud and cam-cream on his cheeks as he swiped at his eyes. He wiped away the grime and sweat in rough motions, scrubbing at the exhaustion etched beneath them.

When he sat up, the tightness in his chest had lessened, but only slightly. It was sufficient, enough to move forward.

That was all he needed right now.

James reappeared in the doorway, now dressed in dark jeans and a loose black hoodie that hung over his broad frame. His white trainers looked scuffed but functional, suitable for blending in. He glanced briefly round the room and then rested his eyes on the MP5 on the sofa. In silence, James lifted it, propping it against his shoulder, fingers hovering on the trigger guard.

"We should get going, Henry," James said quietly. "We can talk enroute."

"Roger," Knox breathed, his voice rough, bracing himself with a measured breath. His eyes rose to meet James's. "Do you know where we're heading?"

James nodded once. "Yeah, it's not far. The theme park is called HippoLand."

Knox's brows lifted. HippoLand?

He found it absurdly incongruous that a place built for families could be the location of such a plan. He straightened his dishevelled shirt, nodding slowly. "Then let us get on with it."

He rubbed the back of his neck and glanced at the rear entrance, remembering Rhys's body that still lay out of sight, blood pooling across the gravel yard in dark rivulets.

"I'll see if Rhys had anything useful," Henry said flatly, "then we can be off. What about the body? We can't just leave him."

His eyes lingered on the door, waiting for James to offer something, anything, that would make this all feel less like leaving behind a train wreck that they had created.

James did not hesitate. "I'll report some shots fired and let the local police handle it. We can't stay here for them; there're more pressing issues at hand. I'm sure they'll pick up the pieces." His tone was matter of fact, though there was urgency underneath. James had seen enough violence to know the aftermath seldom favoured those who stayed around to answer questions.

Knox's gaze grew steely. "What about Cal?"

James sighed, shifting his stance while placing the MP5 back on the sofa. He folded his arms. "He'll be found eventually, I guess. Maybe I should leave instructions on how to open the panic room door? Once free I am sure the police will press him to do some explaining."

Henry gave a curt nod, thinking of the growing tangle of names and lives caught in this net: Michael, Sarah, Jess, and now Rhys... plus Cal. All connected by one person, Gray.

He took a final look at the door, then squared his shoulders. "Roger, let's finish this."

James moved briskly, gathering his laptop bag, the MP5, and Henry's daysack from beside the front door. He carried them outside to the black Range Rover Sport that Cal and Rhys had arrived in, its engine still running in the courtyard, ominous and waiting.

Moments later, Henry came out of the house and walked over to where Rhys's body lay, the blood seeping into the cracks of the gravel in a slow, dark tide. He crouched, patting down the corpse in a familiar search method, the same routine he had performed countless times in Afghanistan, Iraq, and Germany.

Rhys's coat was light, no hidden phone, no documents. Only a counterweight in the pocket and a SureFire torch, standard for men in this line of work.

He left them where they were.

In Rhys' side holster was the Sig Sauer pistol, Knox slide it out and collected the extra magazines and placed them in his map pocket.

Knox stood up, stepping over the body without another glance, and moved to the Range Rover, where James awaited him.

CHAPTER TWENTY-SIX

The wind picked up slightly, tugging at his jacket as he pulled the door open. The day was only just beginning for most people, but to Henry it felt as though it had lasted for weeks.

A moment later, James slid into the passenger seat, adjusting it to accommodate his bulk, then laid the MP5 on the back seat, covering the weapon with a fleece blanket. Knox slipped behind the wheel, the Range Rover's engine already purring quietly, like a patient predator ready to strike.

The interior smelled faintly of gun oil and sweat, layered over the lingering scent of leather. The cup holder held a remote key fob and a black smartphone, its screen faintly lit. Knox glanced at it straight away.

No lock screen.

Knox picked up the phone, scrolling through it with his thumb. He checked recent locations first, finding only the farm. Nothing else. He frowned but was not surprised.

Next, he looked at the call logs, which were empty. Not even a stray misdial. The contact's list was equally devoid of anything. Wiped clean.

Good drills, Knox thought. Cal and Rhys had been thorough, even paranoid. They had done everything right from the technical perspective. No digital footprints, no traceable conversations. They had scrubbed their information before setting out, leaving no clue behind.

Knox wound down the window and flung the phone into the treeline. Keeping it was too risky, since Gray could track it and follow their every move.

Knox's attention moved to the Range Rover's dashboard. Driving this car was obviously a risk. Gray had almost certainly installed a tracker. Yet there was no other option. His own vehicle was miles away, and the police would quickly trace the VRN of James's car, cutting them off long before they arrived at their destination.

At least this way, it would take time and effort for the authorities to link Rhys with James and track the registration. Even then, Knox reflected, there was a good chance the vehicle was not registered in their names. That minor delay was all Knox required to stay ahead for now.

"They wiped everything," he muttered, half to himself.

James smirked faintly, not looking up. "It doesn't really matter, mate. We know where we're going."

Knox shifted the Range Rover into gear, gripping the stick firmly, then pressed his foot on the accelerator. Gravel sprayed from beneath the tyres as the heavy vehicle surged forward, its wheels turning sharply as he pulled the steering wheel to the right. The Rover swung into a tight U-turn, the headlights sweeping across the empty barn and the outline of Rhys's body, now barely visible in the rearview mirror.

James barely reacted, his eyes focused on the sat nav as he keyed in some coordinates. Its glow lit his face.

The vehicle rumbled onto the tarmac, settling into a smooth pace as Knox accelerated along the narrow road. Leafless winter trees blurred past, their branches clawing at the grey sky.

Knox kept his gaze on the road, but his mind was churning. He shot a sideways look at James, his voice cutting above the engine's hum.

"Alright. First things first, what else did you extract from the USB?" Knox asked, his tone neutral, though its gravity was clear. "Then you can tell me about Cal."

James's mouth curved into a slight smile. He shifted in his seat, leaning back against the headrest.

"Well," he began, drawing out the word as though savouring it, "from what I read, Gray had an arrangement with a foreign agent. Some Russian guy working in a sleeper cell in the U.K."

James went on, "Gray told this Russian bloke to target HippoLand. That family theme park, right in the middle of the Christmas holidays. The date was set for today, but there was no specific time mentioned in the email."

Knox spared him a brief look. "HippoLand?" he echoed quietly. Families, children, an easy target.

James noted his expression but did not elaborate. "Yeah, I guess it's a soft target, minimal security, many exits. Maximum damage for minimum effort. Classic move if you want to make a statement."

"There is no strategic gain in it," Henry blurted out.

James turned his face towards Knox. "HippoLand is an easy mark, Henry. If you are someone like Gray, wanting to send a loud enough message to be heard overseas, you do not need strategy. You need vulnerability."

Knox let out a breath through his nose, his hands tightening on the steering wheel.

"Right," he mumbled, mostly to himself. The idea weighed on him, cold and heavy.

"I know HippoLand well enough," James said. "I took the family there a couple of years ago when I was stationed in Catterick. I've walked the grounds. I know some of the weak spots and blind corners. I reckon I know where to set up and stop it before it goes too far."

"You're not going anywhere near this, James," Knox stated, his tone low and firm. "I'll stop this guy, whilst you call Amy, get the police on it, but that is your limit. If they won't handle it, I will."

James turned to him, his face serious though difficult to interpret.

"You're not getting dragged any deeper," Knox continued, cutting him off before he could respond. "I won't let you."

James's slight smirk faded. He leaned back in the seat, arms folded, studying Knox. Although Knox refused to look his way, he felt James's gaze on him.

"You know you can't handle this alone," James said eventually, his voice quieter.

Knox did not reply right away, keeping his concentration on the winding road ahead.

"I've been in deeper trouble before," Knox muttered, though even to himself it sounded hollow.

James let out a quiet laugh. "You never had the authority to tell me what to do when we were in the Army, Knoxy. Why start now?"

Knox said nothing, aware that arguing would only strengthen James's resolve.

James broke the impasse, his voice softer but clear. "You're right about one thing. We should call Amy and let the police know. The threat is real, no question. But I can help, Henry."

Knox glanced at him, already shaking his head, but James pressed on.

"I'm asking permission," James said with a faint, knowing grin. "I know the terrain, exits, the corners they don't show on the map. I can help. You can go and be the hero, charging in and saving the day and I will sit outside, safe and sound, being a good boy."

Knox breathed out harshly, not quite a laugh but close. He remained unconvinced, yet James's stubborn nature was familiar.

James's smile lingered as he slumped back, as though he had already secured the outcome he wanted. "Face it, Knoxy, you're stuck with me."

Knox shook his head, a tiny smirk threatening to appear. "Yeah, lucky me."

He didn't like it. Involving James further felt like inviting more chaos. Yet James was not the type to stand by. That had been clear since the day they met.

Knox finally exhaled, the sound sharp and resigned.

"Fine," he said, voice low with a note of warning. "But you keep your distance. I mean it, James. One false move and I will leave you in the car park with the engine running."

James's grin widened, as though Knox had just handed him the keys. "I would not dream of getting in your way," he said, his tone dripping with mock innocence.

Knox gave him a side glance but let it pass. He was not in the mood to argue over what they both knew would happen anyway.

"Call the local officers, let them handle the gunfight at your place," Knox continued, his voice taking on a harder edge. "After that, ring Amy and tell her what is going on. We have about twenty minutes until we get to HippoLand, and I want a full account of how you outsmarted a former RSM by then."

James chuckled softly, reaching into his pocket for his phone. "You know I love a good war story," he said, unlocking the screen.

The faint glow lit his features as he tapped a few icons. Seconds later, James was calmly reporting a vague but urgent alert about shots fired at a rural property. Knox listened only half-attentively as James relayed the minimum details, emphasising a need for a prompt response.

Once that call was done, James moved on to dial Amy Thornton. Knox saw a flicker of tension return to James's eyes.

This phone call wouldn't be as easy.

James brought the phone to his ear, waiting for Amy to pick up.

CHAPTER TWENTY-SEVEN

The call came through just as Amy was yearning for her bed. Eighteen hours straight was too long, even by her standards of pushing herself beyond reasonable limits. The house explosion the night before had led to a full-scale fingertip search of the scene and a manhunt that ran throughout the night into the morning. She had barely had time to eat, let alone sleep.

Sitting in an unmarked white Ford Focus, she listened to the low hum of the engine and the overworked heater battling the creeping cold that seeped in from outside. Sleet and rain sluiced down the windscreen in thin rivulets, distorting her view of the old police station in front of her, its grey brick exterior solid and forbidding, like a Victorian prison. It was the sort of place that seemed more fitting for gas lamps than CCTV cameras.

Amy slouched in the driver's seat, fatigue pressing down on her.

The phone continued to vibrate.

She glanced at the screen. Unknown number.

Amy sighed, running her hand over her face and then through her damp hair.

"Inspector Thornton," she answered, the weariness in her voice breaking through despite her attempt to remain professional.

"Hi Amy," said a male voice, low and urgent. "James Webster here. We served together in the Army. Catterick. Got a pen? You'll want to write this down."

Her brow knit, and her fingers searched the centre console for a pen.

"James?" she began, confusion in her tone, but he cut her off with brisk insistence.

"No time. I've uncovered a credible threat, a possible terrorist attack at HippoLand Theme Park today. A Russian operative is on the mainland, seems to be targeting the park, but I've no name or description. Just today's date. No further details."

Amy's heart skipped a beat. She fumbled for her police notebook, clicking a pen open one handed, and began scribbling on the thin pages.

"Say that again," she demanded, her voice tightening, slicing through her exhaustion.

"Male, Russian or Russian linked," James repeated steadily. "No ID. If I had to guess, he'll be carrying a rucksack and shying away from cameras, but that is just my speculation. We only have fragments of intel."

Amy's pen halted mid word.

HippoLand.

The family park would be packed at this time of year with parents and children, crowds everywhere. She forced herself to keep writing, despite her mind lagging two steps behind.

"How did you come by this information?" she asked, but the line clicked dead before she could finish speaking.

Amy stared at her phone, hoping to hear it reconnect, but only saw her own frown reflected on the screen.

"Fuck," she muttered, then louder, "Fuck, fuck, fuck."

The patrol car felt cramped, the heater's hum now intolerable. She tossed the phone onto the passenger seat, resisting the urge to smash it against the dashboard.

Her hand hovered over the steering wheel for a moment before she grabbed the phone once more, jabbing at the screen with her fingertip.

She scrolled for her line manager's number, hitting call. It rang once, twice.

On the third ring, the call was answered.

"Amy?" The voice on the other end sounded every bit as exhausted as she felt.

"Boss," she said, urgency sharpening her tone, "there's another situation."

A brief pause. Then his voice steadied. "Well, what is it?"

Amy gazed through the rain-streaked windscreen, watching the old police station's shadow deepen as though it might swallow her whole.

"Somebody just phoned in a credible terrorist attack at HippoLand. Today."

CHAPTER TWENTY-EIGHT

Cal sat in the suffocating darkness of the safe room, the air thick with stillness, so dense it felt as if it might smother him. The blackness enclosed him like a shroud, silencing everything except the pounding of his pulse and the ghostly memory of two gunshots that still rang in his ears. Distant, yet charged with finality. Execution shots. Two rounds, no hesitation.

Knox was dead.

He should have felt relief at such a tidy conclusion. One more loose end tied up, one less threat to the operation. Gray's plan could move forward unhindered. That was the script, the outcome for which the deaths of innocents had paved the way.

Yet relief was the last thing he felt.

Instead, regret gnawed at him.

He shifted uneasily on the concrete floor. It was absurd, he told himself. Sentiment had no place here. People died; that was part of the job. Knox had been an obstacle, like Michael, Sarah, and Jess. Gray had been explicit, and Rhys had followed through.

So why did it feel as if something had gone awry?

He tried to shake the notion away, but the silence in the enclosed chamber was oppressive. Time stretched. The longer he remained in the dark, the gloomier his thoughts became.

He waited, time dragging by, doubt creeping in. Rhys should have returned to free him by now.

His second-in-command would not have hesitated to pull the trigger; Cal knew that. Rhys never balked. Knox was dangerous, a threat who could not be allowed to wander free. Rhys was methodical, steadfast, the kind of operative who never wavered.

But he should have opened the door by now.

Frowning, Cal felt each second lengthen. He imagined Rhys's usual swagger, the smug remark he would have spouted once the job was done, some wry joke about Knox not being so tough after all.

But no sound came.

No footsteps, no voice. Just silence.

And the silence felt wrong.

That thought slid into his brain like a blade, prompting other possibilities. "You slimy little snake, Rhys" he muttered under his breath, coloured with grim amusement.

Perhaps Rhys was not going to free him, not out of betrayal, but because the man wanted to make a statement. That was how Rhys operated, each move layered with meaning. He would not imprison Cal forever, just long enough to prove a point, letting the power dynamic shift for a while. Long enough to remind Cal who was in charge, who stood over Knox's body, controlling the scenario.

Irritated, he realised how he had messed up, and Rhys was rubbing it in. "Fucking crow," he muttered bitterly, no warmth in his short laugh. "Outmanoeuvred by an overweight, desk-jockey SIB Sergeant and a washed-up ex-squaddie."

He appreciated the irony.

His cynical laugh died away, leaving the suffocating silence again, somehow heavier now. Cal tried to steady his breathing, but his fingers tapped restlessly on his leg. Each tap felt amplified in the claustrophobic quiet, stoking the tension beneath his skin.

He thought through the events. Knox was dead, he was certain of that; he had heard the shots. It had all sounded straightforward, clinical, like the final notes of a briefing.

But still he was waiting for Rhys to release him. Second stretched out. He couldn't tell how long he waited, his own tapping the sole punctuation to the dark. Seconds or minutes, all blurred, his mind jumbled with the pointless wait.

He needed action, not to just remain here awaiting Rhys. He needed to seize the initiative.

In the darkness, he pushed himself forward, groping blindly. He remembered glimpses of a desk at the back, recalled from the muzzle flashes he had created earlier, forming a vague mental map of the room.

He remembered seeing rows of servers, small lights blinking, panels humming with power. He assumed there was gear. If Webster had the resources to trap him here, then something in this cluttered space might provide a way out.

Cal's hand slid over the desktop, then into drawers. His fingertips landed on something cold and rectangular. Holding it firmly, he brought it nearer, the shape familiar in his palm.

A phone.

He pressed its power button, and the screen came to life with a faint glow that cut harshly through the gloom. The sudden light stung his eyes, forcing him to tilt it away. Once it had booted, he tapped the screen almost automatically, navigating menus until he found a flashlight icon.

He selected it.

A piercing beam flared, slicing into the dark corners of the room. Everything became abruptly visible under the stark glare.

The room was smaller than he remembered, more cramped.

Steel walls shimmered dully under the beam, giving the space an industrial chill. He played the light steadily across every seam, rivet, and bolt, searching for a weak spot.

Nothing. No cracks, no hidden edges, no easy exploit.

This was more secure than he had feared.

He angled the light upwards without thinking, catching sight of something above the desk: a vent, black metal slats near the ceiling. A ventilation duct.

Cal's eyes fixed on it. It was not guaranteed, but it was something.

He reasoned that a vent was a weak spot. This panic room was designed to keep people out and not designed for keeping someone in. It might be a vulnerability.

Tucking the phone into his waistband, the glow shrinking, he climbed carefully on to the desk. The surface groaned under his weight. The phone's light wavered against his leg. He stretched upwards, feeling for the vent's edges, running his hand around it, seeking any give.

His fingers found the metal frame, and he pulled, arms taut with effort. It did not shift. The screws were tight, set deep.

Dropping back down, frustrated, he grabbed the MP5, examining it. Then he glanced from the gun to the vent, measuring.

He returned to the desk, placed the weapon's muzzle between the vent slats, wedging it into the narrow gap, then pushed and pulled, hoping to lever the frame open.

"Come on," he growled to the silence. Bracing one foot against the desk edge, he forced the weapon forward, his whole body contorting to put maximum strain on the vent.

A tortured metallic squeal echoed, the screws straining. One popped out, clattering across the desk.

"Almost," he grunted, straining harder.

One by one, screws tore free, each pop jarring in the enclosed space. Finally, the entire frame gave a loud rasp and dropped to the floor, clanging.

Cal let the MP5 drop as he stared at the exposed duct: dark, cramped, but open.

He forced his head in first, body squeezing into the duct. Metal dug into him, scraping his back and shoulders. The narrow shaft twisted, making him contort awkwardly, inching forward. Each gain felt fought for. At last, a faint glimmer of light appeared, a pinprick, but unmistakable.

That small hope drove him forward. He climbed into the small vent, inching his way down the claustrophobic tunnel, that felt tight against his shoulders and back, he wanted to expand allow his body to be free, but the tight metal shaft contained him. Finally, he reached the duct's end, slamming his shoulder into the cover with enough force to shake its frame. Another push, and the metal panel groaned and snapped, letting him burst through.

A gush of cold morning air struck him in the face as he toppled out. He hit the ground with a jarring thud, the impact stinging, but he was finally free.

He crouched for a moment, dragging in gulp after gulp of chilly air, the damp seeping through his clothes where he lay. Slowly, he got to his feet, muscles burning from the cramped crawl. Debris clung to him as he stood, gazing up at the dull grey sky. At least he was out.

He looked around, then saw it.

Blood.

It gleamed in the dim fridged light, a thick, dark spread over the frost hardened earth. It seemed to go on forever, creeping into the cracks between paving stones, soaking the ground.

Rounding a corner, he froze.

Rhys's body lay on the ground, limbs slack and contorted, his head tipped at an angle that whispered finality. His eyes were open, blank, staring at a sky he would never see again.

Dead.

And Knox was not dead.

Fuck. The sudden realisation struck him like a blow to the gut. He stared down at Rhys's corpse, lips parted as though to speak, but no words came. The quiet countryside mocked him.

Cal crouched, fingers pressing against Rhys's neck. Cold, lifeless skin, no sign of a pulse. He lingered briefly.

He swallowed, looking to where the Range Rover had once stood. Gone. An empty space.

Good.

The word rose in his mind, sharp and clear, insane as it seemed. But there it was, settled and unshakable.

Knox's escape felt like a victory.

Cal could not fathom why he felt that way, but now he knew what he must do.

He stepped inside the house, passing the door that had been his prison, and entered the kitchen. It looked different, as though the home's normalcy had survived while everything else shifted out of place.

His eyes roamed the area while his thoughts raced, retracing what Knox had left behind. He saw it then, vivid in his mind, like a map unrolling. He knew where Knox was heading.

He just needed a ride to catch up with him.

Fingers glided along the counter edge as he moved around the kitchen, opening drawers. Silverware rattled, receipts rustled, but nothing important turned up. Not until he opened a shallow drawer next to the sink.

He slid it wide and found what he needed.

Keys. Several sets, jumbled on rings and fobs. His fingertips hovered, sifting them out. Then he plucked a black plastic fob bearing a scratched emblem.

Car keys.

He glanced through the window at the low-lying mist thickening in the winter light. Knox was out there, somewhere, moving. Fast.

Cal pocketed the keys. Momentum built inside him, driving him onward.

Maybe this would be the start of something else. A different journey with a different outcome.

CHAPTER TWENTY-NINE

Blue strobes cut through the damp midmorning haze, their relentless rhythm reflecting off the wet, rain-soaked tarmac. The pulses of light scattered over the rows of parked cars, warping into jagged streaks on the waterlogged ground. A once ordinary car park had become a frantic junction of emergency vehicles.

Police units arrived in steady waves, tyres hissing through puddles, engines rumbling with contained urgency. Radios crackled as officers exited their vehicles, boots landing on the tarmac with sharp splashes. The damp air was thick with transmissions laced with static, terse messages bouncing between teams as they coordinated their response.

Despite the influx of personnel, a layer of fatigue clung to the scene. Tired officers peeled themselves from their patrol vehicles as though operating on autopilot. Some had been on shift for almost twenty-four hours, their faces ashen and gaunt with exhaustion, dark circles etched beneath tired eyes. Rain streaked across their uniforms, clinging to high-visibility jackets, but nobody gave it any notice. There was too much work to do.

Beneath it all, resentment smouldered. They had already spent hours sifting through the remains of a burned-out property, pursuing leads in a sprawling manhunt. It had worn them thin, and now this. Another emergency. Another crisis demanding more than they had to give.

They were perilously overstretched, and everyone sensed it.

Reinforcements had been requested from neighbouring forces, but none had arrived. West Yorkshire Police was stretched well past its capacity, left to handle yet another high stakes situation single handedly. Locking down HippoLand was a logistical nightmare: too vast, too many exits, far too many unpredictable elements.

Every unsearched corner held the potential for danger. A suspect might hide undetected, waiting for the opportunity to strike. There was no time to hesitate. They pressed on. Failure was not an option.

Amy parked her unmarked car beside the hastily set up Counter Terrorist Unit command post, which was an Incident Control van adapted for this purpose. It was skewed against the kerb, its side door open, casting harsh fluorescent light onto the wet pavement. The glow reflected on the drenched ground, distorted by shifting puddles.

She stepped out, slamming the door behind her.

It had been less than half an hour since James's frantic call, and she felt in her gut that something was off.

James was connected to Knox. That link nagged at her mind, uneasy and unresolved. The timing of this supposed terrorist threat seemed almost too convenient. Could it be a deliberate decoy? A calculated misdirection?

Her instincts told her the two situations were not unrelated. But instincts were not proof. Right now, she had to concentrate on her job.

James had provided his name freely, a detail he need not have shared, especially not with his number withheld. That single fact was significant, not what someone playing games would do.

It had to mean something.

Her eyes flicked towards the park gates, where more officers moved to secure the perimeter. High-visibility jackets shone beneath the flashing blue lights, forming an unbroken flow of activity.

Beyond the iron gates, though, it might have been another world entirely.

Inside, the park's atmosphere remained unaffected. Families ambled between attractions, faint laughter floated on the drizzle, mingling with the distant jingle of funfair music. Small groups headed from one ride to the next, children grasping fizzy drinks and sweet treats, oblivious to the gathering storm beyond their bright sanctuary.

For them, today was about overpriced entry and exhilarating roller coasters.

For Amy, it was about preventing a catastrophe.

She ducked into the CTU command van, stepping into a stripped back nerve centre of operations. Its design was purely functional, with no adornment.

A folding table ran along one side, covered with half unfurled maps and hastily printed sketches of the park, edges curling in the cold. Each route and potential bottleneck had been circled with a heavy highlighter pen.

At the far end, a row of laptops threw a cool glow, text and data scrolling continuously. Temporary workstations had been thrown together, officers and analysts hunched over them, scanning every feed. Opposite the table, a larger TV flicked through live CCTV views of bustling walkways, dimly lit queue lines, and the busy central square. The park was carved up into small, grainy segments on screen.

Nearby, a pin board displayed the haste of a team under pressure, pinned notes, intelligence files, and photographs overlapping at odd angles. It looked untidy, but it did not have to be neat. Time was not on their side.

Amy took it all in, absorbing the orchestrated chaos.

A cluster of officers stood around the table, heads bent, focusing on updated information and deciding how best to set up cordons.

She spoke above the hum of conversation. “Who’s Silver?”

One of the officers glanced up, still in the midst of fastening another piece of the park map to the board.

“Superintendent Jenkins,” he replied, straightening slightly. His brow shone more from rain than sweat, but tension showed in his rigid posture. “CTU is on its way too, they should arrive soon.”

Amy gave him a short nod. She knew Jenkins’s reputation. Calm under fire, decisive when required. Yet even with his leadership, controlling a potential threat here was like navigating a minefield.

Another officer added new marks to the map, drawing red circles around critical entrances, without looking up. “Jenkins wants a soft evacuation. Low key, keep it quiet. Minimise panic and avoid tipping off the suspect.”

Amy narrowed her eyes. “No helicopter support?”

He shook his head. “Not yet. The bomb squad is on its way, ten minutes out.”

She exhaled, turning the data over in her mind.

“We have begun sealing off the perimeter,” he went on. “My lot are on the exits, low profile.”

Amy nodded. A soft evacuation required finesse. Moving too quickly and overtly could spark chaos, but too slowly and the threat could slip away.

Her gaze shifted to the map’s far side, where open animal enclosures and larger rides sprawled out.

“Get the head ranger or park manager,” she said. “We’ll need their staff as extra eyes and ears. Until a covert team can move in, they are our best resource.”

The officer nodded, already reaching for his Airwave radio.

Amy stepped back out into the cold, bracing against its bite. The sudden shift from the cramped, warm van to the damp, open air drew a shiver from her, but she ignored it. Her suit jacket was woefully inadequate for December. She had worn it since the night before, a light grey trouser suit and blouse, stiff from prolonged exposure to the cold. Possibly enough to pass as a civilian on the street, but it made her stand out here, where families wrapped themselves in thick coats and woollen hats.

She might as well have had the word police written on her.

Behind her, the growl of a diesel engine signalled a new arrival. A black SUV drove through the rain into the makeshift staging area.

Amy turned to watch as Superintendent Jenkins climbed out.

He was tall, standing rigid with an air of command, his full police uniform immaculate despite the drizzle. His polished boots crossed the slick tarmac with confident strides. The brim of his hat cast a shadow over sharp, observant eyes that scanned the scene like a general surveying the battlefield.

In his left hand, he held a tablet, already brimming with scrolling updates.

Officers converged on him as though drawn by gravity.

The hum of controlled chaos flared momentarily as voices overlapped, numerous questions fired in rapid succession. Jenkins raised his hand slightly, his expression calm but unwavering, slicing through the uproar.

His voice was clipped and direct, yet not forceful. Decisive, no pause for indecision.

Amy held back for a moment, watching him manage the situation.

Jenkins had a rare skill: the power to command without shouting, without arrogance. His mere presence in the eye of the storm seemed to bring order, as though he was a fixed anchor point.

She closed the space between them, “Sir,” she called, her voice cutting through the combined hum of engines and distant theme park music.

Jenkins glanced up, his face pale and creased from too many hours without proper rest. Exhaustion showed in his eyes.

“Amy.” He gave a brief nod, acknowledging her presence.

He wasted no time. He never did. “You’re now acting as Bronze for me.”

Amy’s eyebrows rose slightly.

Jenkins continued, “Walk with me.” He said softly, heading towards the CTU, “You’re close to this. I want your full involvement.” His tone carried the quiet assurance of a command.

Amy nodded at once. “Understood.”

Jenkins exhaled, shifting the tablet in his hands. His fingers swiped over the screen, bringing up live CCTV streams from inside the park.

The camera switched to a busy spot near food stalls. Families drifted through the lanes, a father balancing a tray of chips, a child clinging to a balloon.

They had no clue what was unfolding just beyond the gates.

Jenkins’s face hardened. “I want the park sealed in ten minutes. Every entry, every exit.”

Amy's gaze lowered to the screen, her mind already grappling with the logistics of such an order. Ten minutes over such vast and diverse ground. Thick crowds. There were far too many variables.

But ten minutes was all she had.

She nodded sharply. "Yes, sir."

More police vehicles arrived, their doors opening in succession. Officers stepped out with the muted rattle of weapons.

Their rifles hung from slings, hidden beneath wet jackets. Discreet, yet prepared.

Amy turned to Jenkins, reducing her voice a notch. "We've to clear the park zone by zone. If he catches on too soon, we lose control."

Jenkins gave a slight nod, still locked on the live feeds. "Agreed. I've already put plain clothed officers inside. Once we give the signal, they'll guide people out."

They had to strike the perfect balance. If they moved too swiftly, it might push the suspect into panic, leading to catastrophe. If they took too long, they could miss the chance to intervene in time.

She met Jenkins's eyes. "We need speed, but not noise."

Amy glanced at the Ferris wheel, its slow turn barely visible in the damp sky.

"We can't afford a slip up, Amy."

Her gaze returned to Jenkins, her mind racing ahead. "How are we handling public communications?" she asked.

Jenkins paused. They had reached the canopy of the CTU that had been hastily erected at the side of the vehicle. He glanced at a map of the park stretched out on the table in front of him. Although he was looking at it, his thoughts were already beyond the map, examining concerns bigger than simple logistics.

"Officially?" he said, his frown deepening. "We're running a security sweep based on an anonymous tip off. Enough to justify a visible police presence without causing alarm. The press won't pick up on the bomb story unless something actually happens."

Amy nodded slowly. The plan was measured and practical, relying on one crucial factor: keeping the situation contained. That this did not spiral beyond their control.

Yet from her experience, volatile situations rarely follow the plan.

Her voice dropped a touch. "And unofficially?"

Jenkins's expression remained the same, but his stance stiffened.

"Unofficially," he said, lowering his voice, "we are preparing for mass casualties."

The words felt heavy in Amy's chest.

Jenkins continued, grim yet factual. "I've already alerted every local hospital. A&E departments are clearing space, postponing non-urgent cases. They don't know why yet; as far as they're concerned, it's a routine precaution for a potential large-scale incident."

Amy's stomach tightened.

This was procedure, and she knew it would be in place. But hearing it out loud, realising it was happening right now, made it far more real than she wanted.

Amy's eyes turned again to the park entrance.

The colourful archways, usually a joyful sight for families, now felt paper thin, a frail boundary separating normal life from a crisis. All those unsuspecting visitors, she thought.

She looked back at the command table, staring at the map of the park.

"I'll start dividing the park into sectors," she said. Her mind was already splitting the vast area into sections, charting the best evacuation paths.

Jenkins leaned over the table. "You'll take the south." He tapped a zone on the map. "I will handle the north with CTU. We will force him towards the centre."

Amy nodded. Containment. Gradually forcing him inwards.

"If we start clearing people too soon, the suspect will notice," she said. "It needs to appear like natural crowd movements. Maybe fake a power fault or something similar, buying us time?"

Jenkins considered for a moment, then nodded. "We can do that."

He rapped his knuckles against the map in the northern zone. "I want snipers deployed within twenty minutes. The tower and that theatre rooftop both have clear lines of sight over the main square and most busy sections."

Amy stayed focused on the map. Overwatch was crucial, but it would be pointless if they failed to spot the suspect before it was too late.

"Any luck on facial recognition?" she asked.

Jenkins's lips pressed into a tight line. "No, nothing. Not so far anyway." He exhaled through his nose. "We haven't had any hits on our databases. We don't even have a name or face. We're chasing shadows. Unless you know more"

Amy shifted her stance, folding her arms. "I've relayed everything I know", she said.

"Are you sure this is real?" he asked quietly, as if reluctant to voice the question.

She did not falter.

Amy inhaled, eyes narrowing with conviction. "One hundred percent, Sir. This comes from an extremely credible source. One I would bank my life on."

Jenkins nodded.

Amy tapped the map with a fingertip.

"If this man knows what he's doing, he's probably already done a recon. He'll have found the weak spots, the maintenance routes, service gates. He could be out of sight, beyond the crowds already."

Jenkins nodded briefly, glancing at the map again. "I have two teams heading into those tunnels now."

Amy raised her eyes, looking beyond him and the mobile command post, noticing how more cars were still trickling into the car park.

Families, backpacks thrown over shoulders, children tugging parents along by the hand.

Unaware.

Faint Christmas tunes hovered in the drizzle, cheerful yet disturbingly inappropriate.

"Could we station a unit further up the main road?" she asked, forcing herself to remain focused. "Stop more arrivals?"

Jenkins shook his head, resigned. "We don't have the manpower at the moment. We're barely coping as it is."

"Then, maybe we just start quietly moving people out," she replied, her voice steeled.

Jenkins gave her a slow nod. "I must be certain the suspect is not in an area we're emptying," he said. "Without a description, we're working in the dark."

"CCTV is scanning for the device," she said. "If they spot it, we clear that area first. I doubt he will stay close to the IED once he has placed it."

Jenkins studied her for a moment, then looked back at the park itself.

All those people. Hundreds wandering around with no clue, no idea how close they might be to danger.

He let out a deliberate breath, slow.

"Then let's hope you are correct."

Off in the distance, the Ferris wheel turned slowly. The park remained alive with the hum of normalcy, laughter, rollercoaster shrieks, music drifting through the damp air.

Unaware.

CHAPTER THIRTY

Henry brought the Range Rover to a sharp stop, the tyres skidding briefly as he pulled onto a verge in front of a modest red brick building. The place looked forgotten by time, a single storey structure, grimy white framed windows dulled by dirt, and a white wooden door whose paint had peeled long ago. It could easily have passed for a utility shed or an old storehouse.

James was already on the move, unclipping his seat belt in a single fluid motion as the vehicle screeched to a halt.

Knox shifted in his seat, reaching under the fleece covering for the MP5 that rested on the back seat. His fingers closed around the weapon's stock just as James swung towards him.

"You can't take that into the park, mate," James said firmly, his voice cutting through the tension. "The armed response teams will shoot you on sight, and in a place that crowded, you'll put more civilians at risk than you will protect. Leave it in the car, Oxy."

Knox's eyes flicked to James, his hand still on the weapon. For an instant, he hesitated, not wanting to head into the park unarmed.

James held his gaze. "We'll be in the middle of a busy theme park. The last thing we need is stray bullets or you getting shot before you spot the bastard."

Knox's shoulders sagged, accepting the logic. His grip on the rifle loosened, and he reluctantly replaced it under the fleece. "Fine," he muttered, a trace of rebellion in his voice. His hand moved to his belt, drawing a Gerber multi-tool. He held it up, the blade catching what little light there was. "But I am taking this."

James allowed a faint smirk. "Crack on then."

Knox's lip twitched irritably as he stepped out into the freezing air.

James jumped out on the passenger side and headed towards the building. "Turn on your burner," he called over his shoulder. "I will ring you and guide you through it. Now move."

Knox nodded, slipping the Gerber back into its pouch. His breath turned to mist in the cold as he glanced towards the distant lights of the park, the muffled sounds of laughter and music drifting towards him like ghosts.

Without another word, he ran, vanishing into the line of trees, leaving the car and the rifle behind.

Henry soon found the fence line, old but stubborn. He crouched, grasping the wire fencing with one hand, while bringing the Gerber's pliers to it with the other. The metal groaned softly each time he cut it, snapping apart like brittle branches.

Meanwhile, James had reached the grimy window of the old building. He stripped off his hoodie, wrapping it around his forearm. Without slowing, he smashed his arm through the glass, which shattered inwards with a sharp crack, shards clattering inside. Unfazed, James brushed away the larger jagged edges, widening the gap enough to climb carefully through.

The building absorbed him into its dim interior, leaving only the gentle creak of the floorboards behind.

Inside, the room was small and austere. A single desk spanned the back wall, cluttered with dated monitors and tangled cables that snaked towards the floor. Standby lights blinked softly in the gloom. A quiet hum of equipment filled the otherwise silent space.

James pulled on his hoodie again, feeling the warmth return. Using his sleeve, he swept away dust from the keyboard, revealing the unmistakable layout of a CCTV hub. As he had suspected, it was a remote security backup site, connected to the park's main surveillance system. He remembered noticing the building on a previous trip, hidden away like an unused service shed. But James had not been fooled by appearances.

He set his laptop down, flicked it open, and attached it to the network modem with a short ethernet cable and adapter from his bag. As the screen lit up, he retrieved his phone from his pocket and called Henry.

Henry had by now finished cutting through the first fence and had raced through a clump of bushes until he reached a second fence. He knelt, preparing to cut it, but stopped to set up his comms with James. Fishing out the Nokia phone, he removed its back cover, slotted in the SIM card, replaced the battery, and powered it on.

The phone hummed to life, the small screen glowing in the dimness. It felt like a relic of the past, and Henry had to think carefully to use it. He scrolled through its simple menus, fingers moving more slowly than he would have liked.

The phone vibrated, and James's name appeared.

"That was quick, James," Henry said quietly, eyes scanning the shadowy trees on the far side of the fence.

"No sense wasting time," James replied, his familiar dry tone laced with static. "The police are at every entrance. CTU is on site, armed response too. Amy's with them. They're not evacuating yet, meaning they've not spotted the guy or the device. Not yet anyway."

Henry shifted on his knees, swapping which one was pressed into the damp ground. The brightness of the park lights beyond seemed unnaturally vivid against the morning gloom.

"You think you can locate him or the device?" Henry asked.

James gave a brief, scornful snort. "You think I came here to ride the teacups? Yeah, of course I will find him," he said wryly. "First, you need to move. You are hanging around the animal sanctuary side, so you have a bit of cover, but not for long. Head straight in. He will aim for the busiest spot, so that is where you need to be. And don't' go in the wrong enclosure and get eaten by the lions."

Henry looked at the faint trail that led through the trees, heading towards the brilliant lights deeper in the park. The subdued noise of voices and the rumble of machinery drifted on the cold air, growing louder with each step he would take.

"Understood. I'm on my way," he said.

"I'll call when you are in place," James answered. "I need you to get your skates on, Knoxy. We're already behind schedule."

The line died before Henry could respond. With a frustrated sigh, he lowered the phone into his pocket.

Rising from his crouch, Henry grabbed the Gerber again, slicing through the second fence.

Within minutes, he was through and jogging, weaving among the trees. The motion felt second nature, too natural, and with it came the scorching reminder of his wounded leg. The deep cut, hastily packed with Celox, had held up so far, but now, with the sudden burst of speed, it flared with a fresh wave of pain.

He slowed slightly, the pain making his vision blur. Gritting his teeth, he forced it from his mind. No time to stop. No time to think about it.

Keep moving, he told himself.

His breathing took on a stable rhythm, cold air stinging his lungs. He fixed his eyes ahead, following the path through thinning trees as the park's clamour grew nearer.

Muffled rollercoaster screams, heavy music bass, the laughter of crowds, all drew him in, drowning out the ache in his leg.

Knox didn't slow for long. He pushed forward, ignoring the throbbing in his leg, keeping his mind on the device, the threat, and the mass of unsuspecting visitors in the park.

Stay focused. Keep going. Endure.

Bright, flashing lights broke through the branches, and he latched onto the noise, letting it guide him as he ran. His body protested, but he kept pressing on.

Henry hesitated for a moment, his breath catching as he took in the unfamiliar environment around him. Shadows stretched under the trees, and the rumble of rides and crowd chatter floated from the park beyond.

In the CCTV room, James leaned closer to his monitor, clicking through camera views. His fingers flew over the keys, flicking between angles, scanning for anything that seemed out of place: a rucksack left alone, someone loitering where they should not be, anything.

"Come on," James whispered, eyes locked on the grainy footage. "Show yourself."

Henry arrived at a tarmac path marked by a wooden post, its chipped paint bearing arrows. One arrow read Theme Park, so he followed it without thinking.

Gradually, the setting changed from silent, wooded outskirts to a realm of light and colour. Within minutes, Henry was passing under the glow of carnival lights, the grey morning subdued by flashing bulbs and vibrant decorations. Water reflected the neon in small puddles. The smell of grilled food reached him, and his stomach reminded him that it was pretty empty, the aroma of hot dogs and hamburgers filling the air.

His phone vibrated in his pocket, two short pulses. He retrieved it, answering curtly, "Yes?"

James's voice crackled. "You took your time."

Henry surveyed the families strolling by, children darting ahead, enthralled by the rides. He squared his shoulders, trying to blend in as best he could.

"What do you have?" he asked.

James let out a faint breath. "Nothing so far. I've been through the park cameras. If our man is here, he is not shouting about it. I've looked for likely profiles: IC 1 males in their twenties or thirties with backpacks, baseball caps... the usual. But it's like searching for a needle in a haystack. There're just far too many people."

Henry's eyes narrowed as he skirted around a group standing near the ticket booths. It was crowded. Scarves were pulled tightly over faces, hoods raised against the cold, and more bags slung over shoulders than he cared to count.

"There're a lot of covered faces," James added, mirroring Henry's thoughts. "That doesn't help either."

Henry halted briefly near the entrance, his gaze sweeping across the square. "Alright," he said softly. "Keep looking. Something will stand out eventually. It always does."

The line went silent for a moment.

"I'll find him," James said at last, his voice noticeably cooler and more determined.

The bitter Yorkshire morning clung to Knox, intensifying the weariness that had shadowed him since the previous day. His body felt heavier, his muscles stiff and sluggish.

"If this were my job," Henry spoke quietly, avoiding using words that might alarm the nearby crowds, "I would pick somewhere packed with people, a place with limited CCTV coverage. Maybe a dark spot, enclosed, somewhere no one pays much attention."

James's end of the line stayed silent for a second or two, faint typing noises in the background. Henry envisioned him in the cramped CCTV room, bent over the keyboard, eyes glued to screens showing grainy footage, flipping between them faster than most could manage.

"Yeah," James muttered, almost to himself. "That makes sense. There are a few possibilities. There's a café and an arcade just down from where you are. But..." He paused, presumably studying more camera feeds. "There's also an indoor ghost house over on the west side of the park. It is dark, quiet, and nobody looks too closely inside. Could be a good place to hide something without arousing suspicion."

"Yeah, that could work. I'll head to the ghost house and investigate the others on the way," Henry replied, already turning towards the western edge of the park. He quickened his pace. "While I check them, keep an eye out for anyone leaving quickly. If he has already planted the bag, I doubt he will hang about to admire his handy work."

"Understood," James said. "I'll keep you informed."

Henry ended the call and put his phone away. His hands were numb, and his breath formed a faint cloud as he moved, weaving through families clustered by the carousel.

He checked through the café and the arcade, but nothing stood out, so he continued his route to the ghost house. Accelerating along a path that curved slightly and dipped, until at last the ghost house came into view. A flickering sign hung overhead, its paint peeling around the edges.

A queue trailed outside the ghost house, children bouncing with anticipation, parents chatting idly as the line moved slowly. Knox lingered a short distance from the crowd, his eyes scanning the perimeter. It had everything: noise, distraction, an easy place to blend in, dimly lit. Perfect.

He did not join the queue, though. Instead, he peeled away, skirting the building. Following the worn concrete walls, he spotted rusted skips and cigarette butts scattered around the back.

He noticed a maintenance door tucked behind the skips, unmarked and easily overlooked. Knox tested the handle. It resisted a little, but not much. One sharp kick to the side of the frame, placed low and firm, split the wood. The door groaned open and sagged on its hinges.

Knox stepped inside.

Darkness engulfed him, broken only by the occasional flicker of neon lighting. Greens and purples flickered sporadically, illuminating the mud on his jeans and the dried blood on his knuckles. For an instant, he almost looked like part of the attraction, a zombie stumbling through the ghost house's underbelly.

He took out his SureFire torch and let its beam reveal the interior.

It was a maze of tight corners and low-slung props. Knox moved cautiously, senses alert. Animatronics buzzed and lurched to life at intervals, skeletons rattling forward, monstrous faces leaping from behind curtains. He paid them no heed beyond their mechanical rhythm.

Then he saw it.

The torch picked out the strap of a black rucksack. Subtle, nearly lost in the gloom. It caught on the movement of a vampire prop rising from a coffin, hands outstretched, fangs bared.

Knox observed silently, frowning.

That was not part of the scenery.

He waited until the coffin reset and the vampire figure slid back, then he stepped forward. Reaching up, he grabbed the nylon strap and gave it a firm pull.

The coffin shuddered, and something heavy slipped free, landing against his chest. Knox caught it, cradling it with one arm. A rucksack. Plain black, unbranded, easy to disregard.

Which made it all the more dangerous.

He did not hesitate, slipping out through the broken maintenance door and back into daylight. The brightness stung his eyes, and he paused briefly, letting them adjust.

His pulse quickened, not from strain, but from realising he now held a bag that could mean the difference between nothing happening or total catastrophe.

Knox surveyed the area, then moved to a large black bin against the side of the building. He set the rucksack on top, the plastic lid sagging beneath its weight.

His fingers were steady as he grasped the zip. It resisted slightly, challenging him to doubt his intentions. Yet Knox had no illusions; this was no stray bag of clothes or abandoned lunch.

The zip parted with a gentle rasp.

A faint green glow greeted him, soft but distinct, shining inside. It flickered as he widened the opening, then vanished in the daylight.

Knox's eyes fixed on the device lying within.

Basic. Rough. Yet lethal.

A crude weapon for mass destruction, made by someone who blurred the line between makeshift skill and chilling effectiveness.

At its centre was a mobile phone, stripped to essential components, tightly bound to a small electronic relay. Wires wound from the relay to the mechanism's core, coiled as though they were the veins of something both unnatural and deadly. The phone's screen was dark and silent, an inconspicuous trigger awaiting a single command: a phone call, a text, a remote ping. Any could bring the system to life.

Yet the true danger lay underneath the casing.

A sealed, pressurised canister rested at the device's heart, its contents sealed behind a reinforced burst disc. This was not the usual explosive, nor meant for a regular bomb. Instead, it held something far more sinister, an ominous vial that hinted at a chemical payload.

Inside, compressed gas — perhaps CO_2 or nitrogen — kept the agent under consistent pressure. The moment the relay activated, a current would spark the solenoid valve or micro-explosive squib, either of which could rupture the burst disc in a single heartbeat.

Then, terror would begin.

Once punctured, the pressure would blast the chemical through a precisely engineered atomiser. In under a second, the toxic substance would become a vapour, spreading rapidly.

Enclosed indoors, the vapour would flood the area, coating surfaces, skin and lungs in one frantic moment. There would be no way out, no chance for error. One breath would suffice.

In open air, a passing breeze could carry it far beyond the blast's immediate zone, turning a contained strike into a domino effect of misery. The chemical mist would drift invisibly, slipping over an expanding radius, a silent murderer borne on the wind.

Worst of all, there would be no countdown. No blinking lights. No warning.

Just a signal.

A missed call.

A text notification.

Then chaos would unfurl.

Simple. Improvised. Devastating.

Knox's gaze caught the Cyrillic letters etched on the vial clamped inside the canister. The words might as well have been painted in bright red.

Новичóк

Henry's fingers closed around the Nokia phone in his jacket pocket, but he did not move immediately. His gaze remained fixed on the rucksack, now partially unzipped, the canister inside it like a coiled serpent ready to strike.

He swallowed, taking slow, deliberate steps backward, his eyes never leaving the device. Ten feet. Fifteen. His boots scraped quietly on the gravel as he put space between himself and the wheelie bin.

A thought gnawed at the edge of his mind: was the phone in his hand too near the mechanism? Could making a call set off the detonator accidentally? Knox was not about to risk it.

At roughly twenty feet away, he stopped, lifted the Nokia to his ear, and dialled James's number.

The connection was immediate.

"You got it?" James's voice was tense, slicing through the faint hiss of static.

Henry narrowed his eyes, still observing the dark silhouette of the rucksack from across the alley.

"Yeah, I think so," he replied, keeping his voice low. "It's a canister with a vial inside, clear liquid, connected to a mobile phone."

A pause sounded on the other end. Then James exhaled, combining tension and concentration in one breath.

"The phone is the trigger," James said, his tone turning sharper. "Simple but effective. It's probably primed to a call or a text. If it rings, we're in big trouble. Any markings on the bottle?"

"Yeah," Henry replied. "They're in Russian. It looks like... Hob-n-yok, but in Cyrillic. The N is backwards, and the O has a diacritical mark over it."

James did not respond right away. Henry could hear fingers tapping on a keyboard.

"God, Henry, that is Novichok."

Knox's pulse spiked, thudding in his ears, the clarity of that revelation making the risk painfully real.

"Yeah," Henry murmured, forcing his voice to remain steady as he unconsciously took another step back from the device. "I suspected as much."

Henry's eyes returned to the rucksack. Every instinct told him to retreat, let someone else deal with the lethal Pandora's box in front of him, but he couldn't do that. Not yet.

"Okay," he continued, his tone firm. "Here's the plan. Let Amy know. There is nothing more I can do out here by myself. I'll try to secure it, but you must find the Russian. Go through the CCTV footage, find the guy who planted this, and tell me where he went."

James did not pause, speaking steadily despite the urgency in his voice. "Understood."

Knox ended the call and walked back over to the rucksack.

The green light pulsed faintly, the calm, mechanical logic of the device indifferent to the havoc it could unleash.

"What am I going to do with you, eh?" he muttered to the device.

CHAPTER THIRTY-ONE

The fog pressed against the window, thick and unyielding, engulfing the skyline. York's ancient rooftops were reduced to shadows, their edges blurred by the mist. A church spire flickered in and out of sight, like a dying signal.

The fog of war.

Catheryn barely noticed. She stood by the glass, one hand resting lightly against the frame, the chill of the winter morning seeping through the pane and cooling her skin.

She was dressed in the hotel dressing gown, a white cotton robe that almost swept the floor. Its soft fabric felt warm and comforting against her bare skin.

Behind her, the television murmured, looping endless news updates on the neutral hotel walls. A static news presenter, then images of conflict zones. Countless wars raged in the world, yet this one mattered to Catheryn. It was an opportunity.

The presenter continued talking about the Ukraine frontline, about Russia's Special Military Operation. Then the usual talk about NATO strategies, international sanctions, and UN resolutions.

Words that meant nothing in the rooms where real choices were made.

Politicians still played their game, making statements for the cameras, keeping their hands clean while manoeuvring pieces into place as though it were a large chessboard. Trade, wheat, oil and gas. War was an opportunity for everyone to profit.

But ultimately, the peace between east and west would not hold. The world had seen it all before, when politicians hesitated too long, believing they had more time than they truly did, and then someone else moves first, seizing the chance and the advantage.

And when that happens, everything changes.

Catheryn exhaled softly, pressing her palm to the glass. She had always known the world worked like this. She had never needed anyone to explain it to her. That was her burden, knowing more than anyone else by playing them all.

She turned slightly, glimpsing the reflection of the television behind her. The story had moved on, and the presenter on the 24-hour news channel was introducing a new segment.

She looked at the windowpane again. She did not need to look directly at the television. She already knew what was on the screen.

Knox's face.

It was a police-issued mugshot, stripped of everything that had once made him real.

His eyes appeared flat, expressionless.

The story had already been written for him.

FORMER SOLDIER, HENRY KNOX, WANTED IN CONNECTION WITH TWO DEATHS IN YORKSHIRE HOUSE EXPLOSION.

Catheryn's eyes burned, not with emotion nor guilt, but because none of this was necessary.

She had left Knox behind, or at least she had tried. He was never supposed to be near any of this. He should have been occupied with a pointless task of keeping Sophie safe, freeing Catheryn to prepared for what was coming next.

Yet Knox had always been a soldier, who was never able to leave things alone.

Now, he was going to suffer for that mistake.

She drew her arms around her body, gripping the soft material of her robe. Perhaps she still loved him, perhaps she had never truly stopped, but she could not love who he had become.

She had spent countless years hosting officers' wives at their home, acting the role of a Sergeant Major's spouse, observing the protocols, smoothing over the social ranks so he could advance up the ladder.

Only he never had.

He had left the Army, had stopped striving. No ambition, no drive. A man who once occupied rooms where influential decisions were made now traced unfaithful husbands and performed background checks.

What a waste.

She waited for him to awaken, to realise that his potential meant nothing if left unused. But he never did.

So, she moved on. Without him.

And now?

Now he was running for his life, while she was the one orchestrating the storm.

A gentle click behind her made her turn. Archie stepped out of the bathroom, adjusting the cuffs of his shirt. He appeared calm, poised, and entirely sure of himself. She allowed herself a moment to admire him.

Archie had been the one to deliver the news about Henry, when he had brought Sophie back from getting ice cream. Archie had warned her enough times about Henry's inability to sit on the side lines. His moral compass was just too strong.

Now Catheryn observed Archie was almost fully dressed for the day's events, both Catheryn's plan and his would come to fruition today. He stood in his neatly pressed white shirt, and tie. Suit trousers that fit him in all the right places. He exuded confidence and power. But also, his lust intrigued her. Not enough that she fell for him, but enough to keep him interesting. But beneath her admiration simmered quiet calculation. He had opened doors, but he would not define her path. Soon, she thought, Archie would understand that he had underestimated her ambition.

Archie always spoke passionately of possibilities, of shaping events, of restoring Britain's status. It was the very reason she had followed him here, leaving Cyprus behind.

He had introduced her to high-ranking officials, in the U.K. government and abroad. And that's when she had found her next stepping stone.

Normanov.

Archie was a gateway to the rich oligarch, and he was a gateway to real power. Power that is unelected. A power that can't be turned off.

Archie noticed her looking and gave a small smile of amusement. "I told you they would twist the story like that," Archie said, voice measured, gesturing to the news on the small flat screen television. "Everyone prefers a simple narrative: disgraced hero goes rogue, kills his own friends, and the police look righteous."

Catheryn sighed, turning towards the screen. It cut to footage of a press conference in front of a police station, then to an image of a wrecked house. "Yes. You did say they would blame him. I almost wish I could have spoken to him first. He might have stayed away with Sophie, far from all this. Now it will end in tragedy."

She needed to play a game of the pretty prize until she could move on with her next step, but it bored her.

She felt Archie's gaze on her, judging her mood to be about Knox and not her true intention. "Knox made his own choice," he answered calmly. "He refused to aim higher. He is about to learn the penalty for thinking small."

Catheryn's gaze shifted to Archie. He was useful, far more so than Knox had ever been, though even Archie was only a step forward for her. He had the resources she wanted and was offering them freely. Well, not freely, but close enough.

Archie did not grasp that yet, but he would, eventually, once she was finished with him. Once she stepped away from his shadow.

She crossed her arms, tapping the sleeve with idle fingers.

Suddenly, the phone rang.

A harsh, insistent vibration breaking the stillness.

Archie instinctively reached for his phone, then paused, letting the ring continue. It was not for him. It was for her.

Catheryn picked up her device from the bedside table, pressing the green answer button and lifting it to her ear.

A voice spoke clearly from the other side.

"Ms Hale? This is Inspector Thornton, Yorkshire Police."

Thornton. A name she recalled from the past, and she had used Catheryn's maiden name too. Good research, Catheryn was impressed.

Catheryn thought briefly to how she was connect to Thornton, then the connection clicked, Thornton had been one of Knox's former Platoon Commander, a couple of years ago, before he left the forces.

They had not met in person, but she knew enough. Thornton was astute, formidable, the kind of officer Knox respected. Which meant she was not easily fooled.

Catheryn curled her fingers around the phone, keeping her voice steady. "Yes, how can I help?"

"You have seen the news, I assume."

Thornton wasted no time. Direct, no nonsense, but Catheryn was playing her own game. She withheld comment.

A pause.

"We are currently trying to find your estranged husband, Henry Knox. Have you had any recent contact with him?"

Catheryn's eyes slid towards the bed.

Sophie lay quietly, warmth radiating beneath the covers, her little hand gripping a stuffed rabbit.

Catheryn hesitated briefly, neither from remorse nor doubt, just a moment's hesitation.

Then, with smooth composure, she answered.

"No. I have not heard from him in months."

Silence.

Thornton waited, letting the gap stretch. A common police tactic, giving someone space to speak further than intended. Henry did it all the time.

But Catheryn was not that careless.

She allowed the silence to linger, letting Thornton wait.

Finally, the inspector's voice returned. "If he contacts you, you must let us know straight away. It is urgent, Ms Hale."

Catheryn's response was effortless. "I understand. I have your number. I will inform you if I hear anything."

Another pause.

Then the call ended.

She lowered the phone, dropping it on the bed. Archie watched, silent. He asked no questions.

He heard every word; he did not need to ask.

He would not.

He believed he knew the answer, that he understood her, that she was his ally in this.

Catheryn let the moment pass, then turned to the wardrobe, mentally replaying the call as she pretended to review the clothes inside.

Knox. Thornton.

The past inching into the present. She let her fingers glide across the fabrics, the illusion of selection. But there had never been a real choice.

Her eyes settled on the emerald dress, the deep green cloth standing out amid the room's bland décor.

Commanding, poised, yet not over the top. Designed to attract attention but not invite questions. Today was not about Knox, nor about Thornton or the police, and not even about Archie. Today was about placing herself where she needed to be.

She took the dress from the hanger, the material felt cool in her grasp, gliding smoothly over her palm. Everything was in her head already: how she would enter that space, how she would hold attention without demanding it, and how Archie would remain convinced he was in control.

Archie wanted to control the chaos, but Catheryn wanted to rise above it.

She let the hotel robe slide off her shoulders as she stepped into the dress, pulling it into position. It shaped her figure with ease, the folds shining gently as she adjusted the hem.

Fastening a slim gold chain around her neck, she settled the pendant on her collarbone. Subtle, intentional, like all her choices. She caught her own reflection in the mirror, smoothing the fabric again. Poised, polished, unshaken.

Catheryn glanced towards the bed. Sophie lay snuggled under the duvet, her breathing slow and relaxed, tiny fingers clutching a corner of the blanket. A child untouched by the outside world. For a moment,

Catheryn paused, not with indecision or sorrow, but because something about this day pressed on her differently than before, something she set in motion long before now, long before Knox became an inconvenience, long before Thornton's call. A heavy weight bore down on her heart, but she refused to acknowledge it.

Her hand fell gently on the sleeping child, brushing hair aside. Sophie stirred and awoke, slowly emerging from under the sheets, her curls the colour of autumn leaves spilling over her small shoulders.

She stood up, stretching her arms high into the air. She was a slight six-year-old, full of life and fun. She had inherited her mum's looks, the green eyes and beautiful red hair, a rare combination, but took after her dad in her calm under pressure and that inner pull towards solitude.

She reminded Catheryn too much of Henry.

"Is it time for breakfast?" Sophie asked, voice heavy with sleep, rubbing her eyes with a tiny hand.

Catheryn allowed herself a tender smile, smoothing a stray tuft of hair. "Yes, darling. Let's get you dressed first."

Sophie pushed away the covers, stretching her arms before sliding out of bed, the stuffed rabbit clutched in her grip as she padded over to the suitcase by the chair.

Catheryn crouched next to her, lifting out a neatly folded sweater and jeans. She helped Sophie into them quickly, guiding her arms through the wool, adjusting the jeans until they sat perfectly on her child's waist.

Sophie perched on the bed's edge, bouncing slightly while Catheryn slipped on her socks and trainers. She tugged at her sleeves. "Will we see Daddy today?"

The question struck with unexpected force.

Catheryn stood, smoothing her dress before glancing at Sophie.

"Maybe," she said, maintaining a light tone. "It depends if he's available." She looked at Archie, his expression blank, though she could see the sting behind his eyes.

Sophie seemed content, already thinking about breakfast. Sophie and Knox ought to be far, far away from here, Catheryn thought.

CHAPTER THIRTY-TWO

Knox carefully lowered the rucksack into the wheelie bin, holding it by the straps, rising on his toes to avoid dropping it. It settled firmly on the bare, black plastic base. He quickly dropped the lid with a muffled thud and stepped back. He looked towards the horizon, wondering where best, no, where safest place to stash the bin. It needed to be far enough to limit danger but close enough for James to keep in view.

Then, the Russian would be the priority.

Knox sprinted back to the edge of the ghost house and picked up the phone he had left by the wall. It was buzzing as he scooped it up, so he pressed answer, raising it to his ear. His breathing was rapid. "I hope you've found him!"

"I think so," James replied calmly. "There's a big, stocky man in the treeline. Looks like he tried leaving through one of the exits, then saw the police and had the same idea as us, he is currently cutting through the fence."

"Perfect. Where exactly?" Henry smiled. They were getting ahead of this now, he could feel it.

"West of your position," James said. "Keep going straight west. Once you reach the fence line, he is just north. You can't miss him."

Knox nodded as though James could see him. "Roger."

He ended the call without another word, slipping the phone into his map pocket as he rushed back to the bin.

The pain in his leg no longer slowed him. He was in overdrive, refusing to let anything halt his momentum.

Grasping the wheelie bin, he leant heavily against it, pushing it forward like a battering ram across the rough tarmac away the ghost house. The wheels rattled and banged on the uneven surface, scattering stones and debris noisily with each push. Knox did not slow, driving forward the bin as if there were no resistance.

Once he reached grass, the terrain changed. The bumpy tarmac gave way to softer ground, lessening the resistance. Knox accelerated. He steered the bin right to the edge of the park, the distant sounds of laughter and conversation left far behind.

At the fence line, he halted suddenly, breath ragged. He found a large rock and placed it on the lid to keep it secure. His eyes snapped north, searching for any sign of the Russian, but saw nothing, so he set out to find him.

Within minutes of following the fence, Henry spotted an area where the wire had been cut. It drooped on both sides, sagging against the ground.

Got you, he thought, forcing his way through the wide gap. The rough edges caught at his clothes, but he pressed on. There was no time to hesitate.

He ran on, plunging into thick trees, eyes fixed ahead as he scanned the horizon.

Soon, he caught a glimpse of a figure. At first just a dark shape, then it grew distinct: a huge man at the outer fence, crouched as he worked on the wire with a cutting tool. Knox closed in, speeding up, sprinting.

Even crouched down the Russian looked enormous, built like solid rock, weighing well over 20 stone. His close-cropped black hair was neat, and a sharp, clean-shaven jawline added a stark angle to his face, which was partially covered by a thick black moustache. A black bomber jacket stretched across his imposing shoulders, the fabric tight against his chest. His jeans were scuffed and smeared with mud, his trainers likewise, evidence of a rushed and clumsy escape attempt.

Knox did not hesitate. He tucked his head down, bracing his neck for impact, pumping his arms hard as he bore down on the Russian at full speed, hoping to take him by surprise before he had time to react. But the man was not oblivious. The noise of Knox's pounding footsteps must have given him away.

The Russian's head jerked round, his dark eyes locking on Knox with a predator's focus. Without pause, the big man pivoted to charge at Knox, moving with startling agility for someone of his bulk.

They rushed each other, a collision inevitable, two primal forces on a crash course.

Knox tried to lower himself at the last moment, but the Russian mirrored him. They clashed like freight trains, bodies slamming together with a crushing force that knocked both men off balance. Knox felt the air driven from his lungs, yet he stayed upright, using his shoulder to force the Russian back. The larger man snarled, gripping Knox's arms in a vice-like hold, and with a guttural roar, he hurled Knox sideways onto the cold earth.

Knox landed heavily but rolled swiftly to his feet as the Russian charged again. This time, Knox reacted defensively, sidestepping at the final second and driving his elbow into the man's ribs. The grunt of pain was satisfying, but the Russian spun, lashing out a fierce backhand that clipped Knox's jaw and sent him tumbling to the dirt.

Blood-tinged Knox's mouth as he scrambled up. The Russian was already upon him, one huge hand at Knox's throat, the other drawn back for a punch. Knox jerked his knee into the man's gut, loosening the chokehold just enough for him to pull free and smash a fist into the Russian's nose. A sickening crunch followed, blood streaming down his moustache, yet the Russian barely flinched.

The man surged forward, locking Knox in a crushing bear hug and lifting him off his feet. Knox's ribs screamed under the pressure, his breaths short and desperate. In desperation, Knox slammed his head forward into the Russian's nose. The man's grip released, and Knox dropped to the ground, his boots skidding on the damp leaves as he backed away.

Wiping the blood from his face, the Russian sneered. He swung with a quick jab that Knox narrowly dodged. Knox tried a low kick at the man's knee, but the Russian caught his leg and hammered a fist into Knox's side. Knox crumpled, pain bursting through his ribs. He fell to one knee.

The Russian was unrelenting. Standing over Knox, he hammered down punches that Knox barely managed to block. Each impact drove Knox closer to the ground, his body battered and exhausted. Still, he was not finished. He trapped the Russian's arm mid-blow and twisted, dragging the man off balance. Knox lunged upwards, planting a fist in his kidney, then striking his temple.

The Russian reeled but recovered with terrifying speed, throwing a wild swing that connected with Knox's head. Stars flooded Knox's vision as he went down, breath rasping out of him. He rolled instinctively, dirt scraping at him, but the Russian was already on him.

A large hand seized Knox's left arm, twisting it up. The Russian's knee descended like a mallet, cracking Henry's forearm with a horrific crunch that Knox felt more than heard, a deep, nauseating snap that sent white-hot pain through him. The agony was too immense for him to even scream; his lungs seized, his body paralysed by torment.

His vision blurred as tears, sweat, blood and cam-cream mixed on his face into his eyes. He raised his gaze a fraction to see the Russian standing victorious, swaying slightly above him, pulling out a phone. The screen lit up with one command. The Russian's bloody grin grew wider, his finger poised over the call button.

"It is over," he said in a thick accent, triumph rich in his voice. "Fight or not, you lose. Britain will burn, and your people will suffer. One press, and it is done."

Knox lay still, chest heaving, body screaming for action, to jump up and tackle him. But he hesitated, staying on the ground.

The Russian pressed down on the phone's keypad, a cold smile twisting his features as the screen displayed Calling...

Nothing happened.

Knox drew a ragged breath, watching the Russian's face crease in confusion. The man stared at the phone, frowning.

He checked the signal: three bars.

Check.

The battery was charged.

Check.

Everything looked functional. Why was the call not going through?

Irritated, the Russian tried again, pressing hard as if sheer force could make it connect. The screen repeated Calling...

Still no reaction.

Knox smiled faintly. He shifted his weight, his body coiling for the final move, waiting for a chance.

The Russian, consumed by frustration, had lost track of Knox, fixated on his phone.

Henry seized the moment, lunging upwards, channelling all his anger and desperation into a vicious headbutt, using the crown of his skull like a hammer.

The blow was brutal.

Knox's skull smashed into the Russian's open mouth, shattering teeth and snapping cartilage. The man's head jerked back, blood spurting from his lips as he tumbled under the force of the strike.

Knox felt the shock reverberate down his spine, his head throbbing, but he refused to stop. There was no time to stop.

The phone slipped from the Russian's hand, landing in the dirt with a muted thump. Blood gushed from the man's mouth, running in a frothy crimson stream down his chin. His eyes glazed over as his hulking frame toppled, limbs sprawling into the cold grass.

Knox slummed to his knees, rubbing at his pounding head. His scalp stung where it had collided with bone, a dull ache pulsing. He gingerly touched the spot, muttering to himself.

He went for his phone, a trembling in his fingers, the adrenaline fading. He needed to call James, secure the site, get the bomb squad to deal with the wheelie bin and its lethal contents. He tapped the phone, dialling James number, but a sudden movement made him pause.

Someone approached through the trees, cutting swiftly through the undergrowth. Knox's pulse spiked when he recognised the broad shoulders and distinctive stride.

Cal.

Knox instantly assumed a guarded stance, every nerve in his body alert. His mind raced.

Shit!! This isn't over. Not yet.

CHAPTER THIRTY-THREE

Time stretches and contracts in uneven beats, bending to the rhythm of adrenaline and uncertainty. For Amy, this was the cruel paradox of command, the endless grind of waiting paired with the sudden, frantic scramble when the moment arrived. It was a tempo she knew too well. The military had a phrase for it.

Hurry up and wait.

Inside the Command Post was a hive of activity, but no one was any closer to solving the main problem. Where was the bomb? If there was one at all.

Amy was ready to deploy with a team to take the southern part of the park, the team of tired West Yorkshire officers had assembled in the car park and looked thoroughly dishevelled under the dark grey Yorkshire sky.

Then something unexpected occurred. A lifeline, a golden ray of hope.

Her phone buzzed in her pocket, cutting through the hum of voices and radio chatter. It had been buzzing all day, relentlessly demanding attention she didn't have. What now?

Amy fished it out, glancing at the screen.

Unknown number.

Again.

Her thumb hovered over the screen, her mind racing. James? Was it James? Could it be Henry?

She was getting ahead of herself, and tiredness was beginning to play tricks on her mind.

Amy's thumb pressed the screen, lifting the phone to her ear. Her voice was steady, professional, as usual. "Thornton."

James's voice came through the speaker, barely restrained. "Henry found it. He's moving the device now. It's in a black tall wheelie bin near the rear of the Ghost House."

Amy froze, was this truly it? Her mind seized on the words, dissecting them even as she replied. "How do you know all this, James?"

"Here, I'll show you," he said, his tone cold and matter of fact.

Before she could process what he meant, the CCTV feeds on the command van's monitors suddenly flickered and shifted. Every screen now displayed a long shot of the Ghost House. The murmur of voices around her rose into a collective gasp.

Amy's hand tightened on the phone as she stared at the screen. The tension in the command post shifted sharply, the room buzzing with new energy.

"Do you see what I can see?" James asked, his voice calm but urgent.

Amy's brow furrowed, her gaze narrowing on the feed. "Yes," she replied slowly. "Are you controlling our feed?"

"Yeah. Let me zoom in." The camera feed shifted, centring on the area behind the Ghost House. The grainy image resolved, focusing on a figure moving near the wheelie bin. James's voice returned, sharper now. "There. Do you see Henry? He's trying to get the device as far away from everyone in the park as he can. But you need to evac now. It's Novichok, that's the IED." he said bluntly.

Amy's eyes locked on the screen, fear in them. She watched as a dark figure ran a black wheelie bin over the grass area until it rested against the fence line, her brain flooded with the information she had received. She attempted to run a thousand calculations at once. Her free hand moved instinctively to cover the mouthpiece of her phone as she barked over her shoulder. “Get me Jenkins. Now. And start the evac! No one goes near that bin.”

The officers in the command post sprang into action, exploding into motion.

She removed her hand from the mouthpiece. “What about the suspect? Is it Henry?”

“No!” James said, sounding repulsed by the idea. “He’s out there trying to save lives. The suspect is the Russian I told you about, he is currently cutting through the fence line, where your people aren’t stationed. Henry’s going after him.”

Amy attempted to process the information she was receiving, while giving hand signals to the CCTV operatives to get a view of the tree line.

“There’s no CCTV in that area,” James continued, almost second-guessing Amy's thought process. “But I’ll call with an update when I get it. Until then, deal with the device and get those people out of the park.”

The line clicked dead.

Amy lowered the phone slowly, her chest felt heavy, her pulse a steady drumbeat in her ears. Her voice cut through the command post as she turned toward the flurry of activity.

“Where is Jenkins? I need him here now!” she barked.

Amy’s thoughts spun like a turbine. Webster’s intel provided a thin lifeline, a fragment of clarity in a storm of chaos. The device was away from the majority of the civilians in the park. If, of course, this wasn’t a diversion aimed at causing more carnage.

She pushed the thought aside. James was trying to help, but on his terms. If that meant the device was secured and the Russian caught, then so be it. She could live with the compromise.

Before she could take another breath, Jenkins strode into the van, his tall frame commanding as he fixed his gaze on Amy. “What do you know, Inspector?” he demanded.

Amy straightened instinctively. “Sir, I’ll need to give you a full debrief,” she said. “But right now, just trust me. We need the park evacuated immediately, starting at the Ghost House attraction. And I need a CBRN team to disarm the IED. The device is in a wheelie bin near the Ghost House. It’s Novichok.”

For a moment, Jenkins’s expression didn’t change. His poker face was as solid as ever, but Amy caught the faintest flicker of astonishment in his eyes. He hesitated, not because he doubted her, but because what she’d just said was huge, monumental. He had to trust her.

He gave a curt nod, his voice slicing through the command post like a whip. “Alright, you heard Inspector Thornton. Start the evacuation now. Begin with the Ghost House and expand outward.”

The command post erupted into motion, officers moving quickly, relaying the order through Airwave radios. Amy watched as the gears of response clicked into place. Relief did not come, though. Not yet. The risk was still impossibly high, and not all the pieces were on the table.

She met Jenkins’s gaze again, her voice dropping as she leant in. “We don’t have time to second-guess. If my intel is correct, we’re sitting on a chemical time bomb. But if it’s wrong...” She let the implication hover in the air.

Jenkins nodded once, resolute. “This is the job, Amy. We make decisions. People are at risk, and we work with the cards we’re dealt. Trust yourself. Let’s move.”

Within minutes, the CCTV feeds showed the park in retreat. Walkways once swarming with families became eerily void, the festive mood drained into a vacuum of silence. Around the Ghost House, the emptiness was absolute. Only the distant rumble of the RLC bomb disposal vehicle broke the stillness.

Amy stood near the command van’s entrance, arms folded against her chest, her attention on the monitors.

“RLC team in position,” came a disembodied voice through the Airwave handset.

Amy pressed the radio’s button. “Understood. Maintain distance. There’s a westward breeze, so containment is crucial.”

The CCTV cameras made the RLC team look like spectres in the winter fog, wearing heavy DPM charcoal-lined jackets and trousers, huge mark 6 bomb suits fashioned from Kevlar foam and plastic that gave them the look of green Michelin men. GSR respirators masked their faces, lenses reflecting the weak winter light.

The RLC’s 4-tonne Bedford truck was stationed at the outer boundary of the secured zone, its engine humming in the chill. From its rear, a robot emerged, a small track-wheeled device with an articulated arm. It rolled down a ramp, turning on the frosty tarmac that cracked beneath its tracks. The camera feed followed the Remote-Control Vehicle as it crawled across the uneven ground.

A voice crackled on the radio. “RCV deployed,” said the RLC lead operator. “Distance to target is sixty metres. Engaging REMIX for RCIEDS, beginning approach.”

Amy leant closer to the screens, watching intently.

The robot moved steadily on its rubber tracks, grinding over the car park’s cracked surface and onto the grassy slope behind the Ghost House. It advanced slowly, each turn of the tracks imprinting a lined pattern in the mud. A tense hush fell over the command post as it neared the plain, unremarkable wheelie bin brimming with deadly potential.

Jenkins stood at Amy's right, his face unreadable. "This wind isn't helping," he muttered, glancing at the digital anemometer reading on one screen. It ticked up slightly, gusting westward towards the park boundary and beyond.

"I've ordered the estate on the other side of that fence evacuated," he muttered, but Amy didn't answer, her gaze locked on the screen as the robot edged closer.

"RCV is twenty metres out," the RLC operator reported, his voice calm and formal. "No visible sign of leakage."

"Roger," Amy said firmly. "Confirm containment protocol when you reach the target."

The robot arrived at the bin's side. Its mechanical arm stretched out, the camera feed jolting as it zeroed in on the lid. A stone lay on the lid to hold it down. The arm moved with unsettling grace, a careful precision contradicting its metallic frame. Its claw hovered over the stone, poised as the operator manipulated it from within the truck.

"Commencing inspection," the operator said, his words clipped and precise. "No visual anomalies. Proceeding to secure the lid."

Amy felt hot and extremely bothered. Every second felt elongated, stretched thin by the weight of anticipation.

The robot's claw latched onto the stone on the bin's lid, accompanied by the faint hiss of hydraulics.

The claw lifted the stone, the sagging lid lifted slightly and popped back into shape as the pressure was released. Amy let out an audible gasp.

The claw arm shifted, dropping the stone and then returning to its starting position hovering over the bin, the arm juddering and lowering the claw to grasp the handle of the lid.

The claw closed around the handgrip and slowly, it began to lift, the lid rising with agonising slowness. The robot's camera feed zoomed in, capturing every detail of the interior of the bin as it was gradually revealed.

"Lid is up," the operator reported. "Visual confirmation: we have what looks like a black rucksack. There seems to be some kind of tin foil or an aluminium package inside the bag. No visible leaks. No physical damage to the bag. No visual confirmation that this is the device."

Amy exhaled sharply, her breath fogging in the cold air of the van. "Containment team, status?"

"Ready to deploy," the operator replied. "Initiating containment procedure."

Jenkins leaned forward towards the screen over Amy's shoulder, a confused look on his brow, "Is that a faraday bag?" He asked incredulously.

Amy took a closer look at the bag, "Yeah, I think so, and... tin foil!"

Jenkins shook his head, "No wonder it hasn't detonated!"

Amy smiled to herself, bloody Henry had wrapped the device in a faraday bag and tin foil, no signal would be able to get through to the device. No matter how many times the trigger was pressed. Clever bugger!

The robot extended a secondary arm, fitted with a sealed containment canister. It moved toward the device with excruciating precision, its claw gripping the edges of the tin foil-wrapped package.

Even though the device was wrapped in a Faraday bag, any break of the seal would allow the trigger to access the device. It was a delicate moment. "Easy," Amy murmured under her breath, the word slipping out unbidden.

The robot's claw closed around the device and lifted it carefully out of the rucksack and into the containment canister. Once the package was secured, the canister's lid snapped shut with a resounding click. The radio crackled again.

"Device secured," the operator announced. "No leaks. Containment is confirmed."

A collective breath seemed to release inside the van. Amy straightened, her pulse still pounding but steadied by the success. "Good work," she said into the radio. "Now get it out of here."

The robot began its slow retreat, the containment canister held firmly in its grip. Amy's eyes did not leave the screen until the robot disappeared back into the truck, the rear doors sealing behind it.

Amy allowed herself a brief exhale, her grip on the radio loosening. "Excellent work, Captain. What's your next move?"

"We'll stabilise the device in the truck," the RLC Captain replied. "It'll be transported to the nearest CBRN facility for analysis. Local threat has been neutralised."

Jenkins smiled at Amy. "Good work, Amy, good call. But we still have an active suspect. We need to keep the perimeter tight and locate him before he slips out."

Amy nodded, but her focus was momentarily elsewhere as her phone buzzed again. She glanced down at the screen, the now-familiar words: Unknown Number illuminated. Pressing the answer button reluctantly, she lifted the phone to her ear.

"Hello, James," she said, her voice sharp. "Did Henry wrap the device in a Faraday bag?"

On the other end, there was a soft exhale. "So you've got it then? Good," James replied.

"The Russian is now also disabled. You'll find him just north of the bin, in the area between the inner and outer fence line."

Amy's expression turned quizzical as she processed the information, "Henry?"

"Yes," James replied.

"Good work, Henry did well on the device," she replied, a sarcastic edge creeping into her tone. Her lips thinned into a grim smile. "Tell him to come in for his prize."

James chuckled faintly, though there was no humour in it. "I'll pass that along. But don't kid yourself, this isn't over yet."

Before she could respond, the line went dead, leaving her staring at the blank screen with a growing sense of unease. She turned toward the tech team stationed in the corner of the command van.

"Tell me we have a trace on the number that's calling me," she barked, her voice cutting and firm.

One of the techs, a wiry man hunched over a laptop, shook his head without looking up. "No dice," he muttered, his fingers dancing over the keyboard. "He's never on the line long enough, and he's masking his location. Whoever this is, they know what they're doing."

Amy's fingers drummed against the edge of the table, the rhythm betraying the frustration simmering under her calm exterior. Her mind darted through possibilities, none comforting. She turned her gaze to Jenkins, who was leaning over another officer's shoulder, his brow furrowed as he reviewed a live CCTV feed.

"Sir, permission to send a strike team into the wood line," Amy said firmly.

Jenkins straightened, his gaze snapping to hers. Then he nodded, "Find that Russian and drag him in. I want him in custody now."

CHAPTER THIRTY-FOUR

Knox readied himself, his adrenaline increasing again, thrumming through his veins like a war drum. The Russian was down, but it had taken everything Knox had and then some.

Only his sheer will, and a plan cobbled together in desperation had carried him through. Now, standing in the cold light of the aftermath, he faced another threat. Cal. The man who had wanted to end his life back at the farmhouse earlier that morning.

Knox couldn't fathom how Cal had escaped the safe room. Those things were meant to be impenetrable, designed to withstand everything short of an airstrike. But the mechanics didn't matter now. The man himself was here, alive and whole, while Knox was battered, bloodied, and broken. He resolved to have words with James later about the integrity of his handiwork, if he lived long enough to have that conversation.

Knox shifted his weight carefully, mindful of his shattered arm. It hung useless at his side, throbbing with every movement. He tucked it behind his back, his shoulder keeping it pinned in place. He knew what Cal was capable of. If the former RSM got hold of the arm, he'd twist it like a predator worrying a bone, amplifying the pain until Knox crumbled. That kind of agony would be an instant game-changer. Knox couldn't let that happen.

Knox flexed his good hand, his fingers itching for the Gerber knife tucked into a pouch at his waistband.

But then Knox realised something.

Cal was unarmed.

This was a trick, it had to be. Cal wasn't the kind of man to walk into a confrontation unarmed.

But then Cal lifted his hands slowly into the air, the picture of disarming contrition. The broad shoulders of the man who had once been a leader of men seemed to sag slightly.

"I've fucked up, pal," Cal said again, his Scottish drawl sharper than the cold air between them.

"I lost my way. Got caught up in something I shouldn't have, and now..." His voice trailed off, and he let out a shaky exhale, his hands still raised.

"I've messed up badly, Knoxy." He said, nodding slowly, his hands still lifted in the air.

Knox didn't budge, waiting, disbelieving, for the attack that would surely follow. This couldn't be real. Men like Cal didn't walk away from their plans with their heads bowed. They didn't surrender without a fight.

"Why would you do that?" Knox asked, incredulity lacing his tone. His eyes locked on Cal's, searching for the flicker of deceit, the tell that would give him an excuse to strike first, not that he really needed one.

Cal took a slow step forward, his hands still raised, his posture open. "Because I'm in too deep, pal," he said, his voice carrying an unexpected tremor of vulnerability. "And I've got nowhere else to turn."

Knox stepped back instinctively, widening the gap between himself and Cal. His movements careful, the weight of his broken arm hanging like an anchor. He glanced sideways, keeping the Russian's unconscious form in his peripheral vision. If the bastard woke up now, Knox would be outnumbered, and with one arm out of commission, that wasn't a fight he was likely to win.

"Stay where you are," Knox warned, his voice low and even, a predator's growl.

But Cal stepped closer anyway, his hands still raised, his expression strangely earnest. There was no malice in his eyes, no trace of the cold calculation Knox expected. Just a strange, raw kind of regret.

"I gave Michael the thumb drive, Knoxy," Cal said, his voice rough. "It was me. I just didn't know it would lead to this."

Knox's stomach churned, but his face betrayed nothing. He shifted his weight, subtly angling toward a possible escape route. At the same time, his good hand slipped into his pocket and began working the phone, trying to connect a call to James without breaking his gaze from Cal.

"Go on," Knox said, his tone clipped, his mind racing as he weighed his options.

Cal swallowed hard, his shoulders slumping slightly as he continued. "Gray has my family," he said, his voice cracking on the last word. "It's not an excuse, I know that. But when I tried to get out, he... he took them. My wife. My kid. He knew it would keep me in line."

Knox's expression did not change.

"I passed the USB to Michael," Cal said, his voice trembling now. "Hoped it would be enough to expose Gray, to bring him down. But Gray found out, and he killed Michael for it. Rhys was the one who did the dirty work, but it was my fault. I didn't mean for anyone to die, Knoxy, I swear to God. But he has my child."

Knox's fingers stilled on the phone, his heart pounding in his chest. The pieces were falling into place, but they didn't make any of this easier to accept. He stared at Cal, the man who had once stood for everything he'd aspired to be and now seemed to be crumbling under the weight of his own mistakes.

"You expect me to believe that?" Knox said finally, harshly.

"It's the truth," Cal replied, his tone desperate. "I don't expect forgiveness, Knoxy. I just want a chance to set this right. For all of us."

Knox gripped the phone tightly, the sharp edges of disbelief cutting through the haze of adrenaline. His focus split, ears straining for the faint tone of the call connecting in his pocket while his eyes stayed locked on Cal.

"Why should I believe a word you say, Cal?" Knox's voice was rough, teetering between defiance and the desperate need to make sense of the moment.

"Because he has your family too, Knoxy," Cal replied, his tone steady but tinged with something close to pleading. "And together... together, we can get them both back."

The words hung in the air, like smoke after a detonation, thick, choking, impossible to ignore.

Knox froze, his mind struggling to process what he was hearing. "What?" The word fell out of him, flat and hollow.

"Your wife," Cal said, taking a cautious step forward, his hands still raised in surrender. "I know she's been trying to reach you. Her and Gray... it's been going on for a while now. They met in Cyprus. That's why she stayed there."

Knox shook his head sharply, as if trying to fling the idea out of his mind. "What? What are you saying?"

"Catheryn is back in the U.K., Henry," Cal said quietly, each word hitting like a hammer. "And she's with Gray."

Knox stumbled back a step, his body tensing as the revelation tore through him. His world, already unravelled, seemed to collapse further. His wife, a traitor, aligned with a monster.

Blood rushed to his head, a pounding pressure building behind his eyes. He was reeling from the betrayal, unsteady.

"I want to help," Cal said, his voice slicing through Knox's whirling thoughts. "We can work together to stop Gray."

Knox slid his hand from the phone and rubbed his forehead, his mind clouded by confusion, betrayal, and anger. Everything was spiralling too quickly. All he felt was a stinging sense of having been used, a pawn in someone else's game all along.

He kept his gaze on Cal, his broken arm still pressed awkwardly behind his back. He struggled to piece everything together: Gray, Catheryn, the Russian, and now Cal, claiming to be on his side. It was too much, too fast. He felt his composure fraying.

He raised the phone again, pressing it to his ear, forcing himself to concentrate. James's voice came through clearly, urgent and tense.

"Knox! You there?" James's tone was sharp, relief flooding every word.

"I'm here," Knox replied, his own voice dull but steady.

"Thank God for that!" James's relief was palpable but quickly shifted to curiosity. "Who's that with you?"

"Long story," Knox muttered, shutting down further questions. He shook his head, trying to clear it, but kept his eyes on Cal. "Have the police found the device?"

"Yes, they're handling it," James said, his tone touched with admiration. "Wrapping the phone in tinfoil and a Faraday bag was genius. No signal was ever getting through that. Did anyone ever tell you should've joined the SIB?"

Knox let himself smirk briefly. "A couple of times," he said. "The Russian's down. He's in the treeline, between the fences, but I don't know for how long. Send them here now."

James didn't hesitate. "On it. Stay put, mate."

Knox lowered the phone, letting it drop into his pocket.

Cal took a careful step forward, both hands raised in plain sight. His voice was calm, deliberate. "Knoxy, listen to me. I could've killed you if I'd wanted to. I left my weapon in the car. I'm unarmed."

Knox weighed his options, keeping his good hand ready. His tone was cold. "Doesn't mean I trust you, Cal. Not at all."

Cal nodded slowly, staying non-threatening. "I get that. But you know I'm telling the truth. If I'd wanted you dead, you wouldn't have made it here."

Knox's mind whirled, cycling through outcomes, noticing Cal was right. If he had truly intended to kill Knox, he likely would have done so.

Knox moved another step back, finding no comfort in the distance. His voice was bitter. "I don't trust you, Cal. Michael, Sarah, Jess, all dead, and Rhys too. You're the one still alive."

Cal flinched, as though the words had struck him. His voice trembled in confession. "Rhys was told to kill Michael. I swear, I didn't know. I was there for Sarah and Jess, but Rhys jumped early. It... it wasn't supposed to happen that way."

Knox felt rage flare in his chest, but Cal spoke again before he could react, his voice urgent.

"Look," Cal said, hands in the air. "I know where Gray is. Right now. I know where your wife and kid are. Let me help you. We'll fix your arm, then we'll go."

Knox froze, everything else fading at those final words. His wife. His daughter. Sophie.

His mind was a whirlwind. Catheryn was her own person, free to make her choices. The revelation about Gray was a gut punch, sure, but it wasn't something he could fixate on now. But Sophie? His kid, caught in the crossfire of this mess? That was a line too far.

"How do I know you're speaking the truth?" Knox demanded, his voice low and dangerous.

Cal met his eyes, the rawness in his voice unmissable. "You don't. I can't give you proof. But you know I'm not lying, Knoxy. You know I wouldn't use your kid like that."

Knox's one working fist clenched, his broken arm throbbing in protest. He wanted to doubt him, to call it a lie and shut him out completely. But the nagging thread of possibility was there, tugging at him, forcing him to consider the unthinkable.

The air between them crackled with tension. Knox swallowed hard, trying to keep his emotions in check as the realisation loomed larger with each passing second.

Cal's voice was steady, almost resigned. "You don't, mate. I can't offer you anything. What I can do is lie on the ground right now and you can search me. You'll see I've got nothing on me. No weapons. You know damn well Rhys and I had an MP5 and a Sig each. If I didn't bring them with me, it's because I didn't come here to kill you."

Knox didn't respond immediately, his mind whirring through the possibilities. The logic was there, plain and unmissable. If Cal had wanted him dead, Knox wouldn't even have known he was in the treeline. A hundred metres, two quick shots, clean and precise. It would've been over before he'd had a chance to react.

Knox's voice dropped, cold and firm. "Roger, but hear this, Cal, if I get even a hint you're lying to me, I will kill you."

Cal nodded without hesitation, his eyes locked on Knox. "Okay by me."

He moved forward slowly, his hands still raised. Knox stopped him in his tracks, "Where the fuck do you think you're going?" he shouted.

Cal looked alarmed, "I thought that was the signal we were cool. Are we not?"

Knox shook his head. "No fucking way! Lie face down on the ground, with your arms and legs spread, you need to be searched!"

Cal sighed, nodding resignedly, "Ok Knoxy, as you want." He said as he got to his knees and then laid out prone on the ground ready for Knox to be patting him down.

Knox quickly closed the gap between the two men and moved his good hand around all the principal places someone would hide a weapon. Content that he wasn't carrying, Henry offered Cal his good hand. Cal took it and rose to his feet, "We need to splint that arm," Cal said, glancing at Knox's limp, mangled limb.

"I've got a first aid kit in the car. We need to get out of here before the police turn up."

Knox turned on his heel and made his way toward the fence the Russian had been cutting. His able hand reached for the Gerber tool clipped to his pocket, flipping it open. Despite the searing pain in his arm, Knox's grip was firm as he used the tool's pliers to snip away at the remaining wire, widening the gap.

Behind him, Cal crouched beside the fallen Russian, his hands moving swiftly as he searched the man's body. His fingers closed around a phone and a small camera.

Knox glanced over his shoulder, his voice sharp. "Leave them."

Cal looked up, surprised, the objects still in his hands.

Knox's tone hardened. "That's evidence. If he had a weapon, he would've used it on me already. Let the police deal with it."

For a moment, Cal hesitated, his gaze shifting from the items in his hands to Knox's unyielding expression. Then, with a slight nod, he placed the phone and camera back where he'd found them, rising slowly to his feet.

"Fair enough," Cal muttered, following Knox through the fence line, the tension between them a fragile thread stretched thin by distrust.

A black Land Rover slowed to a crawl as it approached the two figures emerging from the tree line, its tyres coming to a stop on the frost-bitten tarmac. James was at the wheel, his face partially obscured by the low winter light. He leaned over and wound the window down with a press of a button.

"How the fuck did you get here, Cal?" James barked, his voice carrying the same disbelief Knox had felt minutes earlier. "Last time I saw you, you were locked in a safe room."

Cal nodded casually, as if the comment wasn't worth the effort of a retort. "You know I could have shot you before you locked me in there, right? I didn't."

James raised an eyebrow, his expression unreadable. "Could've, would've, should've," he replied evenly, his tone dry as a desert. His attention shifted to Knox, the question plain in his eyes. "Knox, why the hell is he here? And why isn't he laid out next to the Russian?"

Knox stepped forward, his face a mask of weary determination. "He's got a lot of explaining to do," he said, his voice low. "But he can take us to Gray and that's why he's not lying dead in the woods."

James's gaze flicked back to Cal, his scepticism still evident. He studied the man for a moment, weighing Knox's judgement against his own instincts. Finally, he gave a brief nod, his trust in Knox's decision overriding the myriad questions brewing in his mind.

"Roger," James said simply, leaning back in his seat. He gestured toward the back of the vehicle with a tilt of his head. "Get in. Both of you. We've got work to do."

Knox and Cal climbed into the back of the vehicle. Knox winced as he manoeuvred himself onto the seat, his broken arm cradled against his chest like a fragile artefact. He reached down, pulling his day sack into his lap, and began rummaging through it with his good hand.

He pulled out a small first aid kit, setting it on the seat beside him. From it, he extracted a pair of field dressings, and a tactical splint rolled into a tube.

Knox ripped the wings off the dressings with quick, jerky movements, laying everything out on the leather seat. He inspected the angry, swelling fracture. The skin around it was flushed, the broken bone beneath an unwelcome bulge distorting his forearm.

Knox pressed two of his fingers against the edge of his palm, checking for a pulse. It was faint but there, for now.

"Okay, Cal," Knox said, his voice hard, "let's establish some early trust. I need you to pull my hand and reset the bone. Pretty sure it's a closed fracture."

Cal shifted in his seat, his eyes flicking to the injury. The former soldier's face remained calm, but there was a grim understanding in his expression.

"Got it," Cal said simply. He reached over, his hands steady as they gripped Knox's forearm below the fracture, pressing his fingers against unbroken flesh and avoiding the swollen area entirely with a firm hold.

Knox braced himself, clutching the grab handle above the car door with his good hand. He looked away, jaw clenched, muscles taut. "Do it," he muttered.

Cal did not hesitate. He pulled hard, feeling the bone shift beneath his grip. The snap was audible, a sickening grind that seemed to echo in the confined space of the vehicle. Knox let out a guttural roar, a sound that was equal parts pain, rage, and pure animalistic defiance. Then, silence.

Knox's chest heaved as he fought to pull air into his lungs. His head dropped forward, sweat beading on his forehead as the searing agony coursed through him.

Cal moved quickly, binding the arm with the field dressings, securing the tactical splint in place. He tied it tightly against Knox's chest.

A packet of pain relief tablets emerged from the first aid kit, Knox taking the packet from Cal. He swallowed two without water.

"Done," Cal said quietly, leaning back. His voice carried no hint of triumph, simply the finality of a job completed.

James glanced in the rear-view mirror, his expression unreadable. "Right," he said, breaking the tension. "Where are we going?"

"Bentley Aerodrome. It's about an hour from here," Cal confirmed.

James gave a curt nod, gripping the wheel. "Then hang on," he said. The engine growled as he pressed the accelerator, the Land Rover surging forward onto the open road.

CHAPTER THIRTY-FIVE

Knox reached across to the laptop on the passenger seat, slow and careful. More hope than certainty. His broken arm pressed against his chest was a dead weight, useless. Any movement sent fire lancing through his forearm, but in truth he had pain everywhere.

A dull roar beneath his skin. The adrenaline was leaving his body, and what remained was raw nerve endings and bruised flesh.

The fight with the Russian had been brutal. Every punch, both given and received, had landed hard. His ribs throbbed with a deep, aching pain, which meant one or two of the bones were probably cracked or worse. His head pounded, a thick, nauseating pressure behind his eyes. His jawline, temples and skull cap burned.

He flipped the screen open with his good hand, fingers settling over the keyboard. One-handed, typed:

Capuchin Security.

The words filled the search engine's bar, and Knox turned his head sharply toward Cal, his expression unreadable but his tone cutting like steel. "Tell me everything about Gray," he said, the words more an order than a question.

Cal met his gaze head-on, his own face a strange mix of resignation and defiance. "Gray and I started Capuchin Security together," he began, his voice low but steady. "It was our plan from the moment we left the service. He was the head of operations, the man with the vision. I handled the teams, the boots on the ground. We tried breaking into the London private security market.

Executive protection, corporate contracts, high-end clients, that kind of thing. But it didn't take off."

"Why not?" Knox asked.

"Too crowded," Cal replied bluntly, shaking his head. "The market was saturated with outfits just like ours, and none of them were willing to share the pie. Every big player already had contracts locked in. We were running on fumes."

Knox's gaze never left Cal. "So what changed?"

Cal hesitated for half a beat and sighed. "We took a job," he said finally, his voice lowering slightly, "for a Russian oil magnate. This was just before the war in Ukraine started."

Knox's fingers hovered over the keyboard. He didn't need to ask where this was going, but he did anyway. "What was his name?"

Cal's reply came quickly, almost too quickly. "Olyaski Normanov."

Knox's fingers flew across the keys, the name filling the search bar. Within seconds, the screen populated with results, a cascade of links and images. Knox leaned closer, scanning the information.

Normanov. Oil tycoon. One of the oligarchs who'd risen from the ashes of the Soviet Union. His wealth had skyrocketed after the fall of the USSR, thanks to a stranglehold on oil and gas reserves. A power player during the Chechnya conflicts, funding private militias that had left a trail of devastation in their wake. He had strong connections to the Kremlin, seen as a close confidant of Putin, with rumours of joint ventures in both legitimate and shadow markets.

Knox continued to scroll, the details darkening with every hyperlink. Arms deals, political bribery, money laundering. The man was a vortex of corruption and power, the kind of figure who operated above laws and above borders.

"And Gray?" Knox asked. "How close was he to this guy?"

Cal's shoulders sagged slightly. "They seemed to hit it off straight away," he admitted. "Normanov liked Gray's style, direct, ruthless, no bullshit, I guess he'd like you too." Cal remarked, but the comment was deflected by Knox's cold steely look. Cal continued, "Gray saw Normanov as a golden goose. The kind of client who could bankroll Capuchin Security for years."

"Keep talking," Knox said coldly. "I want to know every fucking detail."

"We started doing jobs for him outside the U.K.," Cal began, his voice carrying that rough Scottish edge that only seemed to harden the longer the conversation lasted. "Standard protection gigs at first, private compounds, executive escorts. But then Gray started visiting him in Russia. At first, I figured it was strategic, building connections, drumming up high-profile clients. But something shifted. I got left out of briefings, like I was an afterthought. Gray started shutting me out, piece by piece. Suddenly, I wasn't his right hand anymore. I was just another cog."

Knox nodded slightly, a subtle signal for Cal to keep talking, his fingers scrolling through the search results on the laptop. He was staring at Capuchin Security's operational footprint, dozens of countries, spanning continents. The scope was staggering. Africa. Eastern Europe. South America. Deep influences throughout the world, thought Knox.

"Then the Ukraine war kicked off," Cal continued, his tone bitter. "That was supposed to put an end to our dealings with Normanov. Sanctions. Bad PR. The whole lot. But that wasn't what happened. In fact, we worked with him more. Gray doubled down. I told him it was madness, that we were crossing lines we couldn't uncross. But he didn't care."

Cal paused, as he relived the arguments that had defined the unravelling of his relationship with Gray. "I wasn't happy about it, and I made damn sure Gray knew. We fought. Loud, brutal arguments. But Gray... he's not the kind of man you win against, is he? He stopped talking to me entirely. Cut me out. Stopped including me in decisions. I was just a figurehead, left to keep the lower ranks in line while he played kingmaker in Russia."

Knox didn't respond.

"And then Gray started ramping things up," Cal said, his voice dipping lower, his Scottish accent roughening with the strain. "He spent months at a time in Russia. Then he'd fly to Cyprus to meet his connections. That's when he met your ex."

Knox's gaze flicked up, his expression hard, staying silent. He waited for Cal to continue.

"Your wife and kid," Cal obliged, "would go out on Normanov's yacht. Sail around the island. With Gray."

Knox's stomach churned, but he kept his face unreadable. It was a tough listen; he'd known nothing about any of this. Catheryn had avoided telling him.

"It was a whirlwind romance as far as I know," Cal said bitterly, shaking his head. "Then we started operating out of the Crimea, covert, ugly stuff. But by then, I was out. Completely cut off. No intel, no orders. Nothing. And Gray... he kept my family close. Said it was to protect them. Said he was keeping them safe if things went wrong. But that wasn't it, was it? He was holding them over me. Leverage. Making sure I did what he wanted."

Cal's voice cracked slightly, but he clamped down on it. His eyes dropped to the floor, shoulders slumped under the weight of it all.

Knox inhaled slowly, forcing himself to compartmentalise the whirlwind of emotions inside him. Betrayal. Anger. Confusion. But also, clarity.

He closed the laptop, the lid snapping shut. Knox turned his gaze towards James sat in the driver's seat, looking at his through the rear-view mirror.

"When we get there, James, you're not coming in with us," Knox said, his tone brooking no argument. "You've been an amazing pal, I couldn't have got this far without you. But I can't get you involved any further. This isn't your fight."

James opened his mouth to argue, but Knox's stare silenced him before he uttered a word. There was no negotiation, no debate. This was personal now, Knox had to do it on his own, or at least with minimal collateral.

Cal stayed silent, watching Knox with a look that was a blend of respect and resignation. Knox didn't need to say more, but the message was plain.

James nodded, his voice subdued. "Ok, I get it, you're probably right, Knoxy. I'd be useless in there anyway," he admitted, patting his knee.

Knox turned back to Cal. "Smuggle me into the airbase in the boot of the vehicle," he said, calm and unyielding. "I'm guessing they won't search you entering the camp?"

Cal shook his head. "No. I'm still in charge of U.K. operations. They'll wave me through without a glance," he said confidently.

"Once we're in, we confront Gray and end this," Knox continued, his voice dark with purpose.

James hesitated, glancing at Knox in the rear-view mirror. "Shouldn't we call Amy? Get the police to swoop in, arrest Gray? You've already earned enough goodwill from them with the IED and the Russian. I reckon she'd listen."

Knox's eyes locked with James's reflection, hard and unyielding. "Amy will find out when I need her to," he said flatly. "But first, I need my family safe. That's priority one. And what evidence do we even have right now? Cal could confess, but that'd take time we don't have. A warrant to raid the base? That's a process. We're out of time, James. Not if he's got Sophie."

Cal nodded in agreement. "Knox is right. Gray's layered in. He's thought of every angle the cops might come at him from."

Then Cal paused, seeming to weigh his next words. "But there's something else," he said, his voice subdued now, wary.

Knox turned toward him, eyes cold. "What?" he demanded, the single word brimming with menace.

Cal swallowed, glancing between Knox and James. "The HippoLand attack was just a diversion. A smokescreen to drag the police away from what Gray's really up to."

Knox's pulse quickened. "And what's he doing, Cal?" he snarled.

"I don't know," Cal admitted. "But it's big, bigger than this. If he's happy to risk a chemical bomb at a theme park, then whatever he's really planning will be huge."

Knox paused, letting the words sink in. "How many people do you have in your U.K. ops?" he asked, his eyes drilling into Cal.

Cal shifted his posture, "In this country right now? Ten, counting me and Rhys," he said. "But they're not all in Yorkshire. My guess is Gray's only got three guys with him, maybe. They won't be far, but he's not the type to let them hover too close. He hates looking weak or reliant."

Knox's voice carried suspicion. "How come you don't know for sure? Aren't you the head of U.K. ops?"

Cal shrugged, frustration running beneath the surface. "I know where my lads are, Knox," he replied, his tone both defensive and measured. "But not Gray's. He keeps it on a need-to-know basis, and I apparently don't need to know."

Knox studied Cal's face. "So, you're telling me you run the UK side but don't have the full picture?"

"That's exactly what I'm saying," Cal said, unflinching. "Gray keeps his cards close. Always has. But I do know none of my men are near Yorkshire. Now that Rhys is gone, that's it."

Knox nodded, processing. "Alright," he said, finality in his tone. "We get near the airbase, James, we drop you at a service station close by. You lay low and keep the phone on, so if I need you, you're on speed dial."

James nodded, a flicker of relief crossing his features. His knee, the cause of his medical discharge, throbbed with the day's exertion. Driving was one thing, but the rest of the mission would demand more than he could give. "Fair enough," he said softly. "But if everything changes, if you need me, ring me. You still have the burner."

Knox met James's eyes in the mirror, offering a brief nod. Yet his mind was already locked on the task at hand.

Knox turned his attention to Cal. "You and me, we get into the base. Find Gray. End it."

Cal returned Knox's gaze. "Works for me," he said.

Satisfied they had a plan, Knox pulled the fleece blanket around his shoulders, muttering, "Wake me when we get there."

And he closed his eyes, falling asleep immediately.

Sleep when you can, you might not get the chance again.

CHAPTER THIRTY-SIX

The café diner sat hunched at the edge of the service station, beaten by time and weather, a forgotten relic on a stretch of road nobody cared about. Its neon sign flickered weakly against the grey sky, half the letters dead, the other half struggling to stay lit.

The walls were scarred with peeling paint, the car park a mess of potholes and oil stains. No CCTV. No curious eyes. Just empty space and bad coffee.

Perfect.

James pulled in slowly, scanning the forecourt. Remote. Nondescript. A place that didn't ask questions. Exactly what he needed.

The Range Rover came to a stop in the far corner of the parking area, away from the few scattered vehicles and the weather-beaten building. His stomach growled audibly as he killed the engine. It was lunchtime, and he hadn't eaten anything substantial since breakfast, but food wasn't his primary objective.

He was considering how much he could help Knox and Cal from a distance. If he could tap into the air base's CCTV system, maybe, just maybe, he could give Knox and Cal some intel before they walked into what might be a hornet's nest.

The odds weren't great, he knew that. The base, until recently, had been a fully functional RAF installation, part of the country's long-running defence set-up. Military installations didn't have shit security and hacking from afar would be like threading a needle blindfolded. But it wasn't impossible, and James had to at least try.

James reached for the laptop that Knox had returned to the front seat, in a laptop bag. The ageing diner loomed in his peripheral vision, the faint smell of frying grease and burnt coffee drifting in through the cracked window. He reached for his phone and slid it into his pocket.

In the back, Knox was awake now. Stiff, sore, pulling himself out of the car and over to the boot with a low grunt.

James stepped out, limping a bit as he walked around the vehicle.

Knox had the tailgate open, making room inside. A Sig Sauer and an MP5 were laid out. He looked up at James and nodded in thanks.

"I'll call you when I need you James" Knox said. This was as much of a goodbye both men could muster. But nothing more needed to be said.

They shook hands, firm and silent. A nod. Mutual respect, no need for more. Then James turned and hobbled towards the café, laptop bag swinging at his side.

Knox stared down at the open boot. It was big enough, he reckoned, climbing in and drawing his knees up. Bigger than the BMW boot he'd crammed Ronnie into two and a half days ago.

He let out a short huff. Two and a half days. Sixty hours. That was all it had taken for everything to go to hell.

Cal stood at the tailgate, nodding to Knox, then slammed the door shut. Darkness swallowed him.

He rolled onto the rough carpet fabric, lying on his back, head tilted to one side to avoid the wheel arch. His broken arm throbbed with every movement. He tried to keep his mind on what came next, but in the hush of the unmoving car, he couldn't help replaying the chaos that had led him here.

Ronnie, Sarah, Jess, the Russian. The theme park. Sophie. It all blurred together, a mad swirl of danger and heartbreak that threatened to engulf him.

As his eyes adjusted to the dark, he felt the engine roar and then the vehicle jerked forward.

Knox shut his eyes, his good hand resting on the Sig Sauer's grip, the MP5 leaning near his leg. Both guns loaded and ready. One magazine each. Ten rounds in the Sig. Fifteen in the MP5. Not much, but enough for some sort of stand if it all went south.

He shifted, his shattered left arm shrieking in pain, the ache drumming in rhythm with his heartbeat. The conflict had taken its toll, in blood and bone. His leg wound was an echo compared to his arm now, the arm was aflame. He dug into his pocket, took out painkillers, swallowed two without water.

They weren't magic, but they'd dull the worst of it, or so he told himself.

He focused on the plan, aware he was giving Cal a lot of power, a lot of trust. It gnawed at him, forging a partnership with a man whose loyalty had already wavered more than once. If Cal lied, if the talk of family and betrayal was just a smokescreen, then Knox was stepping blindly into a trap, hemmed in and outgunned.

But why would Cal come back for him then? The man could have killed him a dozen times over, in the trees, in the vehicle. He hadn't, and that had to mean something.

Didn't it?

He needed to trust Cal, at least for the moment. But trusting and believing weren't the same, and he wasn't about to forget that.

The engine's vibrations droned, rattling through the boot. The crunch of gravel under the tyres faded as the Range Rover gathered speed for the airbase.

Darkness enclosed Knox, cocooning him in a hush that felt unnatural. Heat spread through the enclosed space, seeping into his muscles, enticing him to let go, to drift. Sleep tugged at the edge of his mind, insistent, like a lover pulling him into oblivion. A familiar state from too many nights on ops, forcibly awake while time crawled. Stags, nightshift, long hours staring at silhouettes in the gloom.

Here, there were no shapes in the dark, just solid black. Knox fought it by slapping his face with his good hand, trying to stay present. Sleep was a weakness he couldn't afford right now.

But the pull was strong, especially in the dark.

CHAPTER THIRTY-SEVEN

The vehicle slowed. Subtle at first, the deceleration barely noticeable. But Knox felt it. The shift in momentum. The slight dip of the suspension. The change in the engine's rhythm, no longer humming at a steady pace but winding down, losing speed.

His body reacted before his mind had fully caught up. A jolt of adrenaline burned through his limbs, snapping him upright, heart pounding against his sore, bruised ribs.

It took a second for Knox to realise where he was.

Had he dozed off? Even for a second?

The movement of the car changed, as did the gears, slowing to a crawl and then the tyres started weaving slightly as the driver navigated the road. Knox pictured it in his mind: the approach to the airbase, the concrete blast walls towering over the roadway, casting long shadows. The chicane of traffic cones designed to force vehicles to slow and zigzag their way through. The guardroom, lit harshly by industrial fluorescents, where a sentry would be stationed. Maybe one of Gray's men. Maybe not.

The car came to a halt, the brakes letting out a soft squeak. Knox held his breath, listening intently. The low hum of the engine thrummed against his back, a steady vibration that drowned out everything but his own heartbeat.

Then he heard voices.

Muffled but distinct, filtering through the car seat. Knox tensed, ears straining. He recognised Cal's Scottish drawl, but something was off. Too high pitched, too exclamatory.

The other voice was sharper, cutting through the faint hum of the idling engine. The sentry. Knox couldn't make out the words, but the tone told him everything, Cal was having his authority questioned.

The exchange escalated. Cal pushed back, his voice rising, trying to reason, to defuse.

The sound of the engine cutting out and then there was movement. The car rocked.

A door opened.

Then shut.

Then silence.

Knox didn't need to see it to know what was happening.

A search.

Knox was in a tight spot. In more ways than one. If they popped the boot, he was exposed, with no cover and no room to move. He was trapped. His grip tightened around the Sig Sauer, the cold steel pressing into his palm.

The faint shuffle of footsteps moved closer, scuffing the ground as they approached the rear.

He shifted in the dark, adjusting himself quietly.

The moment the tailgate cracked open, Knox moved suddenly.

He punched the Sig Sauer forward, locking his good arm straight. The weight and familiar steel felt natural in his hand. His little finger was curled outward, easing the natural pull of a trigger press, compensating for the drag of that first heavy compression.

The first shot was always a bastard on a Sig.

The double action, heavy pull. A built-in safety which was more of a flaw than a feature. Too much weight, too much resistance for an effective first shot.

But Knox had to counter, he did so by lifting his pinky finger from the grip, stopping the stronger pull from leveraging the angle of the barrel away from the target.

The afternoon light flooded into the compartment, blinding him momentarily, but he didn't hesitate. He knew where the target would be.

He fired two rounds. Centre mass. Double tap.

The bark of the pistol was deafening in the enclosed space, a thunderclap reverberating through the boot and pounding in Knox's ears. He felt the shockwave run up his arm, his wrist absorbing the recoil as the rounds found their mark.

The silhouette in front of him collapsed instantly, the body dropping like a marionette whose strings had been cut. Knox blinked against the sudden brightness, his vision adjusting as adrenaline pumped through him.

The ringing in his ears was overwhelming, a high-pitched whine that drowned out all other sound. The smell of carbon hung in the air. Knox loved that smell.

He squinted as light fully flooded in, illuminating the lifeless form sprawled on the ground.

Knox kept his grip on the Sig, arm steady as he slowly released the trigger, the weapon resetting in his hand. Still pointing at the shape on the ground.

His eyes adjusted to the blinding winter sunlight, Cal stepped into view, his face in shadow.

"Good grouping," Cal said, his tone a mixture of exasperation and disbelief. "But that could have been me!"

Knox climbed out of the boot, wincing as the strain tugged at his injured arm. He looked down at the lifeless young man sprawled on the cold ground, his expression unreadable.

"I knew it wasn't you," Knox said, his voice low but firm. "You'd have delayed opening the boot, taken longer, given me time to react. When it opened fast, I knew it wasn't you."

Cal looked at Knox with frustration plain on his face. "Total guesswork, Henry," he snapped. "Once a bluffer, always a bluffer."

Knox turned his head slowly, fixing Cal with a hard, unblinking stare. "It wasn't guesswork," he said evenly. "It was a calculated risk. And I was right. Now help me put this body in the boot, please." His tone softened at the last word.

Without waiting for a response, Knox crouched awkwardly, his single working hand reaching for the limp form on the ground. Cal hesitated for a moment, muttering something under his breath, then stepped forward to help. Together, they lifted the dead weight of the young sentry, manoeuvring him into the boot.

Once the body was inside, Knox began searching it using his good hand, he worked quickly, patting down pockets. He pulled out a folded piece of paper and a small stack of photos, giving them a quick glance before handing them to Cal.

"Take a look," Knox said, his voice clipped. "Are these your guys?"

Cal took the photos, his brow furrowing as he flipped through them. He paused, his expression darkening. "Yeah," he said at last. "They all work for Capuchin Security."

Knox nodded curtly, "Good," he said. "At least we know we're not expecting anyone else today."

Cal slid the note back into the guard's pocket and removed the MP5 from the sling, checking the chamber and magazine before grabbing a second magazine from the sentry's pouch.

Knox shouldered his own MP5, turning to Cal, he said, "I want you to find Gray. If I had to guess, he'll either be in the airbase tower or on the airstrip, waiting to see this plan of his through. Track him down but don't engage, hold him and wait for me. We will take him together."

Knox pulled out a battered Nokia phone from his pocket, its ancient screen glowing faintly in the cold winter light. He held it toward Cal, the number visible on the screen. "Ring me on this number when you've found him," Knox continued.

Cal smirked faintly, shaking his head as he typed the number into his sleek phone. "Nokia, eh? Heard of upgrades, Knoxy?"

"It's served me well these past couple of hours and it works," Knox shot back, his tone as cold as the frost in the air. "Let's hope you're as reliable."

Cal chuckled softly, ignoring the dig, and slid his phone back into his jacket. "Alright," he said, stepping back. "The road up ahead forks about 200 metres from here. The left-hand route leads to the hangars and the stores. The one on the right takes you to the air tower and the airstrip."

Knox nodded. "Roger that," he replied. "Take me to the fork. You go right, I'll go left."

CHAPTER THIRTY-EIGHT

As Cal's vehicle disappeared down the right-hand fork, Knox turned and made a beeline for the dense vegetation lining the road. The undergrowth was thick, tangled with frost-bitten brambles and dead grass, yet it provided the cover he needed. Moving quickly while crouched low, Knox pushed through the brush, his body protesting every step.

He pressed on, the Sig Sauer resting heavily in his right map pocket, while the MP5 hung awkwardly across his chest. He gripped the weapon single-handedly, compensating with his good arm for the lack of support, as the strap dug into his neck at every step.

Knox moved along the roadside, staying low and out of sight. The camp was eerily quiet. Not the kind of quiet that brought peace, but the kind that set nerves on edge, a silence that spoke of abandonment or worse. The usual base sounds were missing, no generators' hum, no distant voices, no boots clattering on parade grounds. Only the faint rustle of the wind against cold metal structures.

As he rounded a bend, the hangars came into view, looming large and imposing, relics from the Cold War at least, maybe older.

Their exteriors were a dull, faded grey, blending into the dreary sky. Corrugated metal walls streaked with rust and grime, the years of Yorkshire rain etched across their surfaces. Single-storey outbuildings clung to their sides like afterthoughts, flat roofs sagging under the weight of moss and debris. It screamed functionality, no charm.

The Russians would feel right at home, Knox thought.

He made for the hangars quickly, keeping hidden. His instincts told him this was where Catheryn and Sophie would be, tucked away and out of sight, waiting for Gray to finish whatever twisted game he was playing. The thought drove him forward, each step faster than the last.

Then a darker thought halted him mid-stride. What if they are not here? The idea slammed into him like a gut punch. What if Gray put them elsewhere, at his own place, or some hotel?

Uncertainty gnawed at his focus. Knox shook it off. He had no time for what-ifs. He couldn't second-guess. If they weren't here, he would deal with that next. For now, this was his only lead.

He reached the nearest hangar and began circling the single-storey building, hugging the wall. He passed broken windows, shards of glass catching the weak winter sunlight and scattering it in jagged patterns on the ground. Knox crouched, peering through one of the smashed panes. Inside was barren, stripped of anything useful, paper strewn across the floor like confetti.

He scanned the empty space through grime-streaked glass. No movement. No sound. Just the echo of what once was. Knox moved on, systematically checking each room in sequence along the outer wall. All the same, empty, deserted, stale. The faint smell of mildew clung to the cold metallic tang of rust. It looked like nobody had been here in months, maybe years.

Stifling the growing frustration, he finally rounded the smaller building. The massive hangar loomed ahead, imposing and desolate. The walls were a patchwork of peeling paint and rust, the once-proud RAF emblem barely visible under decades of neglect.

Knox edged towards the main doors, dwarfed by their

sheer size. One door was partially open, a yawning gap into the cavernous interior. He leaned, angling his body to look inside without showing himself. It took a moment for his eyes to adapt to the darkness, the vast interior stretching out like an empty shell.

About two hundred metres into the hangar were two sleek, black Range Rover Sports, parked side by side, their polished surfaces faintly gleaming even in the dim light. The vehicles radiated wealth and intent. And in front of them stood a single man.

He was tall and solid, dressed in dark clothes that blended with the shadows. His head was bowed, his attention on the glowing screen of a mobile phone in his hand. Knox noticed the lax discipline: no scanning of the perimeter, no checking of angles, just idle phone use. A mind-numbing task, presumably to keep him busy.

Amateur hour.

But amateurs still carry weapons, and an amateur can still kill. The man's lax focus might be an advantage, yet Knox knew better than to rely on it.

Henry unstrapped his injured arm, feeling the weight of his hand as it pulled on his forearm, the pain spiking then settling into a constant throb. Heat coursed through his veins.

He sank to a prone position, aligning himself with the MP5 in his hands. Henry clicked off the safety with a soft snick, thumb brushing the selector switch to single fire. His other hand gave the bolt a quick check, ensuring the bolt was forward. Satisfied, he pressed closer to the cold, damp ground.

Knox leopard-crawled out from the building's cover, trying to keep as low to the ground as possible. His body stretched flat, like a sniper on Otterburn's range.

You could trace a line from the man guarding the Range Rovers, through the muzzle of Knox's MP5, down to the heel of Knox's right boot.

Knox had a perfect, stable shooting platform. Elbows bent at exact right angles, his right hand gripping the pistol grip firmly, trigger finger resting lightly on the guard, poised. His left hand, weak and unreliable from the broken arm, simply propped the muzzle. All the weight, all the control, shifted to his right shoulder and hand, every nerve focused on the gun.

He regulated his deep breathing, letting the rise and fall of his chest steady the sights. Each inhale lifted them slightly, each exhale brought them back in line. He silently counted:

One. Two. Three.

On the third, he held it. His chest stilled, the weapon locked in place, the red dot on the sights drawing a bead on the man's centre of mass.

The target stood unaware, his face illuminated by the glow of his phone. The perfect shot, but Knox didn't rush. He let the weapon's aim settle naturally, the sights finding the exact point he wanted, where flesh and bone would yield to cold steel.

He squeezed the trigger, a slow and deliberate pull.

Targets will fall when hit.

The sound cracked like a whip in the stillness, loud and violent. The sharp crack of the round leaving the barrel shattered the fragile peace of the deserted airfield. The echo ricocheted off the hangar walls and low buildings, bouncing through the emptiness like a ripple in a pond.

Birds scattered from the wet grass nearby, startled by the sudden noise, their frantic wings beating against the air as they took flight.

Knox held his position, the smell of cordite sharp in his nostrils, his body motionless as he waited for the dust to settle. Through the faint haze left by the shot, the man's body crumpled silently, his phone slipping from his grasp as he hit the ground. One clean shot. Immediate. Final.

Knox let out his breath.

Knox remained still, scanning the area for any movement, anyone who might come running. His eyes flicked to the vehicles and back to the surrounding hangar, waiting for someone to appear, or for the man he had just dropped to twitch. A sign of life, a call for reinforcements.

Nothing. No commotion. Only deathly silence, as though the air itself was frozen in that single moment.

Then, with a burst of energy, he launched himself forward.

He sprinted toward the Range Rovers, boots pounding on the hangar floor. Pain flared in his leg and his arm throbbed in protest, but he ignored it all, focusing solely on the vehicles ahead. He rounded them swiftly, MP5 raised, his gaze sweeping for threats.

No one. The man had been alone, as Knox guessed from his lax discipline. No backup, no rotating guard. Just some poor sod glued to his phone, oblivious to the fatal result of his carelessness.

Knox approached the body. Blood pooled beneath him, dark and viscous on the concrete. Knox crouched, his broken arm cradled against his chest. Trying to move the body into one of the vehicles was impossible, no point wasting time. So, he focused on intel.

Knox rifled through the man's pockets. There was nothing noteworthy, no ID, only a phone and two sets of car keys. He quickly examined the phone, but it was pretty clear it held no real data on it. It had been wiped clean of addresses or numbers, the only app was a turn based battle game that the guard had been playing to pass the time.

Knox's focus then changed to the key fobs, where he

pressed the unlock buttons, watching hazard lights blink on both Range Rovers.

He moved to the closer vehicle, opening the door carefully, Sig Sauer in hand, ready to fire at the first sign of danger. The interior was pristine, empty. Knox then checked the second vehicle, opening the driver's door and slipping inside.

This one was different. A thick folder rested on the passenger seat, its corners worn from handling. Knox grabbed it, flipping through its contents.

First, just logistics, numbers, schedules, cargo manifests.

Then his pulse kicked up.

Gray's name. Normanov's name. Again and again, on shipping logs, drone purchase orders, cargo manifests. The paper trail was barely concealed, because nobody outside this operation was ever supposed to see it.

He read on, and it only got worse.

By the time he finished, his gut was hollow.

His face turned to stone.

The plan was simple enough but devastating. Ten drones, each loaded with a one-kilogram payload of Novichok-coated microdroplets, in an ultrafine oil-based solution. Not just a single vial or a crude release attempt. A tactical airborne chemical strike designed for maximum area coverage.

It was all here. Deconfliction routes over the city of York, staggered flight paths below radar coverage, avoiding security intercepts. Pre-programmed dispersal zones above dense population areas. Multiple craft meant at least one would make it, at least.

Knox turned the page to find Gray had considered everything: wind drift, humidity, altitude, to ensure maximum effect, low enough to guarantee exposure.

No fail-safe, no recall. Once the drones were airborne,

it was irreversible.

Gray was overseeing it all. He had bought top-grade drones, stored at the airfield.

Normanov supplied the Novichok, arriving today, at Bentley Aerodrome in half an hour.

The main event, thought Knox, and nobody knew.

HippoLand was the diversion, the sideshow. This was the main act.

Cal had been right.

But why? Why was Gray doing it?

He had served his country, worn the British uniform. Now allied with a Russian. Planning an attack on British soil?

It made no sense.

Not to Knox.

What had changed? What turned a man like Gray into this?

And what had Catheryn pulled Sophie into?

Knox placed the folder back into the vehicle front seat. As it rested on the luxurious leather, it looked bulkier, heavier. As if it was now carrying another secret that Knox had placed there.

He slammed the door, the sound echoing in the empty airfield. He moved swiftly, putting the Sig away in his map pocket, and drew his Gerber, flicking the blade out. In one move, he dropped beside each vehicle, slicing the tyres. The reinforced blade cut deep into the sidewalls.

Then he flipped open each key fob, prising out the tiny batteries with the Gerber's edge. He pocketed them, then tossed the empty fobs into far corners of the hangar. Not foolproof, but it would buy time. The key fobs didn't contain an actual key, everything worked at the press of a button, so this small act of sabotage meant no one would be driving these vehicles any time soon.

Knox straightened, about to move on. His eyes drifted towards the air traffic control tower in the distance, skeletal against the pale winter sky. If Gray were anywhere, it would be there.

Then he heard it, a familiar voice behind him, cutting through the stillness like a chainsaw.

"Henry."

The voice froze him in mid-step, sounding both familiar and utterly impossible. His heart jolted, his pulse hammering as he turned slowly, every sense on edge.

Catheryn.

CHAPTER THIRTY-NINE

Catheryn stood there, framed in the soft glow of artificial light, her emerald dress catching every flicker, every subtle shift in movement. The fabric clung in all the right ways, elegant yet effortless, a statement as much as a choice.

For a moment, she looked perfect. Untouchable.

But then she spoke.

The words tumbled out too fast, her tone sharp, raw, teetering between anger and desperation. There was an urgency beneath them, something unchecked, something slipping.

Her dark hair, usually immaculate, was slightly dishevelled, strands falling loose where she had run her hands through it too many times, too forcefully. It was the only outward crack in an otherwise flawless presentation.

Her eyes burned, green, vivid, alive. The same shade as her dress, but far less composed. They shimmered, catching the light, reflecting the emotions she was failing to suppress. Frustration. Fear. Anger.

And something else.

Something deeper. Something Knox could not name.

It unsettled him. Not because he did not understand emotion, but because it was coming from her, a woman who had always been calculated and composed.

Yet, for the first time, she was not.

"You shouldn't have come!" Catheryn's voice lashed out, sharp and raw. "You're wrecking everything!"

The words fell out fast, too fast, like a confession

forced from her throat. Her hands fluttered at her sides, restless, agitated, as though her body could not contain the frustration twisting through her.

"Why the fuck didn't you answer me?" Her voice cracked, rising, unravelling. "I called you, night and day! And now you turn up here?"

It was not just anger. It was panic, desperation, something fraying at the edges.

Her voice climbed, syllable by syllable, her composure unravelling. Nearly a frenzy now. Almost a plea.

Knox's mind raced, but outwardly he was stone still. His eyes swept the area, marking every corner, every shadow, each possible hiding place. Where had she come from? Could she have been on the building's other side, the one he had not checked? The thought tightened his chest. And who else was here? Where was Sophie?

"Where's Sophie?" His voice was low, sharp, urgent. The words bristled with quiet command, slicing through Catheryn's frantic energy.

He stepped closer, his grip on the MP5 tightening. His gaze held hers, unyielding, demanding an answer. For all the questions crowding his mind, this one eclipsed the rest.

Catheryn froze, her lips trembling slightly as though the answer hovered unspoken. But her hesitation only fanned the fire inside Knox. Time felt dangerously short. Every second of silence too long.

"She's safe, no thanks to you," Catheryn spat, venom lacing her tone. "But you need to leave, right now, Henry. You're making a mess of this, and I want you gone from here and never come back." She demanded.

"Sorry Catheryn," Knox said, her name tasting foreign in his mouth. "Not without Sophie."

Catheryn walked forward towards Knox, her eyes dropping to the crumpled body sprawled by the Range

Rover.

Knox reacted on instinct, closing the gap in a heartbeat. Every warning howling in his mind as he grabbed her, turning her face away from the bloodied corpse. His hands settled on her shoulders, firm but not harsh.

"What have you done, Henry?" Catheryn's voice cracked, her wide eyes on his. Her face turned pale, her breaths shallow. "What have you done?"

Knox's reply was low and rough. "You don't know Gray. The man's a fiend, Catheryn. I've already stopped him killing a load of people today, and I'm gonna stop him now."

Catheryn shoved away from him, breaking contact. She trembled, though she held her ground, her gaze fierce as it locked with his. "You stopped the attack at HippoLand?" she asked, disbelief tinging her voice. "You... you stopped it?"

Knox froze, the impact of her question heavy between them.

"You knew?" he said, the words coming low, almost a whisper, more accusation than question.

"Of course I knew," Catheryn replied, her voice rising, both frantic and sure. "It was my idea. We need to fight back, Henry. This is for our country!" Her words jolted Knox like a blow, halting him, his mind spinning to reconcile the woman he loved with the twisted logic falling from her lips.

His throat went dry, the words failing him as Catheryn stepped closer, her eyes alight with a fiery intensity he'd never seen before. "Archie showed me," she went on, raw and impassioned. "Britain's gone soft since Iraq, since Afghanistan. We lost our edge. We need a spark to become ourselves again."

Knox stared at her, horrified.

"The war in Ukraine is the chance," she said, voice trembling. "We'd be up against a failing superpower, fighting on terrain that suits us and our armour. We'd reclaim our standing in the world."

Knox's forehead creased, disbelief finally finding voice. "But we're not involved in that war," he said, taking a step back.

"Not yet," Catheryn admitted, tone sharp with urgency. "But once news breaks that Russia targeted British people in the U.K., that nobody is safe" her voice faltered briefly, her stare spearing into Knox's, "the government would have no choice but to act. Not like Salisbury, they'd go full NATO. All for the British people. We'd be back in the big league, Henry. People would respect us again."

Knox felt the ground fall away. The woman he'd sacrificed so much for, mother of his child, was now pushing for war on British soil. His voice came out rough with disgust. "You were ready to kill innocents for that? Let Gray profit from it?"

"It's not like that!" Catheryn fired back, her desperation edged with mania. "Archie's doing this for Britain. He's a patriot, trying to save our future! America needed 9/11, so do we. Don't you understand? It's for our greater good!"

Knox's head shook slowly, his hand tightening on the MP5. His heart felt crushed, the pressure of betrayal building in his chest.

"I won't let it happen, Catheryn," he said, voice stiff with resolve. "I won't let innocent people die for Gray. Or you. Or for anyone hoping to cash in on others' misery."

Catheryn let out a cold, scraping laugh that made the hairs on Knox's neck rise. It was not the warm laugh he recalled. This was jagged, cruel, charged with darkness. "So that angle didn't sway you? I should have known better. You're not moved by patriotism," she said, voice even with twisted triumph.

Henry's confusion was plain for a second.

"It was always my plan," she went on, eyes shining with a fanatic glint. "Archie was just a front. He thinks he's in charge, but he didn't spot how I guided him. You? You were another pawn, drifting wherever I nudged you. Both of you, so fixated by your own egos you never saw Normanov was the real brain. I fed him everything he needed, while Archie... was just a fool, believing he was in control. You're all too blind to see the bigger picture. Sacrifice is necessary if we want strength again. Sophie will understand one day, but you never could."

Knox's mind spun, betrayal smashing into him. "What? You think you're using Gray? He's unstable, he needs stopping, not feeding. And I'm not leaving this place without my daughter," he said, voice low, each word solid with intent.

Catheryn arched an eyebrow, which twisted gleam deepening. "You won't see her if you keep meddling. This is beyond you, bigger than Gray. Normanov's plan is in motion, and I'm the one steering it here. So, I suggest you walk away before you lose more than you already have."

Before Catheryn could speak again, a new voice cut through the cold afternoon air.

"Hi, Knox," it said, formal and cold, each syllable laced with condescension.

Knox turned, eyes drawn to the voice's source. Colonel Archie Gray stepped from behind one of the Range Rovers, its tyres slashed and sagging on the frosty ground.

He looked ready for a board meeting, not an abandoned airfield. A tailored navy overcoat, the collar lines crisp around his face, a dark wool suit hugging his lean frame. Polished leather shoes shone in the wan light.

Next to Gray was a huge man, six foot three or more, broad shouldered, dressed in black tactical gear that clung to thick muscle. He had an MP5 at the ready, a close-cropped haircut and dead eyes that spoke of no remorse left in him.

"I was wondering when you'd show up," Gray said, his tone thick with contempt. His cold stare pinned Knox, a smirk just tugging at his lips.

Knox's instincts flared. He raised his own MP5, pressing it snug to his shoulder. Safety off, sights lined up on Gray's chest. The hulking guard matched him instantly, the muzzle aimed at Knox's heart. The standoff was instant.

"Hand over my daughter, Gray," Knox growled, voice slicing through the damp cold. "She has nothing to do with this."

Gray chuckled, a chilling sound that made Knox's teeth clench. "This was never about you, Knox," he said calmly, like explaining something obvious to a child. "You're a soldier, a pawn. People like Catheryn and me... we're reshaping the world in ways you can't begin to grasp."

Something flickered in Catheryn's eyes. She glanced at Gray with undisguised contempt, a slight curl of her lip, but Gray was oblivious. He kept his gaze on Knox, heedless that he himself was but a piece in her game as well.

Knox's heart pounded. He saw Catheryn's face turn to Gray, saw her bury the scorn behind a look of neutrality. She stepped closer to him, a final betrayal. Everything in her demeanour said she was actually the one pulling the strings, even if Gray believed otherwise.

Then, a smaller figure edged out from behind Gray. Sophie. Knox's blood turned ice cold. She looked the same: curls tumbling around her shoulders, a pink coat for warmth, wide, curious eyes. She clutched a stuffed rabbit from her birthday. The same toy she never put down.

Her face lit up with childish excitement. "He did come, Mummy!" she called, voice bright as she dashed forward. For an instant, Knox thought it could all end here. But it happened too quickly.

The little figure sprinting across the concrete broke the deadlock, the guard's peripheral vision seeing the sudden movement. The frantic dash clashed with every lesson about threat identification and reflex. Sophie wasn't in his plan. No orders for a running child. His weapon followed her by reflex, confusion or indecision crossing his face for a split second. But training is a brutal instructor, and his finger tightened on the trigger.

Then Gray spat out a single word.

"Fire."

The next moment seemed to stretch into slow motion. Catheryn's eyes went wide, and Henry felt his heart freeze in his chest. This wasn't her plan, it wasn't anyone's plan.

"No!" Knox shouted, terror stripping his voice raw. "Sophie, no!"

He knew. In that single, agonising instant, Knox understood exactly what was about to unfold. His body acted on instinct, finger squeezing the trigger for a short, precise shot. But he was not quick enough.

The guard had already fired.

CHAPTER FORTY

The crack of the shot shattered the cold air, reverberating off the hangar walls and ricocheting through Knox's chest. His round found its mark almost simultaneously, punching into the guard's centre mass and sending the man sprawling backward, his weapon clattering to the ground. The hulking figure crumpled, but Knox did not care.

His focus was entirely on the small, crumpled figure that lay motionless on the cold ground.

Sophie.

He sprinted, the pain in his leg and arm forgotten, his body driven by sheer, unrelenting panic. His eyes locked on her tiny frame, his mind refusing to accept the brutal reality playing out before him. The stuffed rabbit she had clutched so tightly now lay discarded, lifeless, just a few feet away.

"Sophie!" Knox's voice cracked as he screamed her name, his heart pounding in his ears, drowning out every other sound. The world blurred around him, the edges of the hangar and the parked Range Rovers fading into a smear of muted colours. All he could see was her, lying still on the ground.

He dropped to his knees beside her, the cold biting through his trousers, but he did not notice. His trembling hands reached out, gently cradling her small body. Her pink coat was stained crimson, the bright colour spreading across the fabric in a cruel, vivid bloom.

"Sophie," Knox whispered, his voice breaking as he stroked her face, her cheek still warm beneath his touch.

Her curls framed her face, the colours of light and dark red, soft and cruel in their reminder of the life she had only seconds before. Her blue eyes, his eyes, stared up at him, glassy and unseeing.

"No, no, no..." The words tumbled from him, a broken mantra as he pressed his forehead to hers, his tears falling freely, mingling with the blood on her face. He rocked back and forth, clutching her to his chest, his world falling apart around him.

Time felt as though it had stopped. The cold wind stung his skin, but he did not feel it. The distant sound of Catheryn's scream barely registered, a hollow echo on the edge of his awareness. All he could hear was his own heartbeat, pounding in his ears like a war drum, relentless and deafening.

Knox's grip on Sophie's body tightened, his own trembling with grief and fury. The weight of her in his arms, so small, so fragile, was unbearable. She was never meant to be here. She was never meant to die.

But she had. Because of them.

Knox's head snapped up, his tear-streaked face twisted with anger and heartbreak. His eyes found Gray, who stood rooted in place, his expression unreadable. Catheryn was sobbing, hands over her mouth, face pale as she stared at the scene.

Knox's voice emerged as a low, guttural growl, edged with a grief-fed rage that burned hotter than anything he had felt before. "You did this!" He glared at Gray, his body shaking with anguish. "You killed her!"

For a moment, Gray's mask of composure cracked, a flicker of uncertainty in his eyes, but he recovered swiftly, his tone calm, almost detached. "Unfortunate, Knox, but sacrifices must be made. You should have stayed away."

Time splintered, moving in sharp, uneven fragments.

He laid her on the ground, pressing two fingers to her

neck, desperately searching for any sign of a pulse.

Nothing.

"Come on, Sophie," he whispered, voice ragged and failing. He tugged the day sack off his shoulder and rummaged for his first aid kit, the familiar zip feeling like an insult to what was happening in front of him. He tore open a field dressing, frantically pressing it to the wound, trying in vain to halt the blood that was already little more than a slow trickle. His thoughts sped, body acting on training. He tilted her head back, pinched her nose, and blew air into her lungs.

"Breathe, Sophie," he choked, pulling back to start chest compressions. His arms moved in a steady rhythm, every push a desperate command. "Breathe, damn it!"

He heard only his own ragged breathing, drowning everything else out. He was oblivious to Gray leaving, oblivious to Catheryn. The world had shrunk to this final struggle to drag Sophie back from the brink.

Knox's strength was sapped, each compression taxing him further as exhaustion loomed. His broken arm shrieked in protest, ignored. "Come on, Soph," he muttered, voice near a sob. "Come back to me."

His vision wavered, his pace slowing as realisation crept in. He faltered, then forced himself onward, pressing faster. "Breathe," he pleaded, words shattered by a sob. "Please, Sophie. Please."

But there was no response. No flicker of eyelashes, no gasp, no pulse beneath his touch. Just silence.

And in that moment, Henry Knox allowed a cry to escape him, a sound that laid bare a man who had lost the last thing tethering him to hope.

A hand on his shoulder appeared without warning, Knox reacting on instinct. He jerked away, twisting in a single smooth movement. His good hand yanked the Sig Sauer from his map pocket. The pistol rose as though part of him, the barrel aimed at the figure. His finger poised, only a hairsbreadth away from releasing the final torment he had left.

It was Cal.

Knox froze, the Sig trembling. His red-rimmed eyes locked on the man, not truly seeing him. His chest rattled with harsh breaths, his muscles wound too tight. The world was dead silent. He heard only his hammering pulse in his ears.

Cal raised his hands, palms up, sorrow open in his face. "Knox," he said softly, voice low and strong. "It's me."

The words barely registered. Knox looked at Sophie, her small, bloodied body just feet away. The sight tore at him anew, wave after wave of grief bearing down. His grip on the gun faltered, and the weapon dipped.

"I'm sorry, mate," Cal said, stepping closer. He tried to place his hand on Knox's shoulder again. This time, Knox let him. His strength had gone, utterly drained.

"She's gone," Cal murmured, voice weighed with finality. The words hit Knox like a blow, punching the air from his lungs. His slumped to the ground, the Sig falling beside him with a dull thud.

Knox's head bowed, his body quivering as tears poured unrestrained. He stared at the ground, vision blurred, mind reeling with that one moment replaying over and over—Sophie's excited dash, the shot's crack, and the monstrous quiet that followed.

Cal knelt, his face etched with grief. He laid a hand on Knox's shoulder. "I'm here," he said gently. It wasn't enough, but it was all he could give. For a time, the two men stayed there in the chilling air, united by a grief too profound for words.

CHAPTER FORTY-ONE

The silence in the hangar was oppressive.

Knox managed to push himself upright, his muscles screaming in protest. Blood, sweat, tears, mud and cam-cream streaked his face and clothes, more than a day's worth of stubble on his chin, all remnants of the nightmare he had just endured. He took a slow, shaky breath, turning towards Cal, his voice quieter than usual, edged with a sorrow that cut through the stillness.

"Cal, can I ask a favour?" Knox's words carried the weight of a man who had just lost everything that mattered.

Cal looked at him, his own face etched with exhaustion and grief.

"Of course, Henry. Anything," Cal replied, his voice hoarse but unwavering.

Knox's gaze dropped briefly to the ground before locking onto Cal's. "Stay with Sophie, please. I don't want her to be alone."

The request hung in the air, heavy with all the emotions Knox couldn't allow himself to show.

Cal gave a solemn nod. "Aye, I'll stay."

Knox did not respond. He turned sharply, his body a mix of adrenaline and agony. Fire roared in his veins, anger igniting every nerve, propelling him forward. His heart pounded, his purpose now singular and all-consuming. He sprinted, his strides uneven but determined, chasing the faint glimmer of revenge.

He stripped the MP5 and Sig from his body as he ran, he wouldn't need them to finish this. Shooting Gray wouldn't be enough, he needed to see Gray's fear in his eyes. His leg burned like hellfire, each step a raw, searing ache, but he used the pain, feeding it into the flames of his resolve. His shattered arm throbbed in rhythm with his heart, but it was a distant echo, dulled by emotional torment.

It didn't take long for Knox to find Gray. The man was waiting at the far end of the airstrip, where the flat expanse stretched out like an open wound on the landscape. He was waiting for the aeroplane that tracked towards the runway.

Knox pushed harder, his breaths coming in ragged gasps. The icy wind whipped at his face, biting into the cuts and bruises marking him like a roadmap of his ordeal. Ahead, the shape of an aeroplane descending to the airfield grew larger, its wheels down, engines humming as it closed in on the runway.

It was the cargo. Knox knew it in his gut. The deadly weapon Gray had orchestrated this entire nightmare for.

"Gray!" Knox roared, his voice tearing through the wind. "You fucking murderer! You fucking traitor!"

The words carried across the empty airstrip, heavy with raw fury and heartbreak. Gray slowed, turning to face him. His silhouette stark against the pale sky, the cold wind tugging at his coat. Behind him, the plane neared, the ultimate prize in Gray's twisted plan.

"That was your fault, Knox," Gray sneered, his tone dripping mockery, not a trace of remorse. He stood poised, eyes gleaming with cruel satisfaction. "You should have joined the team. Instead, you came looking for trouble. Your daughter would still be alive, safe with her new stepdaddy."

The words slammed into Knox like a grenade blast, obliterating what remained of his control. Rage flared, wild and boundless, coursing through him like wildfire.

He roared, a guttural sound from the depths of his soul, charging at Gray with reckless abandon. His moves were fuelled by blind fury, his coordination slipping as raw emotion overwhelmed him.

Gray smirked, sidestepping Knox's ragged blows with ease. Knox swung wildly, a haymaker aimed at destroying Gray's face, but Gray ducked and countered with a crisp right hook that connected with the side of Knox's face like a sledgehammer. Blood sprayed from Knox's split lip and burst nose, flecking the cold air with red. He stumbled, the world tipping sideways, but forced himself upright, spinning to meet Gray again.

Gray was ready and confident. Knox's next punch, thrown in desperation, was blocked easily. Gray aimed a blow at Knox's broken left arm, the savage jolt of pain tore a guttural cry from Knox's throat. His guard fell, and Gray exploited the opening, firing a brutal uppercut that crashed into Knox's jaw. His head snapped back, his left eye immediately swelling, purple, as blood oozed from a fresh cut below it.

Knox staggered, legs threatening to collapse, but he gritted his teeth and refused to drop. He tried to reset, to find some footing, but Gray was relentless, unleashing a flurry of blows on Knox's battered face. Knox's vision blurred, his body trembling under the weight of pain and exhaustion. He had already endured too much, the house explosion, the leg wound, the shattered arm, and now a merciless beating that pushed him beyond reason.

Gray kicked out, boot hammering into Knox's thigh. Knox crumpled to his hands and knees, arms shaking as he struggled to rise. He gasped for air, shallow and ragged. Gray pounced again, stepping in and slamming another vicious kick into Knox's ribs, the force reverberating through his ravaged body, toppling him onto his side.

Knox rolled instinctively, his good arm clawing at the tarmac. Survival drove him, his mind racing through every scrap of training. As Gray stepped in for another blow, Knox lashed out, catching hold of Gray's leg and twisting with his remaining strength. Gray crashed backward, landing hard with a jolt.

Knox scrambled upright, lungs heaving, muscles screaming. His left eye was swollen shut, leaving him half-blind, while blood trickled steadily from his face. Every fibre of his being demanded he yield, but he couldn't. Not after everything.

Gray climbed to his feet, brushing himself off. Seeing Knox's wretched state, he laughed, a cold echo rippling through the empty strip. Knox swayed, his body near collapse. Gray moved in again, emboldened by Knox's obvious weakness.

"You're done, Knox," Gray jeered, his voice thick with contempt. "A valiant effort, but you're out of your depth. You're just a tired, broken old man clinging to a fight you've already lost."

Knox's breathing was ragged, his body burning, but he forced himself to speak, his voice rough. "You always did talk too much."

Gray launched another storm of punches, each blow smashing into Knox. He did his best to defend, but Gray was fresh, his strikes precise. Every jab connected, temple, jaw, ribs, sending Knox sprawling on the frosty ground.

Gray stepped back, panting lightly with exertion, releasing a cruel laugh that cut like a knife. "Like I said, Knox. Brave, but pointless," he said, his voice mocking, Canadian accent emphasising each syllable. "I dare say you'd have been a decent CP operator, but in the end, you've wasted your potential. Utterly pointless."

Knox rolled onto his back, every muscle shrieking. His

face was swollen and bloody, left eye all but sealed. Yet, somehow, behind the agony, a slow, defiant grin tugged at his battered lips. Blood coated his teeth as he let out a soft, rasping chuckle. "Finally," he breathed, voice laced with pain, "I get to wipe that fucking smug grin off your face, Gray, you pompous twat."

Gray's composure cracked, his sneer morphing into outright anger. He leaned down, driving a vicious punch into Knox's face. Blood burst from Knox's mouth and nose, metallic tang choking him. Gray sneered, his tone riddled with scorn. "And how do you plan on that, Knox? Tell me."

Knox coughed, spitting a mix of blood and saliva onto the tarmac beside him. Despite the torment, his gaze never left Gray, a shred of defiance kindling in his eyes. "The police are on their way," he said quietly, voice steady, a faint smile in the corner of his ruined lips. "You're not getting away with this."

Gray snorted derisively, shaking his head. "The police? They don't have enough to touch me. They can't even get onto this airbase, let alone stop me. No warrant, no jurisdiction. Once that flight lands—" He gestured toward the distant aeroplane, its wheels just touching the tarmac. "I'll be gone, cargo and all. In minutes, Knox. Minutes. And you?" He crouched low, levelling his gaze with Knox's. "You'll take the fall."

Gray leaned back and drove another punch toward Knox's face, but this time, Knox anticipated it. He tilted his head forward at the last moment, catching the blow on his forehead. The impact sent a sharp jolt of pain through Knox's skull, but it was nothing compared to the look on Gray's face as his fist met solid bone.

A sickening crunch echoed between them, and Gray staggered back, clutching his hand. His fingers curled awkwardly, his face distorted with pain. "You fucker,"

Gray hissed through clenched teeth, shaking his hand as though trying to rid himself of the burning ache in his shattered metacarpals.

Knox pushed himself up into a seated position, wiping the blood from his mouth with the back of his hand and grinning, the expression as much defiance as it was a disguise for his own pain. "You never did learn to punch properly," he said, voice edged with bitterness.

Gray's eyes flared with anger. "Fuck you, Knox," he spat, voice dripping venom.

Knox tilted his head, his grin broadening despite the blood trickling down his chin. "The police might not have enough to arrest you, but they certainly have enough to come on here to arrest me," he said, his words carrying a cryptic note.

Gray froze, rage giving way to confusion. He stared at Knox, his mind racing. "What the hell are you talking about?" he demanded.

Knox leaned back a fraction, his bloody smile unwavering. "I guess you saw the news, an arrest warrant has been issued for me," he said in a mock-casual tone. "And I just finally turned my phone on and left it sitting in your Range Rover. If I know Amy, and I think I do, she's already triangulated the location. A murder suspect of three people would certainly be enough to enter the camp and I wouldn't be shocked if she's already here. And when she comes, she'll have half of West Yorkshire's Armed Response Teams with her. She'll arrest me, sure. But when that door is opened she'll also find plenty of evidence to bury you for life."

The colour drained from Gray's face, his arrogance evaporating at the faint sound of sirens rising in the distance. Fear crept into his eyes, it was just the fuel Knox needed.

Henry cocked his head slightly and smiled, as if

savouring the noise. "Hear that, Gray? That's the sound of your freedom melting away."

Knox spat a thick gob of blood onto the concrete, the crimson stark against the grey surface. He forced himself upright, every movement agony. The pain had become a steady roar in his mind, yet he shoved it aside. "Still waiting for that plane to land, are you?" he rasped, scorn saturating each syllable.

Gray's gaze darted to the taxiing aircraft, wheels squealing on the tarmac. The wind whipped around them, carrying the smell of jet fuel and the chill of the open runway. The plane slowed, its hulking shape an ominous outline against the bleak horizon.

Knox watched Gray's face churn with fast computations, seeking an exit. The former officer stepped back carefully, torn between fighting or fleeing. But Knox would not let him go. Not after everything.

Knox hurled himself at Gray, his fists thrown in a rush of desperate strikes. Gray deflected most of them, but the onslaught rattled him, forcing him to defend rather than retreat.

Gray swerved around a sweeping kick meant for his legs and answered with a cutting punch that clipped Knox's battered ribs. Knox hissed in pain, but pressed on, relentless. Each blow a mix of precision and rage, designed not just to overwhelm Gray but to keep him from running.

The roar of the jet's engines intensified, the craft looming behind them. Gray glanced at the plane, then at Knox, desperation fuelling every step. But Knox gave no ground, raining punches until Gray had no option but to stand his ground.

Then came the noise. The rising wail of sirens, each second louder. Blue and red lights flickered at the airfield's edge, slicing through the drear. Gray's face darkened, his composure faltering as the reality of his predicament set in.

Knox saw the lights as well, the swirling presence of police vehicles skidding to a halt behind them. One black SUV led the charge, its tyres screeching before armed officers poured out, weapons at the ready.

Knox held his position, chest heaving, one arm limp at his side. He didn't flinch when a shout came from one of the vehicles, a voice resolute and commanding.

Amy.

"Down on the ground! Both of you! Hands where we can see them, feet wide!"

Knox paused, eyes on Gray's, he smiled and slowly eased to the ground, eyes never leaving Gray. He spread his arms and legs, feeling the cold, unforgiving surface beneath him. From the corner of his swollen eye, he watched Gray hesitate, his fingers twitching before he too complied, lowering himself bitterly. His polished façade cracked.

Their gazes locked again, two enemies at the climax of their conflict. Knox's bloodied face worn with grim vindication, while Gray's eyes flicked about anxiously, his mind realising that all his careful planning was unravelling.

The armed officers advanced, on Knox who remained motionless, silent. He only stared at Gray, the man who had destroyed everything dear to him, now also prone on the floor, his entire scheme collapsing around him.

CHAPTER FORTY-TWO

Two days later, Knox stepped out of the narrow confines of a police cell into the glaring, sterile light of a custody suite. The sudden brightness made him squint, his body instinctively recoiling from the contrast. A uniformed police sergeant sat at the high desk to his right, sorting paperwork, his presence barely registering with Knox.

Amy Thornton stood waiting for him, poised and sharp in a tailored pinstripe suit and crisp white blouse. Her hair was swept back into a neat chignon, not a strand out of place. She exuded authority and composure, but her eyes softened when they met Knox's battered form.

Knox managed a faint smile, though the motion tugged painfully at his swollen lips. His left arm hung in a cast and sling, held awkwardly to his chest. The wedding band that he had once worn was now absent. His dark combat trousers and scuffed boots, though cleaned, bore evidence of his ordeal. His black T-shirt, emblazoned with a faded Counting Crows logo, seemed out of place against the station's clinical backdrop.

Amy stepped forward, her polished heels clicking softly on the tiled floor. She extended her hand. "Thank you, Henry. Good work," she said, her tone firm but threaded with genuine respect. As their hands briefly clasped, she added, her voice quieter, "I'm sorry for your loss."

Knox nodded, her words washing over him like distant waves. "What happens now?" he asked, his voice quiet but steady.

Amy hesitated, her gaze flicking to the documents she carried before refocusing on him. "With the evidence, your testimony, and Cal's statements, we can charge Gray with terrorism offences. The Russian and the pilot too." She paused, her voice dropping. "We didn't find your ex-wife at the airfield, but when we do, she will be charged with aiding and abetting. As for Cal... the CPS will probably show leniency thanks to his confession and cooperation, but he'll still do time. At least his family are free."

Knox stayed silent, letting her continue.

Amy went on, "And Normanov? He wasn't on the plane. An international warrant's out for him now. Waiting game." She tilted her head, her sharp eyes scanning his face. "What about you, Henry?"

Knox's eyes grew distant, and for a moment, he said nothing, the past days had been an ordeal, and he craved normality. Eventually, he exhaled. "I have a funeral to plan," he murmured.

Amy offered no reply, her expression sombre as he walked past her and headed toward the exit.

Moments later, he emerged into the blinding winter sunlight of Yorkshire. He paused, blinking at the sudden brightness, the chill stinging his skin. The black stone façade of the 19th-century police station loomed behind him, weathered by time, like a relic from another age. Its shadow stretched across the old cobbles.

Knox descended the steps slowly, using the blue handrail to steady himself. In the crisp light, his silhouette cut a stark figure, carved by grief.

James waited for him at the kerb, dressed in a hoodie and joggers. He leaned against the door of a brand-new matte black Range Rover, its sleek lines unmistakably familiar.

"Well, we won't be seeing Cal or Gray for a while,"

Knox said grimly as he approached, his voice loaded with finality. He winced as he adjusted the sling supporting his left arm, the sharp pain a persistent reminder of the physical cost of the past days.

James nodded. “What about Catheryn?” he asked carefully.

Knox stopped, meeting James’s gaze. His eyes burned, dark and resolute, the edges of his expression turning to steel. “She’s dead to me,” he said, his tone abrupt and definitive.

James did not blink, his face calm, nodding almost imperceptibly. “Understood,” he said, his voice unfazed. “How about breakfast? We can talk about what happened in the last 48 hours.” His voice lightened slightly, though his concern stayed clear.

Knox shook his head. “I want to see Sophie first,” he said firmly.

James paused, his own expression softening with understanding that needed no words. “Alright,” he agreed at last, a single word carrying a depth far beyond mere consent.

He opened the passenger door of the Range Rover with a fluid motion, stepping aside for Knox, who climbed in carefully, then settled into the seat.

James hobbled round the vehicle, dropping into the driver’s seat. The engine purred, ready to roll.

As the Range Rover glided out onto the frost-dusted street, Knox’s phone vibrated in his pocket, breaking the hush. He frowned, fumbling awkwardly to retrieve it with his good hand. After some difficulty, he pressed answer and lifted it to his ear.

“Knox Investigations,” he said into the handset.

ABOUT THE AUTHOR

Pete Briggs, the acclaimed author of the **Henry Knox** detective series, brings an unparalleled authenticity to his gripping novels, drawing from a lifetime of extraordinary real-world experiences. A veteran of the British Army's Royal Military Police, **Pete** served for more than two decades in high-stakes environments across Northern Europe, the Balkans, Iraq, Canada, and Oman. His military career honed his expertise in leadership, team dynamics, and operational effectiveness, imbuing his stories with a depth and realism that only firsthand experience can provide.

As a trained private investigator, **Pete** combines his military background with a sharp eye for detail, crafting narratives that capture the precision and nuance of investigative work. His career extends into leadership, project management, and security management, fields that further enrich his novels with intricate plots and multidimensional characters.

Blending his professional expertise with a gift for storytelling, **Pete Briggs** creates novels that are as thrilling as they are thought-provoking. The **Henry Knox** series goes beyond mere entertainment, offering vivid explorations of resilience, ingenuity, and the relentless pursuit of truth. A testament to **Pete's** remarkable life, his books transform personal experience into unforgettable fiction.

PETE'S OTHER PUBLICATIONS:

SQUADDIESAURUS

A whimsically imagined dictionary and thesaurus that brings British Army Slang and terminology to life.

Dive into the brilliantly chaotic and endlessly entertaining world of British Army slang with The ***Squaddiesaurus***. More than a dictionary, this vibrant, unapologetic collection celebrates the humour, camaraderie, and sheer inventiveness that define military life. From the ritual of "NATO Standard" tea-making to the darkly funny phenomenon of "Pavement Pizza," this book is your passport to a world where language serves as a bond and a survival tool in equal measure.

Looking for an insider's guide to the **Henry Knox** novels? The ***Squaddiesaurus*** is the key to decoding the lingo and immersing yourself in the culture that shapes their world. Don't wait, grab your copy and step into the heart of squaddie life, one hilarious definition at a time.

Beneath The Red Cap

In ***Beneath The Red Cap***, author **Pete Briggs** offers an unflinching, deeply personal account of his extraordinary career in the British Army's Royal Military Police. With over 20 years of service, **Pete Briggs** takes readers on a journey from the disciplined training grounds of Chichester to the high-stakes frontlines of Northern Europe, the Balkans, Iraq, and beyond. Through unvarnished storytelling, he reveals the intense challenges and unparalleled camaraderie that define life in military policing.

Essential reading for fans of military history and deeply human stories, ***Beneath The Red Cap*** also acts as a prequel to the **Henry Knox** novels. While **Pete Briggs** is not **Henry Knox**, many of the experiences and challenges described in the memoir mirror those faced by the fictional character, offering an even richer perspective on the world that inspired the novels.

For up-to-the-minute news about Pete Briggs and his character Henry Knox, find us on X

/PBriggs_Author

Or YouTube Channel

YouTube/CSMTAC

Printed in Dunstable, United Kingdom

63414188R00180